APPLE TURNOVER
MURDER

Books by Joanne Fluke

CHOCOLATE CHIP COOKIE MURDER

STRAWBERRY SHORTCAKE MURDER

BLUEBERRY MUFFIN MURDER

LEMON MERINGUE PIE MURDER

FUDGE CUPCAKE MURDER

SUGAR COOKIE MURDER

PEACH COBBLER MURDER

CHERRY CHEESECAKE MURDER

KEY LIME PIE MURDER

CARROT CAKE MURDER

CREAM PUFF MURDER

PLUM PUDDING MURDER

APPLE TURNOVER MURDER

Published by Kensington Publishing Corporation

APPLE TURNOVER MURDER

JOANNE FLUKE

KENSINGTON BOOKS
http://www.kensingtonbooks.com

KENSINGTON BOOKS are published by

Kensington Publishing Corp.
119 West 40th Street
New York, NY 10018

All Kensington titles, imprints, and distributed lines are available at special quantity discounts for bulk purchases for sales promotion, premiums, fund-raising, educational, or institutional use.

Special book excerpts or customized printings can also be created to fit specific needs. For details, write or phone the office of the Kensington Special Sales Manager: Attn. Special Sales Department. Kensington Publishing Corp., 119 West 40th Street, New York, NY 10018. Phone: 1-800-221-2647.

Kensington and the K logo Reg. U.S. Pat. & TM Off.

ISBN-13: 978-0-7582-4745-2
ISBN-10: 0-7582-4745-1

First trade paperback printing: March 2010

10 9 8 7 6 5 4 3 2 1

Printed in the United States of America

This book is for Ruel.
Thanks for Breakfast in a Muffin, honey!

Acknowledgments

Big hugs and kisses to the kids and the grandkids.

Thank you to: Mel & Kurt, Lyn & Bill, Lu & Sheba, Gina, Adrienne, Jay, Bob, Laura & Mark, Lois & Neal, Amanda, John B., Judy Q., Dr. Bob & Sue, Richard & Krista, Mark B., and Suzy & her remarkable Steelie.

Special thanks to my extraordinary Editor-in-Chief and long-time friend, John Scognamiglio.

Many thanks to Walter, Steve, Laurie, Doug, David, and Maureen.

Thanks to Hiro Kimura for the delectable Apple Turnover on the cover.
And thank you to Lou Malcangi for designing the gorgeous dust jacket.

Thanks also to all the other talented folks at Kensington who keep Hannah sleuthing and baking up a storm.

Thank you to my friend, Trudi Nash, for convincing me that she actually enjoys going along on book tours!
And thanks to David for getting along without her while she's gone.

Thank you to Dr. Rahhal, Dr. and Mrs. Line, and Dr. Wallen.

Thanks to John at Placed4Success for Hannah's movie and TV spots.
(And for knowing which wires go to which plugs on my computer.)

Thanks to Ken Wilson for remembering everyone at every bookstore in L.A.
Hugs to superb food stylist, Lois Brown, for making my recipes look yummy on TV.

Thanks to Jill Saxton, the best copy editor I've ever met.

Thank you to Sally Hayes for sharing loads of recipes and baking stories. Are you sure your real name isn't Hannah?

Many thanks to Terry Sommers for testing recipes in her Wisconsin kitchen.

Thank you to Jamie Wallace for keeping my Web site,
MurderSheBaked.com
up to date and looking great.

And big hugs to everyone who sent favorite family recipes for me to try.
In a perfect world, Hannah and I would have an extra day every week just for baking.

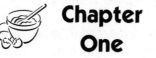 # Chapter
One

"'Til death do us part."

The words echoed in the hushed flower-scented air and Hannah Swensen shivered in her bridal finery. The church was filled to capacity on this Sunday afternoon in early June and sunbeams streamed through the stained glass windows that lined the nave, transforming the dust motes that floated on lazy air currents into bits of vividly colored confetti.

'Til death do us part.

The words were simple, the sentiment was true, and Hannah knew that marriage was supposed to last a lifetime. But hearing such grave words on this joyous occasion always reminded her of an opening line in a television murder mystery. In the next shot, the groom would kiss the bride and the whole congregation would mirror their happy smiles. Then the camera would pull back, and the music would change to a minor key. Something was about to happen, something ominous. Someone was going to die before the first commercial break, and you could almost bet that the victim would be one-half of the bridal couple, most likely the actor or actress who was lesser known and lesser paid.

But not today and not here in Lake Eden, Hannah told herself, feeling a bit silly for her dark thoughts on this happy occasion. She could probably blame her overactive imagination on too much work and not enough sleep. Hannah and her partner, Lisa, had put in long hours at The Cookie Jar, their coffee shop and bakery, and their jam-packed schedule was far from completed. They'd baked scores of cookies for graduation celebrations, bridal and baby showers, engagement parties, and school picnics. They'd even baked their signature wedding cookies for this wedding, Old-Fashioned Sugar Cookies topped with glittering crystals of granulated sugar and decorated with the initials of the bride and the groom in frosting, enclosed in a frosting heart. Once the reception line had come to an end, everyone would mingle in the church garden to enjoy iced lemonade and The Cookie Jar's wedding cookies.

Hannah was attempting to count the wedding celebrants that filled the pews to make sure they'd brought enough cookies when a warm hand reached out to clasp hers. The hand belonged to Norman Rhodes, son of the bride, Carrie Rhodes, and one of the men she was currently dating. Norman was smiling and he'd told Hannah that he was pleased his mother was marrying a man they all knew and liked, Earl Flensburg.

As Carrie and Earl turned and began their first walk down the aisle together as man and wife, Hannah caught a glimpse of her own mother's face. Delores Swensen was a study in contrasts, smiling and dabbing at her eyes with a lace handkerchief at the same time. Weddings always made Delores cry. She'd once admitted to Hannah that she'd cried at her own wedding and, much to her embarrassment, smudged her mascara in the process.

Hannah followed Norman out of the pew and down the side aisle toward the front doors of the church. "Are you going to stand in the reception line?"

"I'll congratulate them later when I make the first toast." Norman waved and Hannah turned to see Mike Kingston, the other man she occasionally dated, standing on the steps that led up to the church doors. He was still wearing his Winnetka County Sheriff's Department uniform and that probably meant he was still on duty. Mike waved back at them and Hannah and Norman went down the steps to greet him.

"Sorry I missed the wedding," Mike said when they arrived at his side. "I was supposed to be off work an hour and a half ago, but there was a robbery. You'd think in heat like this, the criminals would stay home and fan themselves."

"What did they steal?" Norman asked.

"A couple of fans?" Hannah guessed, earning long-suffering looks from both men.

"You're close," Mike told her. "They stole a truck loaded with one of those above-ground swimming pools."

"That's a pretty big thing to steal," Norman said. "Did you catch them?"

"Sure. The pool was still in the bed of the truck and they were trying to fill it up in the parking lot at the Eagle. You know where that is, don't you?"

Both Hannah and Norman nodded. They'd rescued Hannah's youngest sister, Michelle, from the country-western bar last summer when she'd helped them substantiate a suspect's alibi.

"They were trying to set up the pool at the Eagle?" Hannah asked him.

"*Trying* is the operative word. Since they didn't have a hose, they recruited everybody at the bar to carry out beer mugs filled with water and dump them in the pool. Lonnie and I figured it would have taken them at least four days to fill it up enough for a swim."

"So you caught them and arrested them?" Norman asked.

Mike shook his head. "It seems they were drinking buddies with the owner of the truck. And once they agreed to help him unload the pool at his house, and he agreed to let them go for a swim, everybody went off happy. But I missed the wedding and I'm sorry about that." Mike turned to Norman. "Give your mother and Earl my apologies, okay? And tell them I'll see them later."

"Let's head out to the Lake Eden Inn," Norman suggested after Mike had left.

Hannah glanced at her dress watch, squinting a bit to read the tiny numbers. She was used to the big dial on the watch she wore at work where time was of the essence and a minute or two more could turn a boiled frosting into concrete. "If we leave now, we'll be an hour early for the reception."

"Good. I want to check my video equipment to make sure everything's working right." Norman stopped speaking and frowned slightly. "Did I give you the bag of cat treats and toys I bought?"

Hannah turned to smile at him. "Yes, you did. But there's enough in that bag for a month and you're only going to be gone for three nights."

"I know. It's just that I've never left Cuddles before and I wanted to make sure she had everything she needed."

"But how about the time Marguerite took her up north?" Hannah asked, remembering the vacation Cuddles and her former owner had taken last summer.

"That's different. I didn't leave Cuddles. Cuddles left me." Norman was silent for a moment and then he began to grin. "That sounds a little crazy, doesn't it?"

"Not a bit. I'd feel the same way."

Hannah reviewed the plan in her mind as they walked to Norman's car. Once the reception was over, Norman would be driving his mother and Earl to the international airport in Minneapolis where they would catch a midnight flight to Rome. They were touring Italy for their honeymoon, somewhere Carrie had always wanted to go. Norman would see them off and then he'd drive to the hotel where he'd be staying for three nights. On Monday he'd meet up with some friends from dental school who were opening a clinic in St. Paul, tour the building they'd chosen for their clinic, and then they'd all go out to dinner together. On Tuesday he'd attend the grand opening, stay over that night, and drive back to Lake

Eden Wednesday morning in time for his first appointment. He'd pick up Cuddles that night after work, and his cat would have almost seventy-two hours to spend playing with her best friend, Moishe.

"Do you think we should check on the cats before we drive out to the reception?" Norman asked.

"We can stop at the condo if you're worried about them, but I'm sure they're fine. I filled the Kitty Valet with food before we left and Moishe's always been a real gentleman about letting Cuddles eat first. They're probably snuggled up on the couch together, watching the Animal Channel."

"You're right. No sense in disturbing them." Norman opened all four doors of his car to let the heat out before he gestured for Hannah to get inside. "I'll get the air conditioning on right away," he promised.

It was a hot afternoon and Hannah was glad that the air conditioning in Norman's sedan was better than the air conditioning in her cookie truck. Even if she turned it on full blast, someone blowing over the top of an ice cube would be more effective. Riding in Norman's well-maintained car was a welcome treat, and by the time they pulled out of the church parking lot, cool air was already beginning to pour out of the vents. "I just *love* your car!" she said with a sigh, leaning back against the headrest.

The moment the words were out of her mouth, she regretted them. They'd just come from a wedding and that meant both of them had weddings on the mind. It would be natural for Norman, who really wanted her to accept the proposal he'd tendered over a year ago, to say, *Marry me and I'll buy you one just like it.* Or, *Just say yes and I'll make everything easy for you, Hannah.* Or even, *Did you see how happy Mother was? I'd make you even happier if you'd marry me.*

But Norman didn't say any of those things. Instead, he just laughed. "You don't love my car. You love my air conditioning."

"It's true." Hannah hung her head in pretended shame. "I'm just a fool for a good-looking condenser and powerful vents."

Norman chortled. There was no other word for it. It was a sound that was midway between a chuckle and a gurgle and it made Hannah smile to know she'd caused it. There was no greater gift than making someone laugh. People who laughed were happy.

It was a huge party. Almost everyone they knew in town was there, but the Swensen sisters had found each other and snagged a table. Hannah, Andrea, and Michelle were seated at a rectangular table at the edge of the dance floor. Their mother, Delores, sat at one end, looking no more than a decade older than her daughters.

"And you're going to fill in at Granny's Attic while Carrie's on her honeymoon?" Hannah asked Michelle.

"That's right." Michelle turned to smile at her mother. "I've got a whole month before I have to be back at Macalester, and Mother's promised me a commission on any antiques I sell."

"And an hourly wage on top of that," Delores amended her youngest daughter's statement, and then she turned to Hannah. "Michelle will be able to stay with you for a while, won't she, dear? I'm having the hardwood floors redone and it could take several weeks."

"Not a problem. Michelle can stay with me anytime she wants."

Michelle turned to give Hannah a grin. "Thanks!"

"I should be the one to thank *you*. The last time you stayed over, you made breakfast for me. And the day you left, you stripped your bed and washed the sheets. Not only that, you emptied the drier and folded all my clothes. I *love* it when you stay with me."

All four Swensens looked up as a man stopped by their table. It was Lonnie Murphy, the deputy sheriff Michelle dated when she was in town. "Hi, Shelly. Do you want to dance?" he asked.

"I'd love to!" Michelle smiled, got up from her chair, and took Lonnie's arm. She looked genuinely delighted to be asked as they stepped out onto the dance floor.

Hannah hid a grin. Michelle hated to be called Shelly. It was the name her fourth grade class had given to the box turtle they kept in their terrarium. She'd once told Hannah she thought that Shelly was a great name for a turtle but not for her, and she'd engaged in several hair-pulling fights on the school playground with anyone who'd dared to call her by that nickname. Obviously things had changed. When Lonnie called her Shelly, Michelle just smiled at him. Hannah figured that must be love, or at least a close facsimile.

"Delores. Just the person I wanted to see." Bud Hauge approached their table. He owned the welding shop in town and Hannah knew he'd worked on several broken antiques for her mother.

"Bud." Delores acknowledged him with a nod. "Don't tell me you can't weld the rocker on my treadle sewing machine."

"Okay. I won't tell you I can't weld your sewing machine."

"Bud!" There was a warning tone in their mother's voice and Hannah exchanged grins with Andrea. Delores had gone to school with Bud and he loved to tease her.

"Just kidding. It's all ready for you, good as new. I'll drop it by Granny's Attic tomorrow morning."

"Thank you, Bud. That's perfect. I'd like you to take a look at something else we bought. Have you ever done any restoration on grave art?"

Bud gave a little shrug. "I don't know. They bring it in, I weld it. What's grave art?"

"It's a tribute for a grave, a statue or some kind of decoration chosen by the family. Commonly they're made of marble or granite, but this one is metal."

"What is it? An angel or something like that?"

"No, it's a fish."

"A fish?" Both Andrea and Hannah spoke at once since Bud appeared to be rendered speechless.

"I believe it's a walleye pike. It's not so unusual if you consider that families like to personalize the graves of their dearly departed."

Dearly departed? Hannah stared at her mother in shock. She'd never heard anyone use that phrase outside the walls of a church. "So some dead person inside, whoever he was, liked to fish?"

"I assume so, dear. We have several examples of grave art at the shop. They're from the family mausoleum section of Spring Brook Cemetery and they date back to the eighteen hundreds."

"They're tearing down part of that section, aren't they, Mother?" Andrea asked.

"They're relocating it, dear. The city council feels that the crypts are in such bad repair, they could be dangerous."

"How could they be dangerous if everyone who's in them is dead?" Hannah asked.

Andrea and Bud burst into laughter, and Hannah noticed that Delores did all she could do to keep a straight face. "That's not very nice, dear," she chided her eldest daughter.

"But it's funny," Bud said, still chuckling.

"And it's true," Andrea added.

"Well, be that as it may, the council decided to take down the crumbling mausoleums and relocate the . . . um . . . contents."

"All of them?" Hannah asked, remembering how she used to ride her bike out to the old part of the cemetery and walk past the giant stone angels and carved headstones. "I used to love the pink granite mausoleum with the columns in the front."

"That belongs to the Evans family and Florence has agreed to repair it. Four generations of her family are buried there. The problem the council had was with some of the other mausoleums. At least a dozen were unclaimed. Either the families moved to parts unknown, or there are no living relatives."

"Those are the ones they're tearing down?" Bud asked.

"That's right. But some of the grave art can't be moved to the new gravesites. Either it's in bad repair or it's simply too large. Carrie and I are taking whatever we can salvage to sell at Granny's Attic and we'll donate the proceeds to the relocation fund."

"That's nice of you, Mother," Andrea said. "But do you really think that anybody will buy a walleye for a grave?"

"It's already sold, dear. Winnie Henderson is buying it for her family crypt. She's kept it up over the years, but she never got around to ordering any kind of decoration."

"And she wants the walleye?" Bud looked astonished.

"Yes. One of her husbands just loved to hunt and fish. I think it was the third one?"

"I thought it was the fourth," Hannah said.

"Whatever. Winnie said his fishing buddy wanted all his fishing tackle, so she couldn't put any inside. All she had were his hunting things."

"She put those inside?" Andrea asked.

"Yes, and that's why she wants the walleye. Winnie wants everyone to know that he was a great fisherman as well as a good hunter."

"Sounds like what the Egyptians did with the pyramids," Bud commented. "Does Winnie believe he'll use them in the afterlife?"

"I don't know, Bud. Winnie has some strange notions and I didn't really get into it with her."

"Wait a second," Bud said, looking a little worried. "She didn't put any guns in there, did she?"

"Heavens, no! She kept the guns. She said you never know when you need firearms out on the farm. She shot a lynx last year, right before it attacked one of her calves."

"Is a lynx the same as a wildcat?" Andrea turned to Hannah. "I always get those two mixed up."

"A lot of people do. The bobcat's genus is lynx, but if you're thinking of the Canadian lynx we see here in Minnesota, they're twice as big as bobcats, and they have snowshoe paws."

Delores laughed. "I don't think Winnie got close enough to examine its paws."

"But was the bobcat Winnie shot a Canadian lynx?" Andrea asked.

"Probably," Bud answered her question, "especially if it was attacking something as big as a calf."

"Maybe it was a cougar, or a . . . a mountain lion." Andrea was obviously struggling with the nomenclature. "Or don't we have any of those here?"

"I think cougars are another name for mountain lions," Hannah told her. "And if I remember correctly, they're lumped in there somewhere with pumas and panthers."

"But do we have mountain lions here?" Andrea repeated her question. "We don't have any mountains in Minnesota."

"You're right," Bud said. "Most of them are farther west, but they migrate over here once in awhile. They're adaptable, and if there's not enough food where they are, they go in search of it."

"Then you think the big cat that Winnie shot might be a mountain lion?" Hannah asked him.

"I doubt it. If you spot a big cat here, it's probably a Canadian lynx." He turned to Delores. "Tell me more about that walleye. What's wrong with it?"

"It's missing one of its fins. That's why I asked if you'd ever done any restoration work. Do you think you could fabricate a fin and weld it on?"

"Yes, but only if you dance with me."

"What?!"

"Only if you dance with me. This is our song . . . remember?"

Delores didn't say a word, but she got to her feet and took Bud's arm. Hannah noticed that her mother's cheeks were bright pink as Bud led her to the dance floor and took her in his arms.

"I wonder if Bud's an old flame," Andrea mused.

"He could be. Mother told me she dated a lot in high school."

"You mean our mother played the field?"

"You could call it that, I guess. I know she wasn't serious about anyone until Dad came along."

Both sisters were silent as their mother danced by with Bud. Then Andrea turned to Hannah. "I wonder if she feels lonely now that Carrie's married again."

"I don't know. She hasn't said anything about it. Then again, she probably wouldn't. Do you want me to ask her?"

"No! That'll only make her think about it, if she's not thinking about it already. It's just that . . . I was wondering if we should keep an eye on her . . . just in case."

"Just in case what?"

"Just in case she falls in love again. Remember what happened with Winthrop?"

"I'll never forget it, but I really don't think that'll happen again."

"Why not?"

"Because Mother's wiser now, and there aren't any new, fascinating men with British accents who've moved to Lake Eden. Mother's known all the eligible local men for years."

"I know that, but . . ."

"Besides," Hannah went on, "Mother doesn't seem interested in anything but friendship. And the men seem to feel exactly the same way."

"Really?" Andrea nudged Hannah and gestured toward the dance floor. "Take a good look and tell me that again."

Hannah scanned the couples on the floor and located Delores dancing with Joe Dietz. Their mother was looking up at

Joe and smiling in what Hannah thought could be a mildly flirtatious way. "What's Mother doing with Joe Dietz? I thought she was dancing with Bud!"

"She was, but not anymore. Joe cut in on Doc Knight."

"Doc Knight? How did Doc Knight get into the picture?"

"Doc cut in on Bud."

"But it can't be more than a minute since Mother left the table! Are you telling me that she's had three dance partners already?"

"Yes, and number four is on the horizon and approaching fast. Look to your left."

Hannah followed Andrea's direction and watched as Pete Nunke walked out on the dance floor and made a beeline for Delores and Joe Dietz. There was no doubt that Andrea was correct when Pete tapped Joe on the shoulder.

"See what I mean?" Andrea asked.

"I see."

Both sisters watched as Joe tried to wave Pete away. There was a moment of good-natured banter between the two men and then Delores said something to Pete. His response caused her to throw back her head and laugh in obvious delight, leaving no doubt that she relished being the belle of the ball at her best friend's wedding.

"Mother's very popular tonight," Andrea said as Delores went into Pete's arms.

"Yes, she is."

"From where I'm sitting, she looks as if she's enjoying every minute of it," Andrea commented, "and it looks like it could be a little more than simple friendship to me."

Hannah sighed. Her sister was right. "I guess it wouldn't hurt to keep an eye on Mother . . . especially since all the bachelors and widowers in Lake Eden seem to be doing the same thing!"

Chapter Two

She was being crushed between two boulders . . . except they weren't boulders. They couldn't be boulders. Boulders were hard and cold. These were softer, and they were warm. She couldn't be certain what material they were made of, but she was totally restrained by whatever it was.

Her arms must be bound, or perhaps wedged at her sides, because she couldn't move them. Her legs also seemed to be trussed or contained in some manner. Why was she imprisoned like this? She couldn't remember, and she wasn't even certain that she'd ever been told.

There was a noise in the dark, way in the distance. She struggled to identify it for a moment, and then her mind, which seemed to operate in slow-motion, latched onto an image of a truck. It was the sound of a motor running, perhaps several motors running. Was she about to be moved from this place of confinement and transported to another location?

The rumbling continued, echoing around her, filling her head with questions. How had she been brought here? Who was responsible? And when there were no answers to those questions, her mind turned to others.

How high was high? What made the wind blow? No one could disagree that she was thinking. Did that mean that she existed? But this line of thought was not productive in her current situation. She ought to attempt to find a way to break out of her confinement and not waste time woolgathering.

Woolgathering. The words swirled in her mind, back and forth, around and around. The letters were made up of little puffy balls of cotton wool and it reminded her of sheep the size of kittens. And there was something about kittens, something about the fog creeping in . . . but that was cats. And these sheep were . . . cats!

"Off!" Hannah ordered, startling the two cats and sending them leaping from the bed. No wonder she'd dreamed about being wrapped up like a mummy! It had gotten cold and damp in the wee hours of the morning. Moishe and Cuddles must have felt the chill, because they'd moved from the living room couch to her bed. There they'd climbed up on her pillow, Moishe on the left and Cuddles on the right, moving closer and closer to her as they slept. For all intents and purposes, she'd ended up with two cats glued tightly to either side of her head.

A glance at the clock on her bedside table made Hannah groan. It was already a quarter to four and she had to get up in forty-five minutes. By the time she made a trip to the bathroom and got back in bed, only forty minutes of sleep time would be left. And by the time she actually calmed down, gave the cats several scratches behind the ears to apologize for startling them, and got back to sleep, it would be almost time to get up again.

And now, just thinking about it and figuring out the times, she was wide awake. No sense even trying for the few additional minutes of sleep that she might possibly gain. It was better to get up and try the recipe her college friend, Beth, had sent her for Vanilla Crack, to see if they could use it at The Cookie Jar. It certainly seemed easy to make and they had nothing else like it on the cookie menu.

By the time the little hand was a smidgen short of the four and the big hand was flirting with the eleven, Hannah emerged from the bathroom squeaky clean. She dressed quickly in the clothing she'd set out the previous night, and before the second hand could tick off the remaining three clicks to the hour, she was ready for the day that had not yet arrived.

"Thanks a lot, guys," she said to the two felines who were now nestled on her pillow, sound asleep, and walked down the carpeted hallway toward the kitchen. As she passed the closed guest room door, she listened for any sound that might indicate Michelle was awake. Her youngest sister had come home just as Hannah was going to bed, and both of them had been too tired to do more than say goodnight.

When she got to the kitchen, Hannah flicked on the banks of fluorescent lights that turned the white-walled room into the luminance of day, and re-read the recipe she'd received in the mail. It was even easier than she'd remembered, and she had all the ingredients on hand, including a fresh box of soda crackers. Then she set the recipe down on the counter and completed the first step toward a successful baking experience. She poured herself a cup of coffee to wake up.

The first sip was heaven. Hannah gave a deep sigh of pleasure and sank down on one of the plastic-covered chrome tube chairs that would eventually become antiques. Could anything be better than the first cup of coffee in the morning?

Hannah sat there relishing the experience, concentrating on the dark, rich taste. It was full-bodied but not bitter, and that meant the beans had been roasted to perfection. She definitely liked the new coffee Florence Evans, owner of Lake Eden's Red Owl Grocery Store, had ordered for her. It was called Silver Joe's, and they were trying it out at The Cookie Jar this morning. If their customers liked it, they'd switch. And that just went to prove that there was an upside to keeping in touch with old classmates. Who would have guessed that Pat Vota, the bratty boy who had pushed her off the dock every time they'd gone swimming at Eden Lake, would end up as a top executive at a gourmet coffee company?

Once her cup was empty and the morning caffeine had performed its miraculous cure, Hannah poured a second cup and began to gather ingredients. The list was short and consisted of only four items: butter, white sugar, vanilla, and salted soda crackers. Since there was a variation called Chocolate Crack, Hannah also carried a canister of brown sugar and a bag of chocolate chips to the counter. She had just filled a saucepan with butter, sugar, and vanilla when the phone rang.

Hannah turned to glance at the clock. It was four thirty-five. Who would call her this early? Visions of crippling auto accidents, life-threatening medical emergencies, and violent crimes befalling friends and family filled her mind with dread as she rushed over to answer it.

"Hello?" Hannah answered, hoping it was a wrong number. Anything else was likely to announce a disaster.

"Good morning, Hannah."

"Norman?" Hannah could scarcely believe her ears as she recognized the cheery voice. It was Norman, calling her on his cell phone, and he sounded alert and wide awake. "Is everything all right?"

"Yes, but I woke up too early. I couldn't sleep without Cuddles."

And I couldn't sleep WITH Cuddles, Hannah thought, but of course she didn't say it.

"So how did she sleep?" Norman continued.

"Cuddles slept just fine. So did Moishe," Hannah replied, deciding not to tell him about her rude awakening with both cats plastered to her head.

"Good. Well . . . I'd better let you go then. I know you're probably just getting ready for work."

Hannah gave a little smile. "Actually, I'm baking. I'm testing a new recipe a friend sent me for Vanilla Crack."

"Is that a cookie?"

"Not really. I guess you could say it's a cross between a cookie and a candy."

"Sounds interesting. Will you save one for me when I come to pick up Cuddles on Wednesday night?"

"Of course I will."

"Okay then. I'd better try to catch a little more sleep. I'm meeting the old gang to take a tour of the clinic this afternoon, and then we're all going out for dinner."

"Have fun."

"I will. It's been three years since I've seen these guys. We'll probably spend most of the night playing catch-up."

Hannah said goodbye and hung up the phone feeling envious. Norman was going back to bed. She wished *she* could go back to sleep and get up much, much later.

It didn't take long to boil the butter and sugar the required amount of time. Hannah had just added the vanilla and poured it over the bed of soda crackers she'd arranged on a cookie sheet when her phone rang again.

It only took a moment to sprinkle on a few pieces of salted nuts, slip the pan into the preheated oven, and set the timer. Hannah managed to answer the phone on the third ring. "Hello?"

"Hannah!" It was Andrea's voice and she sounded anxious. "I'm sorry to call so early, but I knew you'd be up and I really need to talk to you. It's about . . . oh drat! Bill's out of the shower and I can't talk now. I'm showing two houses this morning, but I'll come in this afternoon, okay?"

"Fine, but . . ." Hannah stopped talking when she realized that her sister had hung up. She stood there staring at the receiver for a moment and then she returned it to the cradle. Andrea was usually a late riser. What had happened to get her up before dawn? Or had she been sleepless all night, worrying about something?"

The timer dinged and Hannah removed the pan of Vanilla Crack from the oven. It smelled marvelous. She removed the pieces from the cookie sheet on a wire rack to harden and gave a little smile of satisfaction.

"What smells so heavenly?"

Hannah whirled around to see her youngest sister standing in the kitchen doorway, wearing a red and black checkered nightshirt and pink bunny slippers.

"It's a new cookie called Vanilla Crack."

"Vanilla *Crack*?" Michelle's eyebrows approached the edge of her honey-brown bangs. "Do you know what *crack* is?"

"Of course I know what *crack* is."

"But you're still going to call this cookie Vanilla Crack?"

"Yes, I am. There's no way I'm going to let a slang term invented by a scroungy dope dealer spoil my friend's cookie name. They're called Vanilla Crack, and Chocolate Crack, because the syrup is poured on crackers. And anybody who objects to the use of a perfectly good English word because illiterate criminals use it is an idiot!"

Michelle backed up a step and held up her hands, palms facing Hannah. "Okay. Forget I mentioned it. You're absolutely right. I just didn't know if you knew that it might have negative connotations. It smells divine, though. I think I'll try a piece for breakfast, if that's all right with you."

"For *breakfast*?!" Hannah heard her own words, more than a little censorious, echoing back to her. It wasn't that long ago that she'd been a college student like Michelle, and she'd eaten cold pizza for breakfast. On the scale of nutritional correctness, was a piece of Vanilla Crack that much lower than a piece of cold pepperoni pizza?

"Hannah? Can I try a piece of Vanilla Crack for breakfast?"

"It's *may* I. And yes, you may. Let me know how you like it while I start on the Chocolate Crack. And be careful. It hasn't had long to cool and it could be too hot to eat."

Michelle reached out to touch the confection on the cooling racks while Hannah arranged graham crackers on another cookie sheet. Then she put butter and brown sugar into her saucepan and brought it to a boil. She boiled it for the required five minutes, poured it over the graham crackers on the cookie sheet, and slipped the sheet in the oven. She'd just measured out the chocolate chips she'd need once it finished baking when she noticed that there was a large empty space on the cooling rack. "You've already eaten a quarter of a pan?" she asked Michelle.

"I guess I was hungry," Michelle said a bit sheepishly. "It was great, Hannah. It's just like a flaky candy bar. Is the Chocolate Crack almost done? I'd like to taste that, too."

"Ten minutes in the oven, five minutes to cool, and you can have a taste . . . or maybe another quarter-pan. You're pretty wide awake for someone who didn't get home until after midnight last night. I thought you said Lonnie had to work a swing shift."

"He did work a swing shift. And before he went to the sheriff's station, he dropped me off at the community college. It was jazz night at the Cave," Michelle named the little bistro on campus that hosted student entertainment in the evenings, "and I met some friends. I caught a ride here with one of them."

"Oh." Hannah turned away to hide her worried expression. She hoped the friends Michelle had at the college didn't include Bradford Ramsey. She'd been meaning to warn Michelle about the unscrupulous professor ever since her youngest sister had invited him to Christmas Eve dinner, but the time had never seemed right. Hannah supposed now was as good a time as any, but the thought of imparting such an embarrassing confidence at shortly after five in the morning made her courage shrink up and her voice turn mute.

"What is it?" Michelle asked, locking eyes with Hannah. "You look . . . pained. Is it the coffee on an empty stomach?"

"Heavens, no!" Hannah said, and changed the subject quickly. "That reminds me . . . what do you think of the coffee? We're trying a new brand at The Cookie Jar and I brought some home to test."

"It's really good. I like it better than the old kind. But you haven't told me what's wrong?"

Hannah sighed. She supposed she really should answer Michelle. She steeled herself to introduce the subject, but just as she was about to speak, the phone rang. "Oops. I'd better get that," she said, and grabbed the phone. "Hello?"

"Hi, Hannah. It's Mike. I'm not calling too early, am I?"

"I've been up for an hour, Mike," Hannah answered, using his name deliberately so that Michelle would know who it was.

"Tell him hi from me," Michelle said, hopping up from her chair. "I'm going to go get dressed. By that time, the Chocolate Crack should be cool enough to try."

"Did she say Chocolate *Crack*?" Mike asked, and Hannah could hear the shock in his voice.

"That's right. It's a new recipe. And I do know what *crack* is. This crack refers to one of the ingredients, crackers, and I'm not about to change the cookie name because some criminals use it for drug slang."

"Okay. Okay. I just wanted you to know, that's all." Mike backed off quickly. "Have you heard from Norman?"

"Yes, at four thirty-five this morning. He told me he couldn't sleep well without Cuddles."

"That figures. It's all a matter of habit. When I was growing up, I slept in a room with my older brothers. When they moved out, it took me a week before I could sleep through the night. It was just too quiet, you know?"

"I *do* know. So what's up, Mike? You don't usually call this time of the morning just to chat."

Mike gave a little laugh. "You know me too well, and you're right. Do you know where Norman is staying in the Cities?"

"No, and I didn't ask him when he called. I should have, but I guess it was just too early to operate on full brainpower."

"I know what you mean."

"Do you want me to ask if he calls again? He'll probably get in touch with me sometime this evening."

"That'll be too late. I need to call and ask him where he hides his extra key."

"Which key?"

"His house key. I know he hides one somewhere outside."

"Did Norman tell you that?"

"No, but almost all the homeowners do it. It could be nasty if you got locked outside by accident in the winter."

"True," Hannah said and then she was silent. She wasn't about to give away Norman's hiding place until she knew more about why Mike needed that information.

"So do you know where he hides it?"

"Yes. Why do you want to know?"

"One of Norman's neighbors was driving by on her way to work the early shift at DelRay this morning, and she saw a light flick off upstairs. She knew that Norman was gone, so she called the station to report it."

"That was nice of her."

"Yes, it was. It's probably a light on a timer or something like that, but I'm driving out there to check it out. I'll jimmy a window or something if I have to, but it'd be a lot easier if I had a key."

"Of course it would. I've got a key here, but it'll be a lot faster if you drive straight out there and use Norman's hidden key. There's a concrete statue of a moose under the pine tree to the left of the front door. The key's in its mouth."

"Wow!" Mike was clearly impressed. "That's a great hiding place. I never would have thought to look there. Most people hide their keys under flowerpots on the front porch, or they've got one of those silly little rocks that's hollowed out to hold a key."

Hannah frowned. Mike had just described the rock she had in her planter by the front door. "Do criminals know about those rocks?"

"Sure they do. And just in case they're not smart enough to figure it out, all they have to do is flip the rock over and it says, *Hide-A-Key* on the flap that slides over the hole." Mike stopped speaking for a moment and then he chuckled. "Don't tell me you've got one of those!"

"Not anymore."

"Good. Thanks for the information, Hannah. I'll check out Norman's house right away."

"I'll be leaving for work in just a couple of minutes. Will you call me on my cell phone if there's anything wrong?"

"Sure, but you'll have to remember to turn it on."

"I'll turn it on," she promised, more than a little amused. She had a habit of turning off her cell phone when she didn't want to receive calls and forgetting to turn it back on again.

"Do you want to go out for a burger tonight after I finish my shift?"

An outsider to their complicated relationship might have thought that Mike was following the old adage, *Make hay while the sun shines*, and taking advantage of the fact that Norman was out of town. Hannah knew that simply wasn't true. If Mike felt like asking her to go out for a burger, he'd ask her whether Norman was in town, or not.

"That sounds nice," she responded. "What time?"

"I'll pick you up at your place at six, and we'll run out to the Corner Tavern. They've got a new burger with peanut butter and peppers inside. It comes with something called an onion bouquet, and I want to try it."

Hannah said goodbye, and when she hung up the receiver, she was smiling. She was still smiling after she'd taken the Chocolate Crack out of the oven, sprinkled the top with chocolate chips, and spread them out into a frosting with a spatula. When she'd first met Mike, she'd suspected that he was a meat and potatoes man, a typical Midwesterner who hadn't strayed far from the cuisine his parents and grandparents had enjoyed. And then he'd met her and his world had changed, although the jury was still out on whether it was for the better, or the worse.

It had all started with the Jalapeno Brownies she'd baked for him and left on his desk at the sheriff's station in retaliation for saying that someone else's brownies were the best he'd ever tasted. But like many attempts to retaliate, this one had turned out to be a joke . . . on her! Mike had loved the brownies and Hannah credited them for opening up his eyes to the exciting possibilities of unorthodox food combinations. On the other hand, her fiery hot brownies could have permanently shocked his taste buds into complete passivity, leaving him completely open to sampling any gastronomic innovation, worthy or not.

VANILLA CRACK

Preheat oven to 350 degrees F., rack
in the middle position.

1 box salted soda crackers. (*I used Saltines*)
2 sticks salted butter *(1 cup, 8 ounces, ½ pound)*
1 cup white *(granulated)* sugar
2 teaspoons vanilla extract
½ cup salted nut pieces

Line a 10-inch by 15-inch cookie sheet with heavy-duty foil. If you have a jellyroll pan, that's perfect. If you don't, turn up the edges of the foil to form sides.

Spray the foil with Pam or other nonstick cooking spray. *(You want to be able to peel it off later, after the cookies harden.)*

Cover the pan completely with a single layer of soda crackers, salt side up. *(You can break the crackers in pieces to make them fit if you have to.)* Set the cracker-lined jellyroll pan or cookie sheet aside while you cook the topping.

Combine the butter with the white sugar and vanilla in a heavy saucepan. Bring it to a full boil over medium high heat on the stovetop, stirring constantly. *(A full boil will have breaking bubbles all over the surface of the pan.)* Boil it for exactly five *(5)* minutes, stirring it constantly. If it sputters too much, you can reduce the heat. If it starts to lose the boil, you can increase the heat. Just don't stop stirring.

Pour the mixture over the soda crackers as evenly as you can.

Hannah's Note: I start by pouring the mixture in lines from top to bottom over the length of the pan. Then I turn it and pour more lines over the width of the pan. Once the whole pan is crosshatched with the hot toffee mixture, I pour any that's left where it's needed. If it doesn't cover the soda crackers completely, don't worry—it'll spread out quite a bit in the oven.

Sprinkle the salted nut pieces over the top.

Slide the pan into the oven and bake the cookies at 350 degrees F. for ten *(10)* minutes.

Remove the pan from the oven and let it cool on a wire rack.

When the cookies have thoroughly cooled, peel off the foil and break them into random-sized pieces.

CHOCOLATE CRACK

Preheat oven to 350 degrees F., rack
in the middle position.

1 box graham crackers. *(I used Nabisco Honey Maid)*
2 sticks salted butter *(1 cup, 8 ounces, ½ pound)*
1 cup brown sugar *(pack it down when you measure it)*
2 cups semi-sweet chocolate chips *(12-ounce package)*

Line a 10-inch by 15-inch cookie sheet with heavy-duty foil. If you have a jellyroll pan, that's perfect. If you don't, turn up the edges of the foil to form sides.

Spray the foil with Pam or another nonstick cooking spray. *(You want to be able to peel it off later, after the candy hardens.)*

Line the pan completely with a single layer of graham crackers. Cover the whole bottom. *(You can break the crackers in pieces to make them fit if you have to.)* Set the cracker-lined jellyroll pan or cookie sheet aside while you cook the toffee mixture.

Combine the butter with the brown sugar in a saucepan. Bring it to a boil over medium high heat on the stovetop, stirring constantly. *(A full boil will have breaking bubbles all over the surface of the pan.)* Boil it for exactly five *(5)* minutes, stirring it constantly. If it sputters too much, you

can reduce the heat. If it starts to lose the boil, you can increase the heat. Just don't stop stirring.

Pour the mixture over the graham crackers as evenly as you can.

Hannah's Note: I start by pouring the mixture in lines from top to bottom over the length of the pan. Then I turn it and pour more lines over the width of the pan. Once the whole pan is crosshatched with the hot toffee mixture, I pour any that's left where it's needed. If it doesn't cover the crackers completely, don't worry—it'll spread out quite a bit in the oven.

Slide the pan into the oven and bake the cookies at 350 degrees F. for ten *(10)* minutes.

Remove the pan from the oven and sprinkle the chocolate chips over the top. Give the chips a minute or two to melt and then spread them out as evenly as you can with a heat-resistant spatula, a wooden paddle, or a frosting knife.

Slip the pan in the refrigerator to chill.

When the pan has chilled, peel the foil from the cookies and break them into random-sized pieces.

Chapter Three

"Nothing succeeds like excess," Hannah said, looking up from her position behind the counter at The Cookie Jar as Mayor Richard Bascomb and his wife, Stephanie, came in the door.

Hannah's partner, Lisa, took one look at the female half of Lake Eden's first couple and burst out laughing, a gaffe she quickly covered by pretending to cough. Stephanie Bascomb was resplendent in a bright blue suit of raw silk with a stylish blue hat. Her frilly blouse matched the blooms on her hat, which Hannah identified as slightly more purple than the cornflowers growing wild in Winnie Henderson's back forty. The first lady's gloves were bright-blue leather and her chic leather pumps were of the same hue. A large sapphire surrounded with diamonds graced her right hand and she wore a matching set of necklace and earrings.

"Hannah! And Lisa!" Mrs. Bascomb greeted them with the same surprised tone she might have used if she were traveling and happened to run into them at a Buddhist monastery in Sri Lanka.

Hannah exchanged puzzled glances with Lisa. Where else would they be during the hours The Cookie Jar was open for business?

"Good to see you, Mayor," Hannah said, and then she turned to the woman who spared no expense buying herself a stunning new outfit every time she found out about one of her husband's dalliances. The mayor's last peccadillo must have been particularly flagrant to warrant a suit, hat, gloves, shoes, and a fortune in gemstones. "You're a vision in blue, Stephanie."

"Do you like it?" Stephanie asked, twirling around so that Hannah could see the flared skirt below the impeccably tailored jacket.

"I just love that color," Hannah answered truthfully, neglecting to mention that it was indeed possible to get too much of a good thing. Stephanie was living proof that the concept of overkill could be applied to fashion.

Stephanie turned to Lisa. "How about you, Lisa? Do you like my new outfit?"

Hannah waited breathlessly for Lisa's answer. Her partner, well known for hating to hurt anyone's feelings, would have to think fast on this one.

"It's stunning," Lisa said, and Hannah mentally congratulated her young partner for choosing a word with several shades of meaning. "Wherever did you get it?" Lisa continued breathlessly. "Unless, of course, you're keeping that secret to yourself."

"Well . . ." Stephanie considered it for a moment. "It's a new, very exclusive shop at the mall. You have to know someone to get in. Everything they have is incredibly expensive . . ." Stephanie turned to her husband. "But I do think it's worth it, don't you, Richard?"

"Yes, definitely worth it," the mayor pronounced, smiling at his wife. "Aren't you going to tell them the secret about your charity gala, my sweetness?"

My sweetness?! Hannah stared hard at their town's most indiscreet Romeo. Although she didn't usually place much credence in gossip, she might have to ask her mother about the mayor's most recent transgression. Delores was the founding member of what Hannah called *The Lake Eden Gossip Hotline*, and in a town the size of Lake Eden, everyone knew everything about everybody. It was possible to keep a three-way secret, but only if two of the three people were permanently billeted at Spring Brook Cemetery.

"I might just tell them," Stephanie answered playfully, "but only if we can have some of their fabulous cookies and coffee."

Hannah poured the coffee while Lisa took cookie orders from Lake Eden's first couple. When they'd seated themselves at a table near the back of the coffee shop, Hannah opened the discussion with a question. "What's all this about your gala, Stephanie?"

"I'll tell you, but only if you promise to keep the details a secret." She turned to Lisa and Hannah. "Girls?"

Although Hannah hadn't been called a girl in a month of Sundays, perhaps even much longer, she nodded. It was what Stephanie expected. Lisa did the same. and both the mayor and his wife gave them smiles of approval.

"I'm sure you've heard that I agreed to chair the Lake Eden Combined Charities Drive this year," Stephanie said.

"We knew that," Hannah told her. "It was in the *Lake Eden Journal* last week."

"But here's something that wasn't in the papers." Stephanie leaned across the table. "I managed to book Samantha Summerfield as the guest speaker at the opening luncheon."

"The same Samantha Summerfield who's on *Hello Handsome?*" Lisa asked.

"That's right. She's in Minneapolis visiting her family while the show's on hiatus. Isn't that exciting?"

"Very exciting!" Lisa's eyes were like saucers. "But why would she come here? To Lake Eden?"

"Because she wants to help our charities." Stephanie looked smug. "She believes she can help us raise money for a worthy cause."

How much of a cut are you giving her? Hannah wanted to ask. And if that wasn't it, her second question would be, *What bargaining chip do you have to hang over her head?* But she asked nothing. Stephanie and the mayor wouldn't tell them anyway. Instead, Hannah locked eyes with Lisa. Her glance said, *Watch out! She wants something!* And Lisa's return glance replied, *Thanks for warning me. I'll be careful.*

"Now, not a word to anyone," Stephanie went on, "not until the news breaks on KCOW television tonight. Agreed?"

"Agreed," Lisa breathed.

"Fine," Hannah said, not particularly impressed with the sitcom actress who was gracing their charity luncheon with her presence.

"The charity drive is incredibly important this year," Stephanie went on. "We need to raise more money than we've ever raised before. We have six projects that are red-flagged and we simply have to find the money to fund them!"

Hannah and Lisa listened as Stephanie gave them an overview. It seemed that the Children's Home needed a new roof; Jordan High had to update their computer equipment; The Senior Center had a budget that was much too small for their needs; and the Piggy Bank, a fund that provided clothing and school supplies for underprivileged children, had completely run out of money. Marge Beeseman, their volunteer librarian, had requested several reference works and a microfiche reader, and although Janice Cox's preschool, Kiddie Korner, was self-sufficient, she'd asked the combined charity for the money to put in a small kitchen so that she could serve a hot lunch to her students.

"And that's just the tip of the iceberg," Stephanie told them, ending her recital with a dramatic sigh. "I know times are tough right now, but my goal is to present a truly gala event, a three-day happening that everyone in the Tri-County Area will want to attend."

"Attend *and* pledge to the cause," Mayor Bascomb added.

"Exactly right. Of course we can't use the Lake Eden Community Center as a venue. It's just too small, especially with the crowd that Samantha is bound to draw. Richard and I considered holding it at the Lake Eden Inn, but Dick and Sally are completely booked. I'm just so lucky my Richard came through for me. He spoke to Ken Purvis and since summer school doesn't start for another two weeks, he's agreed to let us use the Jordan High auditorium, all the grounds including the football field and the baseball stadium, and the entire parking lot."

"Do you really think there'll be that many people?" Hannah asked.

"I *know* there will be. I've already received over five hundred reservations for the opening day luncheon, and more are pouring in every day. And this is before I told anyone about Samantha Summerfield."

"So how many are you expecting?" Hannah asked.

"At least a thousand. I arranged for party tents to be set up on the football field, and the Lake Eden Nursery on Old Lake Road has agreed to bring live plants and flowers to decorate the area. It'll be like a garden party. And after the luncheon is over?"

Stephanie turned to her husband and the mayor continued. "Personnel from the nursery are going to sell the plants and give fifty percent of the profits to Stephanie."

"Well, not to me personally," Stephanie gave a tinkling little laugh. "It's for the Lake Eden Combined Charities."

"That's very nice," Hannah said, still waiting for the second shoe to drop. Stephanie wanted something from them and she hadn't asked for it yet.

"This is going to be a spectacular party." Stephanie looked from Hannah to Lisa and then back again. "That's why I wanted to talk to you today, before you got too busy. I'm going to need over a thousand sugar cookies."

"*When* do you need them?" Hannah asked, knowing that Stephanie's answer would dictate theirs. June was their busy month with bridal showers, weddings, graduation parties, family reunions, and barbecues galore. Everyone wanted cookies, and Hannah and Lisa provided them. It was also a busy month for non-work obligations. Both Hannah and Lisa were in-

vited to a series of parties and barbecues to celebrate the beginning of summer.

"The luncheon is on Wednesday afternoon. We're having
raspberry sorbet for dessert and we were planning to serve it
with a chocolate leaf garnish. Isn't that clever?"

"Chocolate and raspberry go well together," Hannah said,
wondering what was so clever about the combination that
had been around for years.

"I'm talking about the leaf design. The theme of my charity event is *Turn Over a New Leaf*. I want everyone who at-
tends to turn over a new leaf and pledge twice the amount
they pledged last year."

"Oh. Of course," Hannah said, although she hadn't known
about the theme. She wasn't about to admit that she'd received information about Stephanie's charity event and it was
still sitting on her desk at home, waiting to be opened.

"I contracted with the little chocolate shop I frequent when
I'm in Minneapolis. They assured me that they could make the
leaves, but the owner called this morning to say they couldn't
fill the order. It was something about not being able to get
supplies. And that's why I'm here. I need twelve hundred sugar
cookies by noon on Wednesday for the luncheon. You can
decorate them with a leaf made out of chocolate frosting, can't
you? I know it's late in the day, but just an outline of a leaf
would be all right."

Hannah began to frown. The cookies themselves were no
problem, but Lisa would have to decorate each cookie and
that would take time. It was time they didn't have, not with
all their other orders. And Stephanie probably expected them
to donate the cookies for free!

She must have sensed Hannah's reluctance because Stephanie
held up her hand. "I know you probably won't charge me
since it's for such a worthy cause, but I insist on paying you
for the ingredients. That way you won't have any out of pocket
expenses."

But you won't pay us for our time, and that's the most ex-

pensive variable in the equation. Any time we spend on your order is less time we can spend on the customers who actually pay! Hannah didn't voice her thoughts. It wasn't politic to alienate the female half of Lake Eden's first couple. But before she could tell Stephanie that they couldn't possibly take on a project that large with such short notice, Lisa spoke up.

"We can't fill your order, Mrs. Bascomb. There just isn't enough time to decorate all those cookies. It's very labor intensive. But we can give you chocolate sugar cookies to go with your raspberry sorbet."

"I've never heard of chocolate sugar cookies," Mayor Bascomb commented.

Neither have I, Hannah added silently, hoping that Lisa had a recipe for the treat she'd just promised to bake.

"And I have another dessert idea for you," Lisa continued. "It's something that fits right in with your theme, *Turn Over a New Leaf*. Hannah and I could bake apple turnovers for you to sell during the events. Everyone loves apple turnovers."

"Perfect!" Stephanie breathed. "You're a genius, Lisa!"

"Thank you. You can set up a booth, man it with volunteers, and heat the turnovers in a toaster oven so they're warm and smell divine."

"We could do that," Stephanie agreed, nodding quickly.

"Hannah and I will provide the turnovers and we'll follow Lake Eden Nursery's example. We'll donate fifty percent of our profits to your charity drive."

"Wonderful! But how about coffee? Could we have your coffee for sale, too?" Stephanie glanced down at her cup. "This is simply marvelous coffee."

"Thank you." Hannah took the hint and reached out to refill Stephanie's cup. "It's a new kind of coffee from my high school friend, Pat Vota."

"Vota . . ." the mayor repeated, looking thoughtful. "If I'm remembering right, he was a heck of a basketball player. Maybe I should give him a jingle and see if he'll donate some of this coffee to the cause."

"That's a wonderful idea, dear!" Stephanie praised him. And then she turned to Hannah. "Do you think he might send us a case or two?"

"I don't know," Hannah said. There was no way she'd make any sort of commitment for a classmate she hadn't seen since the summer after they'd graduated.

"Well, look who's here," a voice called out and Hannah turned to glance at the customer who'd come in the door and was headed straight for their table. There was no way she could mistake his lean, well-muscled body, his glossy brown hair worn slightly longer in front, and his remarkable brown eyes with sprinkles of gold in their depths. It was Bradford Ramsey and he'd clearly impressed Lake Eden's first couple with his handsome, talented, sensitive and caring professor act. What was *he* doing here in her cookie shop?

"Bradford!" Stephanie turned to greet him. "You know my husband, of course."

"Of course. It's a pleasure to see you again, Mr. Mayor."

"This is Lisa Beeseman," Stephanie went on with the introductions. "She's married to our town marshal. And this is Hannah Swensen."

Bradford turned his thousand-watt smile in Hannah's direction. "Hannah and I have met . . . haven't we, Hannah?"

Hannah's mouth went suddenly dry, as parched as a nomad caught in a desert sandstorm without benefit of water. She managed to nod, but all the while her mind was screaming out a warning. *He knows! It took him a while, but he remembered me! And now he's going to tell everyone here about us!*

"You know Hannah?" Stephanie asked him, completely oblivious to Hannah's inner distress.

"I certainly do! And I'll tell you a little secret about her."

Hannah prayed for a loud clap of thunder to drown out his words. Or a tornado to touch down and whirl her away to another land, like Dorothy in *The Wizard of Oz*. Any sort of major disaster would do as long as it would keep him from revealing her painful secret.

Bradford leaned closer and gave her a little wink. "You might not know this, but Hannah makes the best plum pudding I've ever tasted. I'm her sister's faculty advisor and I had the pleasure of joining the whole Swensen family for dessert on Christmas Eve."

He didn't remember! Hannah felt weak with relief. He hadn't remembered on Christmas Eve and he still didn't remember. She was safe! He had no idea she was the naive graduate student who'd fallen under his spell while they were in college. But he would remember . . . eventually. That knowledge was like the sword of Damocles suspended over her head.

"Nice to meet you, Lisa," Bradford continued, "and it's good to see everyone else again. I just stopped in for a quick hello when I saw you through the window. Now I've got to run back out to the college. There's a department meeting I can't miss."

As the front door shut behind Bradford, Hannah felt her composure begin to return. The crisis was averted . . . for now at least. She took a few deep breaths, pasted a pleasant expression on her face, and began to listen to the conversation again. With a little luck, no one had noticed how distressed she'd been.

"We'll leave the pricing of the turnovers up to you, Mrs. Bascomb," Lisa was saying. "All you have to do is tell us what day you want us to deliver."

"All three days," the mayor answered quickly. "They'll be a big hit during intermission at the talent show on Wednesday night."

"You're absolutely right, Richard!" Stephanie beamed at her husband.

"There's a talent show?" Lisa asked, and Hannah hid a grin. It was clear her young partner hadn't opened her charity information packet, either.

"It's a show for local talent in the Tri-County Area," Stephanie explained. "We're going to poll the audience and give cash prizes to the top three acts of the evening."

"Thursday night is Casino Night," Mayor Bascomb explained. "We'll be playing for prizes that are donated by local merchants, and people will be walking around from table to table." The mayor turned to his wife. "I think you should sell turnovers during Casino Night too . . . don't you, my sweetness?"

"Yes, I do. We can set up a little bistro in a corner of the auditorium. We'll put out chairs and little tables and people can wander in for coffee and turnovers."

"How about during donkey baseball on Friday afternoon?" the mayor asked her.

"That's a natural, Richard. We'll be right there on the school baseball field and we can use the snack shack to sell them. Actually . . . we could send the volunteers into the stands to sell coffee and turnovers the way they sell peanuts at major league baseball games."

Hannah risked a glance at Lisa. Her partner didn't look at all worried. Hannah hoped that was because Lisa had baked apple turnovers hundreds of times at home. Hannah had made plenty of pies, but she'd never even tried to make a turnover!

"Is there still time for people to enter the talent show?" Lisa asked, and Hannah assumed she was asking for Herb's benefit.

"I have room for five more contestants, and all you have to do is pay the twenty-five dollar entrance fee," Stephanie told her. "Will you be singing? Or dancing?"

Lisa gave a little laugh. "Oh, not me! I don't have any talent like that. I was asking for my husband. Herb's an amateur magician and he's really good."

"That's right! Someone told me he was fabulous at the Tri-County Fair. We'd love to have him enter. We don't have any other magicians and everyone loves a magic show."

"Then I'll pay his entrance fee right now," Lisa said, rushing behind the counter to get her purse. "Herb just loves to perform his illusions."

Hannah watched as the deed was accomplished. Lisa handed

over the money, Mrs. Bascomb assured her that every cent of it would go to charity, and then she wrote out a receipt on a napkin.

"You'll just love the talent show," Stephanie commented, handing over the napkin. "Perry and Sherri Connors are dancing right after the intermission."

"Perry and Sherri are in the talent show?" Lisa asked, her voice high and strained.

Hannah read her partner's expression and she could tell exactly what Lisa was thinking. Why had she just paid twenty-five dollars to enter The Amazing Herb in a talent contest he couldn't possibly win? Perry and Sherri were world-class dancers. They'd won every competition they'd entered, and just last week the *Lake Eden Journal* had run an article announcing that the Connors twins would be showcasing their dancing talent in a live television special that would air Christmas Day. The twins would be reprising famous dance routines that Fred Astaire and Ginger Rogers had performed during their long careers.

"Oh, they're not talent show contestants," Stephanie explained. "They're just going to demonstrate one of the routines they learned for the television special. I thought it would be a real treat for the audience."

"I'll look forward to it," Lisa said with a smile and Hannah could see her visibly relax.

"I have another treat, too," Stephanie said. "I snagged the most wonderful person to be the host."

"Not Samantha Summerfield!" Lisa looked astounded.

"No. She'll be commenting from the audience during the first half of the show, but her driver is picking her up during intermission. It's Bradford Ramsey. He agreed right away when I asked him to host the show. He told me he really loves performing in front of an audience and he's very eager to help our charities."

"That's nice of him," Lisa commented.

"He seems like a great guy," Mayor Bascomb gave his opinion.

Hannah said nothing. Instead, she busied herself by adding more cookies to the plate on the table. Bradford was neither a nice man nor a great guy, and she knew that for a fact. He was a skunk, a snake, and a lying, cheating, totally unredeemable jerk. To think that she'd once been in love with him was even worse than embarrassing. The less the mayor, Stephanie, and Lisa knew about her unhappy past with Bradford Ramsey, the better!

 **Chapter Four**

"Tell me you know how to make chocolate sugar cookies and apple turnovers," Hannah said to Lisa the moment the door had closed behind the mayor and Stephanie.

"I know how to make chocolate sugar cookies. I found a recipe in one of Mom's boxes and I made them for Herb's birthday. Everybody really loved them."

"Great. How about apple turnovers?"

"I don't know how to make apple turnovers."

Hannah let out a groan that would have awakened a hibernating bear. "But you promised Stephanie we'd make them."

"I know. Don't worry, Hannah. Marge makes the best apple turnovers I've ever tasted, and she told me it's easier than making pies. She baked over a hundred for our family reunion last year."

Hannah began to feel better immediately. Lisa's mother-in-law was an excellent cook and baker who never did anything fancy. She'd grown up on wholesome home-cooked meals and if she'd baked that many apple turnovers, it couldn't be that difficult to do.

"Will Marge teach us how to make them?" Hannah asked.

"I'm sure she will. I'll give her a call right now and ask. Knowing Marge, she'll probably offer to help us bake them and talk Aunt Patsy into coming along, too."

"That would be great. I'd feel a lot more confident if *some-body* knew what they were doing."

"Me too." Lisa gave a little smile. "Now I want you to stop worrying about the recipes and the baking, and think of all the money we're going to make on a gazillion apple turnovers!"

It was two in the afternoon and everything was coming up roses. Or at least it was coming up daisies, Hannah amended the old adage. There still weren't enough hours in the day to get everything done to her satisfaction, but Marge and Patsy had offered to help with the turnovers. They'd even suggested a plan. Since Marge's turnovers froze beautifully, they were going to start baking them tonight, right after The Cookie Jar closed for business. Jack, who'd convinced Marge that he was the fastest apple peeler in Minnesota history, would come with them to operate the old-fashioned apple peeler, corer, and slicer that his grandmother had used in her farm kitchen. Hannah would leave once everyone had arrived and drive to her condo to check on the cats and go out to The Corner Tavern with Mike, who'd stopped in at The Cookie Jar to tell her that no one had broken into Norman's house. What his neighbor had thought was a burglar was actually only a burned out lightbulb that Mike had replaced.

"I've got something for you to taste," Lisa called out, emerging from the kitchen with a plate of cookies.

"Chocolate Sugar Cookies?" Hannah guessed, gazing down at the sparkling grains of sugar on the dark chocolate cookies.

"Right. I called Dad and he read the recipe to me over the phone. I just thought I'd try them to make sure they were as good as I remembered."

Hannah bit into one of the still-warm cookies and gave a little sigh of contentment. She was about to take another bite when Jon Walker, the local druggist who'd come in for his early afternoon break, tapped her arm to get her attention.

"How about us?" he asked, making a sweeping gesture that included everyone seated at the counter. "We'll help you test those cookies."

Both Hannah and Lisa laughed. Their customers were always ready to critique new cookies. "Here you go," Lisa said, passing the plate to Jon so that he could distribute them.

Stan Kramer, Hannah's accountant, was the first to comment. "Good crunch," he said.

"They're nice and buttery," Bertie Straub, owner of Lake Eden's beauty parlor, the Cut 'n Curl, gave her assessment.

"And the chocolate is just right," Jon said. "It's dark, and sweet and . . ."

"Yummy!" Hannah finished the sentence for him.

Father Coultas, who was sitting at the end of the counter, gave Lisa the high sign. "I'd give it a ten out of ten," he said. "You'll bring some to our next bake sale, won't you, Lisa?"

Just then the bell on the front door tinkled and Andrea stepped in. As usual, she could have stepped off the cover of a fashion magazine. Her makeup was perfect, and her shining blond hair was caught up in a barrette, a hairstyle that exposed the back of her slender neck and was perfect for a warm summer day. She was wearing a mint green dress with a full skirt that was decorated with wide black rickrack around the collar and hem. A black leather belt with a rickrack design nipped in Andrea's slim waist, and black leather sandals with tiny heels completed the outfit.

"What an adorable outfit!" Bertie said by way of greeting.

"Thanks, Bertie." Andrea gave her a smile that didn't quite reach her eyes, and then she turned to Hannah. "Could I see you in the kitchen for a minute?"

Uh-oh! Hannah's mind shouted as her sisterly radar went on high alert. Something was definitely wrong. Although Andrea was smiling as she led the way to the kitchen, Hannah could tell by her sister's stiff posture that she was barely holding herself together.

"What is it?" Hannah asked, the moment the swinging, restaurant-style door had closed behind them.

"It's Bill!" Andrea took a deep breath and tried to control herself, but she seemed unable to keep up the façade and she dissolved in tears.

Hannah imagined the worst. "He's all right, isn't he? I mean . . . he didn't have an accident or anything, did he?"

Andrea shook her head, but she was crying so hard, she couldn't speak.

"You're shaking your head no." Hannah could have kicked herself for asking two opposing questions. "Does that mean no, Bill's not all right? Or no, Bill didn't have an accident?"

Andrea took another deep breath and swallowed noisily. "Bill didn't have an accident. And he's all right . . . but I'm not!"

"What's wrong with you?" Hannah asked, her anxiety growing. It was obvious that Andrea was very upset.

"I'm afraid Bill will make the wrong decision. Or maybe it'll be the right decision for him, but it'll turn out to be the wrong decision for me." Andrea sniffled and wiped her eyes with a tissue that was so wet and ragged, it was almost unrecognizable.

"Here," Hannah said, grabbing a stack of napkins from the supply cart against the wall and handing them to her sister.

"If he says yes, there aren't enough tissues in the whole world!" Andrea wailed, grabbing several napkins from the top of the stack and wiping her eyes.

This was a crisis of the highest magnitude. Hannah knew that because Andrea had just smeared both eyeliner and mascara. "Hold on," she said. "We need coffee."

It only took a moment for Hannah to fill two cups from the kitchen coffee pot and carry them to the workstation. Then she made another trip to the baker's rack beside the oven, scooped up a half-dozen of Lisa's Chocolate Sugar Cookies, and transferred them to a plate.

"Eat," she ordered, setting the plate in front of her sister.

"I'm not h . . . hungry."

Hannah could tell that more tears were imminent by the quaver in her sister's voice. "You don't have to be hungry. Just eat a cookie. It's medicinal."

The *I'm-your-big-sister-and-I-know-best* tone in Hannah's voice must have been convincing, because Andrea picked up a cookie and ate it. When the first cookie had disappeared, Hannah pushed the plate closer, and Andrea took another.

"Coffee," Hannah instructed, pointing to the mug she'd set in front of her sister. "Take a sip of coffee to wash down that second cookie, and then tell me all about it."

Andrea didn't argue. She just did as Hannah directed. And then she let out a quavering sigh. "It's Bill," she said, repeating what she'd said earlier.

"You told me that. What about Bill?"

"He's been . . ." Andrea stopped and cleared her throat. "He's been offered a new job!"

"As Managing Sheriff of the Tri-County Area?" Hannah hazarded a guess.

"No! That'd be wonderful. If they offered him that job, I'd want him to accept right away. But they didn't. And this job isn't wonderful. This job is just . . . just awful!"

"If it's that awful, he shouldn't take it," Hannah said reasonably.

"I know that. But I'm not sure *Bill* knows that. You see, it's almost double the money, and he'd have his own practically unlimited expense account. And the benefits are even better than the ones he has now."

Hannah began to frown. "I must be missing something here. What you just described sounds like everybody's dream job. What's so awful about it?"

"It's not the job that's so awful. It's just that it's for Tachyon."

"What's Tachyon?" Hannah asked, managing, somehow,

to curb her impatience. Getting information from Andrea could be a long, painful process.

"It's a big security corporation. Bill got a call from them this afternoon and they offered him a job heading up their quality control division."

Hannah felt a bit like someone trying to put a jigsaw puzzle together without the picture on the cover of the box. Andrea was feeding her pieces of information, but she was far from seeing the whole picture. "Why is Tachyon interested in Bill?" she asked, hoping for another piece to help her complete the puzzle.

"They liked the work he did for them last year. Tachyon makes security devices, and they test them by sending out samples to law enforcement agencies all across the country. The feedback they get tells them how to make the products better."

Hannah remembered the security cameras that Mike had been testing. "Did Tachyon make the security cameras that Mike was testing for the department?"

"Yes. They make all sorts of things for home and office security. Bill brought home one of their touchpad locks, but that didn't work out for us."

"Why not?"

"Peanut butter gums up the whole thing and there's no good way to clean it out. Bill put that in his notes. *Not recommended for families with small children.* He was in charge of compiling all the reports from the Minnesota law enforcement agencies and transmitting them to Tachyon. They were so impressed with his suggestions they called him up to offer him the job."

"He didn't accept, did he?"

"No, but he hasn't turned them down yet, either." Andrea's eyes began to glisten and she blinked back fresh tears. "I know it's a great opportunity, but I don't want to move!"

She'd finally struck pay dirt with her questions! Hannah

came close to shouting *Eureka!* but she managed to restrain herself. Instead she posed a question. "Why would you have to move if Bill takes the job with Tachyon?"

"Because they want him to work at headquarters, and Tachyon headquarters is in Fort Lauderdale, Florida. I don't want to move away when my whole family is here in Lake Eden!"

"Of course you don't." Hannah reached out to pat her sister's hand.

"And . . . and besides, they've got crocodiles in Florida!"

"Alligators, not crocodiles," Hannah corrected her.

"Whatever. They're slimy green things with big teeth, and sometimes they even knock on the door. I saw that on the news. A woman went to answer the door and when she opened it, there was a big crocodile!"

"Alligator. I saw that, too."

"Then you can understand how I feel. What if Tracey answered the door. Or Bethie. She can turn the knob now, and Grandma McCann can't kept an eye on her every minute of the day. If we moved to Florida, Bethie could end up being some crocodile's dinner!"

"Take it easy, Andrea." Hannah didn't bother making the alligator correction a third time. It didn't really matter what Andrea called the carnivorous swamp dweller. It was still scary, and Hannah could understand why Andrea was upset.

"You understand, don't you?" Andrea paused to take a deep breath. "I don't want to move. I just know I'd hate it there. But at the same time this could be a big career move for Bill, and I don't want to stand in his way."

"I understand perfectly," Hannah said, wondering what she'd do if she were faced with a similar dilemma. Andrea was caught between husband and family, torn between her duty and her desire. Hannah hadn't thought it could ever happen, but it made her own dilemma of trying to choose between the two men she loved seem practically trivial in comparison.

CHOCOLATE SUGAR COOKIES

Preheat oven to 325 degrees F., rack
in the middle position.

2 cups melted butter *(4 sticks, one pound)*
4 one-ounce squares semi-sweet chocolate *(I used
  Baker's)*
2 cups powdered sugar *(not sifted)*
1 cup white sugar
2 eggs
2 teaspoons vanilla
1 teaspoon orange zest *(optional)*
1 teaspoon baking soda
1 teaspoon cream of tartar *(critical!)*
1 teaspoon salt
4¼ cups flour *(not sifted)*
½ cup white sugar in a small bowl *(for later)*

Melt the butter and chocolate squares in a saucepan
over low heat, stirring constantly, or in the microwave. *(I
melted mine in a quart measuring cup in the microwave
on HIGH for 3 minutes.)* Once the butter and chocolate
are melted, stir them smooth, transfer them to a large mixing bowl, and add the powdered and white sugars. Stir
thoroughly and set the mixture aside to cool.

When the mixture is cool enough so it won't cook the
eggs, add the eggs, one at a time, stirring after each addition.
(You can use an electric mixer at this point if you like.)
Then mix in the vanilla, orange zest, *(if you decided to use*

it) baking soda, cream of tartar, and salt. Mix it all up together.

Add flour in half-cup increments, mixing after each addition. You don't have to be precise—just divide your flour into roughly 4 parts. *(One very important reason for adding flour in increments is so that the whole mountain of flour won't sit there on top of your bowl and spill out all over the place when you try to stir it in.)*

Once the dough has been thoroughly mixed, roll one-inch dough balls with your fingers. *(You can also use a 2-teaspoon scooper to form the dough balls).* Dip the balls in the bowl of white sugar and roll them around until they're coated.

Place the dough balls on a greased cookie sheet, *(I usually spray mine with Pam or another nonstick cooking spray,)* 12 dough balls to a standard-size sheet. Flatten the dough balls a bit with your impeccably clean palm so that they won't roll off the cookie sheet on the way to the oven.

Bake the Chocolate Sugar Cookies at 325 degrees for 10 to 15 minutes. *(Mine took 12 minutes.)* Cool them on the cookie sheet for 2 minutes and then remove the cookies to a wire rack to finish cooling.

Yield: Approximately 7 to 8 dozen fudgy, melt-in-your-mouth, sugar cookies.

Chapter Five

"Remind me not to order that again," Mike said, pulling into the alley that ran past the back of The Cookie Jar.

"You didn't like your peanut butter pepper burger?"

"It was . . . interesting."

Hannah laughed. "That word covers a multitude of put-downs."

"That's true." Mike pulled into the parking lot at the back of The Cookie Jar, parked next to Hannah's cookie truck, and grabbed the bag of burgers they'd brought for what Hannah thought of as the Beeseman-Herman clan. "Beautiful night," he said, looking up at the night sky.

"Yes." Hannah looked up at the myriad of stars shining brilliantly overhead. After a day that had topped the eighties, the temperature had dropped to the low seventies and the air felt cool, a rarity in Minnesota where the difference between the high and low in the summer was seldom more than a few degrees.

There was a low sound as Hannah passed Herb's cruiser. It was midway between a whimper and a bark, and she moved a few steps closer. The windows were down, and she could see Herb and Lisa's puppy on a rug in the back bench seat. "Hi, Dillon," she said. "What are you doing out here all alone?"

Dillon stared at her with sad puppy-dog eyes, and Hannah would have reached in to pet him, but she knew that Herb was training him and she didn't want to break any rules. "I'll come back with a treat," she promised, "if Daddy says it's all right."

"Poor little guy's probably lonely out here," Mike said. "Why don't you ask Herb if he can come in?"

"I would if you weren't here. It's against health board regulations."

"I'm not the health board."

"Then it's okay?"

"It's okay by me. Besides, Herb's training him to be a police dog. Police dogs can go anywhere they're needed."

"And Dillon is needed inside?"

"I'd say so. Somebody might break in and try to steal those apple turnovers you're making. If that happens, Herb and I might need a little police dog assistance."

Hannah gave Mike an approving look. When he'd first come to Lake Eden, he'd been a "by-the-book" cop. He'd moved here from Minneapolis, and big city police departments had to be stricter and their officers were expected to follow regulations to the letter. It had taken quite a while for Mike to learn that things were more relaxed in Lake Eden, and the rules were tempered by common sense.

When Hannah and Mike opened the back door of The Cookie Jar, a delightful scent rolled out to meet them. Hannah identified cinnamon, cardamom, and apples baking in what she was sure was a buttery crust.

"Mmmm," Mike said with a sigh, taking a big gulping breath of the heady scent. "Nothing smells better than apple pie in the oven."

"They're apple turnovers," Marge corrected him.

"I know, Mrs. Beeseman. Hannah told me. But it smells like my mom's kitchen during apple-picking season. She used to make at least a dozen pies a day."

"Did she sell them?"

"No, they were for the freezer. Apple pie was my dad's favorite and he always wanted it for Sunday dinner."

"Your Mom must have used cinnamon, nutmeg, and cardamom," Lisa told him. "That's what Marge uses."

Mike shrugged. "I guess she must have because it sure reminds me of home. My mouth's watering and my stomach's growling, and I just had a full meal."

"My stomach's growling and my mouth's watering, too," Jack Herman, Lisa's father, spoke up. He was a tall, silver-haired man in his sixties who'd been diagnosed with Alzheimer's disease a little over two years ago. When Lisa had married Herb, Marge had given them her house as a wedding present. She'd moved in with Lisa's father and had become his primary caretaker so that Lisa would be free to enjoy married life with her son.

Normally, in a small town the size of Lake Eden, people would have voiced loud disapproval of a widow who moved in with a widower without benefit of marriage. In Jack Herman and Marge Beeseman's case, there wasn't a breath of censure, or even gossip. Everyone in Lake Eden liked Herb. He was their town marshal in charge of parking enforcement. And everyone thought Lisa was a sweet, selfless young woman for giving up her college scholarship to stay home and take care of her dad. Both Jack Herman and Marge Beeseman were respected members of the community, and if they wanted to share a house, that was fine with Lake Edenites.

"Your stomach's growling because you haven't had supper," Marge said, smiling at Jack. Then she turned to her sister Patsy, who also lived with them. "Don't start thawing that next batch of puff pastry. We'll take a break to eat and then we'll get right back to it."

Hannah handed the bag of burgers to Marge, and then she turned to Herb. "How about Dillon? Is it okay if he comes inside for a cookie?"

Herb glanced at Mike. "How about the health regulations?" he asked.

"They don't apply to special needs dogs or police dogs," Mike told him.

"Great! Will you open the door, Hannah? I'll call him."

"Sure, but he's inside your cruiser."

"That's okay. The windows are down. Just open the door and watch what happens."

Hannah opened the back door. "What now?" she asked Herb.

"Now I call him." Herb pulled a silver whistle from his pocket and put it to his lips. Hannah listened but the whistle didn't make a sound.

"Is it broken?" Patsy asked.

"No, it's a dog whistle. It's such a high frequency humans can't hear it." Herb raised the whistle again. "Step aside, Hannah. He'll come barreling in any second."

Herb blew the whistle again and Hannah heard a thump outside as Dillon hit the ground running. A second later he raced in the door, skidded to a stop in front of Herb, and sat down on his haunches.

"Good boy!" Herb praised him. And then he patted Dillon on the head and scratched him behind the ears.

"Impressive," Mike said. "There's only one thing I'm wondering about."

"What's that?"

"Will Dillon come to anybody who blows a dog whistle?"

"No, not unless they know the code."

"This little dog knows codes?" Jack asked, looking astounded.

"Just one, and I guess it can't hurt to tell you. It's three blasts on the dog whistle, a pause, and then two more blasts. That's the only thing he responds to. Any other combination of whistles and he just sits there waiting."

"Smart." Mike said.

"Very smart," Jack agreed, eyeing the bag of hamburgers on the counter. "Is there a hamburger for . . . what was his name again, son?"

"Dillon," Herb told him.

"Right. And it's for Marshal Dillon. I keep thinking it's Field Marshal Montgomery, but he's British and my grand-dog's not British. Dillon's foreign, but he's from Labrador."

Herb and Lisa laughed, and Jack looked pleased. "But he's only half Labrador. The other half's . . . what is it again?"

"Jack Russell Terrier," Lisa told him, "and heaven only knows what else is in there."

"It doesn't matter. He's a handsome guy." Hannah went to the kitchen cabinet and took out a box of dog treats. "Can he have one of these, Herb?"

"Yes, but he won't take it."

"Why? Jon Walker's dog, Skippy, just loves them."

"Oh, Dillon would love one, but he won't take it unless I say it's all right. Go ahead and try to give it to him."

Hannah walked over to Dillon with the dog treat and held it out. "Here you go, Dillon. Have a treat."

Anyone watching could tell that Dillon wanted the treat. He gave a soft little whimper, but he turned his head away.

"Try again," Herb said.

"Here, Dillon." Hannah waved the treat under his rose. "It's really good and it's yours."

Dillon turned his head away for the second time, and Herb gave a proud smile. Then he said to Hannah, "Okay, try it again. This time I'll tell him it's okay."

Hannah held out the treat. "Do you want this?"

"It's okay, Dillon," Herb said, and Dillon gently took the treat from Hannah's hand.

"That's *really* impressive," Hannah said. "Do you train cats?"

Everyone laughed, including Herb, who finally stopped chuckling enough to speak. "If you're talking about Moishe, the answer is no. Moishe's a very smart cat. If I tried to train Moishe, he'd end up training *me*!"

"What's the count?" Hannah asked at a few minutes past ten.

"Two hundred forty," Lisa answered, picking up the last tray to come out of the oven and carrying it to the baker's rack. "Do you think I should freeze these while they're still warm?"

"Wait until morning," Marge told her. "They'll get ice crystals if you freeze them while they're warm. Cover them with a sheet of wax paper until morning, and then wrap and freeze them."

Hannah stood up and stretched her back. "You're the boss, Marge," she said, wiping down the work surface. She stopped as she came to the apple peeler that Marge and Jack had brought with them. "Do you want to take this home with you?"

"No sense in that," Patsy said, also standing and stretching. "We're just going to use it tomorrow night. Can you stick it in that industrial dishwasher of yours and save it for us when we come down here tomorrow night?"

"Sure, but are you sure you want to do this again tomorrow?"

Patsy laughed. "We'd better. Mrs. Mayor said she needed turnovers for the talent show, Casino Night, and Donkey Baseball. I figure that's got to add up to seven hundred, maybe even a thousand."

"You're right," Mike offered his opinion. "Anybody who eats one at intermission tomorrow night is going to want another one on Casino Night and another at Donkey Baseball. People are going to be talking about how good these turnovers are. That's word of mouth and it's going to send sales through the roof."

"So you like my apple turnovers?" Marge asked him.

"They're even better than my . . ." Mike stopped and looked as guilty as a small boy with his hand caught in the cookie jar. "Don't tell anybody I said this, okay? Mom's apple pie is great. I love Mom's apple pie. But your apple turnovers are even better!"

MARGE'S APPLE TURNOVERS

Hannah's 1st Note: Marge uses commercial puff pastry dough for her turnover crusts. She says life's too short to spend all day making puff pastry. She buys it frozen in sheets and thaws it as she needs it. One batch makes 8 turnovers, and Marge uses one 17.5-ounce package. Florence down at the Red Owl carries Pepperidge Farm frozen puff pastry dough and it contains 2 sheets.

If you'd rather, you can use pie crust dough. Just remember to roll it out a little thicker than you would for a regular pie since it won't be in a pie pan.

The Crust
　　One 17.5-ounce package frozen puff pastry dough
　　1 egg
　　1 Tablespoon water
　　White *(granulated)* sugar to sprinkle on top

Apple Filling:
　　4 and ½ cups cored, peeled, sliced, and chopped
　　　　apples *(I used 2 large Granny Smith apples and*
　　　　2 large Fuji or Gala apples)
　　½ cup sweetened dried cranberries *(I used*
　　　　Craisins)
　　1 Tablespoon lemon juice
　　⅓ cup white *(granulated)* sugar
　　¼ cup flour
　　¼ teaspoon ground nutmeg *(freshly ground is best,*
　　　　of course)

¼ teaspoon cinnamon *(if it's been sitting in your cupboard for years, buy fresh!)*
¼ teaspoon cardamom
¼ teaspoon salt

Thaw your puff pastry dough according to package directions. Do this on a floured board.

While your pastry is thawing, core and peel the apples. Slice them as you would for a pie and then cut the slices into 3 pieces. Place the apples in a large mixing bowl and mix in the sweetened dried cranberries. Sprinkle the fruit with 1 Tablespoon of lemon juice to keep the apples from browning. Toss the mixture around with your fingers to make sure all the apples are moistened.

Mix the sugar, flour, spices, and salt together in a small bowl.

Dump the bowl with the dry ingredients on top of the apples and toss them to coat the apples. *(You can use your fingers – it's easier)*

Preheat the oven to 400 degrees F., rack in the middle position.

When your puff pastry has thawed, roll half of it out to a twelve-inch square on a floured board. Use a sharp knife to make one horizontal line through the middle of the square and one vertical line through the middle of the square. This will divide it into 4 equal *(or nearly equal)* pieces.

Break the egg into a cup. Add 1 Tablespoon of water and whisk it up. This will be your egg wash.

Line a cookie sheet with a piece of parchment paper.

Transfer one square of puff pastry dough to the cookie sheet.

Use a pastry brush to brush the inside edges of the square with the egg wash. This will make the edges stick together when you fold the dough over the apples.

With a slotted spoon, pick up approximately ½ cup of the filling (*¼ cup for the smaller turnovers*) and place it in the center of the square.

Pull one corner of the square over the filling to the opposite corner of the square, forming a triangle. Press the edges together.

Use the tines of a fork to seal the edges together.

Coat the top of the turnover with egg wash, using a pastry brush.

Cut two slits in the top of the turnover with a sharp knife. The slits should be about an inch long. *(This is a very important step. Not only does it let out the steam when the turnovers bake, releasing a delicious aroma that'll have the neighbors knocking at your door, it also gives everyone a peek at the delicious filling when it's time to serve dessert.)*

Follow the same procedure to fill and seal the remaining three turnovers.

Roll out the second sheet of puff pastry and cut it into squares. Transfer the squares to the baking sheet, and fill and seal the remaining turnovers.

When all the turnovers have been filled, sealed, and brushed with egg wash, sprinkle the tops with white sugar.

Bake your turnovers at 400 degrees F. for 25 minutes, or until they're golden brown on top.

Remove the cookie sheet to a wire rack and let the turnovers cool for 5 minutes. Then pull the parchment paper and the turnovers off the cookie sheet and onto a waiting wire rack.

These turnovers are delicious eaten while slightly warm. They're also good cold.

If any turnovers are left over *(fat chance at my house!)* wrap them loosely in wax paper and keep them in a cool place. The next day you can reheat them in the oven.

Chapter Six

The dimly-lit garage smelled of wet concrete blocks, soaked by yesterday's midafternoon rain shower, lingering exhaust fumes from recently departed vehicles, and a potpourri of coffee grounds and old orange peels from the dumpster that sat against the far wall. It wasn't the stuff that perfumes are made of, but to Hannah it smelled like home.

Mike took her arm and walked her to the set of steps leading up to ground level. This took them past the dumpster and Hannah noticed that he wrinkled his nose. "Tomorrow's garbage day?" he asked.

"That's right. Every Tuesday morning."

"I thought so. Something's getting a little ripe in there." Mike walked her to the covered staircase that led up to her second-floor condo.

"Coffee?" Hannah asked when they arrived at her door, even though every tired muscle in her body was screaming for the comfort of a soft mattress and as many hours sleep as she could get. The last thing she wanted tonight was company, but it was only polite to offer.

"No coffee for me, thanks. It's almost eleven and you need your sleep. I just want to make sure everything's okay inside and you're locked in safe for the night."

Hannah felt a warm glow start at her toes and move up

her body to the top of her head. That was nice of Mike. Ever since she'd almost been killed six months ago, he'd been acting as her protector. And she could swear that he was making a real effort to curb his self-centered tendencies and put her concerns first. In her uncharitable moments, she thought it was probably because he was between girlfriends. And in her generous moments, she was sure that he really did love her to the exclusion of all others. Since she was a level-headed woman who saw the glass as neither half empty nor half full, but rather a glass with something in it and room to pour in more, she figured Mike's true motivation was somewhere between the two extremes.

Mike took the keys she handed him and unlocked the door. They both prepared to catch Moishe as he hurtled through the air into waiting arms, but no orange and white cat leaped through the doorway.

"He's probably snuggled up on the couch with Cuddles," Hannah said.

Mike stepped in and turned back to her. "You're right. Neither one of them is moving an inch. They're too comfortable."

"They certainly are!" Hannah followed Mike inside, and they stopped to pet the cats and scratch them under their chins. When both Moishe and Cuddles were purring blissfully, Mike moved on and Hannah stayed a few steps behind him.

"It was great the way you helped Jack with the apple peeler," Hannah said, once Mike had checked the guest bathroom.

"That used to be my job when Mom made pies." Mike opened the door to the guest room and bent to check under the bed. He made a move to open the closet, but Hannah grabbed his arm.

"Don't!" she said.

"Why not?"

"Because something will fall out. It's overflowing with stuff I should have packed off to the thrift store years ago."

"But someone might be . . ."

"Hiding in there?" Hannah gave a little laugh as she interrupted him. "Impossible. There isn't room for one more thing."

"Okay. If you say so." Mike moved on to her bedroom. The first thing he did was head for her closet. "Is it okay to check in here?" he asked.

"Yes. Everything I cleaned out of here is in the guest room closet." Hannah was silent as Mike opened her closet and checked for intruders. When he'd slid the doors closed again, she followed him to her bathroom and waited while he checked that. "You made Jack feel good, asking him about the little animals he carves."

"It was interesting. He knows a lot about wildlife."

"Well, thank you for being so nice to him. Everybody there appreciated it."

As they walked back down the hallway, Mike slipped his arm around her and gave her a little hug. "You don't have to thank me for being nice to Jack. I like Jack. It's true he's losing it a little, but he's still got more on the ball than a lot of people."

"That's true."

"I like everyone who was at The Cookie Jar tonight. Lisa's like the girl next door. She's sweet, and nice, and . . . and wholesome. And Herb's a true-blue Minnesota guy. He'd give you the shirt off his back if you needed it. And then there's Marge. She's got a big heart and she wants to help everybody. And I think Patsy's the same way. It makes me feel good to be around people like that."

Hannah smiled. "So you changed your mind about living in Lake Eden?"

"What do you mean?"

"When you first moved here, you thought it was too small, that it would be like living in a fishbowl."

Mike shrugged. "Well, it *is* like living in a fishbowl. But I really don't mind. I like almost everybody here in Lake Eden."

"Everybody?" Hannah couldn't resist teasing him a little.

Mike shrugged. "I said almost everybody. I even like Bertie Straub . . . in small doses."

Hannah laughed. Bertie wasn't shy about giving people advice, and she didn't have a tactful bone in her body. She'd decided that her niece was the right woman for Mike even though Mike wasn't interested. And every time she saw Mike, she tried to force the issue.

Mike opened the hall closet, glancing inside, and shut it again. Then he checked out the kitchen and the laundry room. "Everything looks good," he told her.

"Great. Thanks for coming in to check." Hannah led him to the door, but she didn't open it. Instead, she stepped closer and gave him a little hug. It was intended as a thank-you hug, the kind of hug you'd give your brother-in-law if he'd just fixed your garbage disposal. But Mike must not have recognized the imaginary blue band around the generic hug, because he pulled her up tight against him and tipped her face up to kiss her.

Uh-oh, he's got the wrong idea, Hannah thought as their kiss deepened. And a few seconds later, she thought, *Uh-oh, he's got the RIGHT idea!* And she knew she'd better break things up quickly.

"Sorry," Mike said, stepping away before she could even consider how to achieve the same result.

"That's okay," Hannah said, hoping the little quaver in her voice didn't give away how captivated she'd been.

"I'd better go now, while I still can." Mike walked to the door and turned. "You know I love you, don't you?"

Hannah nodded. She knew Mike loved her . . . in his own way. She loved him too, but Mike's love wasn't exactly monogamous. Of course her love wasn't exactly monogamous either since she also loved Norman. It was . . . complicated. Very complicated.

"I've got no right loving you. Not when I'm such a jerk." Mike stopped speaking and sighed deeply. "I don't know what's wrong with me, Hannah. You're the best thing that's happened to me since my wife died, and I keep goofing it up right and left. It's like I don't want to succeed in love again. And as long as I'm fickle, I don't have to try."

Hannah didn't know what to say. Mike was being brutally honest. Everything he'd said was true. "I . . . I think I understand," she said.

"You're too good for me, Hannah. If you hook up with me, I'm just going to break your heart. You should marry Norman. He loves you. I'm sure about that. Norman's a really nice guy and he'll treat you right."

Again, Hannah was at a loss for words. She just stared at Mike, wondering what he'd say next. And then she realized what he'd already said. "You want me to marry *Norman?*"

"No! It's not what I want, that's for sure. But I think you *should* marry Norman. I know you want to get married. I've seen you with Tracey and Bethie, and I can tell you want kids of your own. Norman would make a great father."

"True," Hannah said, giving a tight little nod. "But I don't want to get married to *anyone!* Not now. Maybe not ever. And you can't palm me off on Norman like I'm some kind of bad poker hand!"

"I wasn't . . ."

"Yes, you were!" Hannah interrupted him. "You were being all selfless and sweet, and trying to pull the wool over my eyes."

"What wool? What are you talking about?"

"You don't want to marry me anymore, and this is a good way of breaking up with me. It makes you look like the good guy. Why don't you just come out and say that you don't want to marry me anymore?"

"But I *do!* I just don't think I'd do right by you, that's all." Mike put his hand on the doorknob, but he didn't open it. Instead he turned back for a final word. "I'd be the happiest man in the world if you'd marry me, Hannah. I can't think of anything that would be better for me. But it wouldn't be better for you. You'd be miserable if you married me. Every time I turned around to look at a pretty woman, you'd wonder if I was going to make a move on her when you weren't around. Think about it, Hannah. I've already let you down a couple of times in the past, and you'd have to be the biggest fool on earth to take a chance on me."

And with that said, Mike pulled her into his arms and kissed her until her mind was spinning with joyful abandon.

There was no way of telling how long the kiss lasted. And there was no way of doubting that Mike desired her. It was a lover's kiss, a way of communicating the closeness they both felt. Hannah reveled in the feeling for breathless moments and then . . . suddenly . . . Mike was gone, and she realized that she was standing there alone with her fingertips touching her lips, swaying slightly, savoring the memory.

"Oh," Hannah gave a soft little cry. Mike was willing to sacrifice his own happiness to keep her from making what he thought would be a dreadful mistake. She felt like running after him, throwing her arms around him, and . . .

The feel of warm fur brushing against her ankles brought her out of her imaginings and back in touch with reality. Was Mike putting her on? Was this a little game he was playing? Did he want her to feel so sorry for him, she'd race after him, tell him it didn't matter, and melt into his arms?

Hannah pondered the questions for a moment, and then she sighed deeply. There was no way she could know for sure. Thank goodness Norman was coming back soon! Of course she'd never ask Norman for advice on her relationship with Mike, but just knowing that Norman was there, steady and loving, gave an anchor to her confused emotions.

And that was when she saw that the red light on her remote phone was blinking rhythmically. She'd missed a call working late at The Cookie Jar and she hadn't noticed it when she'd come in with Mike.

Hannah took time to reach down and pet the two cats, and then she headed for the end table by the couch to play back her message on the remote phone system she'd bought when her old-fashioned answer machine had finally given up the ghost.

"Hi, Hannah. It's Norman." At the first sound of Norman's voice, Cuddles jumped up on her lap and tried to lick the phone. "It's your daddy," Hannah said, holding the phone a little closer so that Cuddles could hear.

"It's almost seven and I guess you're out somewhere for dinner. I'm just getting ready to leave the hotel and meet my friends for dinner."

Hannah frowned slightly. Norman's voice sounded strained, but perhaps that was the connection.

"If it's not too much trouble, can you keep Cuddles for another night? I'm going to stay over one more day. I have a couple of things I have to do and it's going to take me longer than I expected. I'll be back on Thursday and I'll pick up Cuddles on Thursday after work." There was a pause and Norman cleared his throat. "Oh, yes. I already talked to Doc Bennett and he's coming in to work for me, so you don't have to worry about that."

Hannah's frown deepened. Perhaps it was just her imagination, but Norman didn't sound very happy. And he should have been happy meeting up with all his friends from dental school again.

"I guess that's it." Norman cleared his throat again. "Have a nice evening. 'Bye."

No *I love you*? No *I miss you*? No *I'm thinking about you and I wish you were with me*? Hannah replaced the phone in the charging station with a frown. She wasn't sure what had happened to Norman in Minneapolis, but something was definitely wrong.

Of course she couldn't go to bed, not with one boyfriend confusing the dickens out of her by wanting to marry her but claiming he was saving her from herself by pushing her into another man's arms, and the other boyfriend suffering with an unknown problem in Minneapolis, a problem that made him sound like a stranger instead of a man who could hardly wait to get back to her. In a situation like this, there was only one thing to do and she knew exactly what it was. She had to bake.

Hannah hurried to the kitchen and opened the pantry to survey the ingredients she had on hand. She'd received a recipe last month from a friend she'd known in college. History major Katie Strehler had always attended class with a to-go cup of coffee in her hand. She'd been an even bigger coffee drinker than Hannah, and if Katie said her Mocha Nut Butterballs satisfied that coffee urge, Hannah certainly wasn't about to doubt her. She'd already stocked up on the ingredients she needed to make Katie's cookies. They were on the top shelf, along with the recipe. Hannah read it through again to make sure she had everything, and then she carried it all out to the kitchen counter.

It didn't take long to mix up the dough, and within five minutes Hannah had the first pan in the oven. Since it was silly to try a new recipe without at least tasting it, she put on a fresh pot of coffee and sat down at the kitchen table to wait for the cookies to come out of the oven. She'd just slipped the second pan into the oven and was preparing to roll the cooled cookies in powdered sugar when the door opened and Michelle came in.

"It's almost midnight!" Michelle said, spotting Hannah at the kitchen counter. "Can't you sleep?"

"I can't sleep quite yet. I have to wait for another couple of pans of cookies to come out of the oven."

Michelle sniffed the air appreciatively. "They smell great. What are they?"

"Mocha Nut Butterballs. Do you want to try one?"

"Sure." Michelle tossed her purse on the table and went to the coffee pot to pour herself a cup. "I'll help you bake the rest. I'm too mad to go to sleep."

"Why are you mad?"

"It's Lonnie. He's being a real pain about wanting to get engaged right away. I think he's afraid I'm going out with someone else."

"Are you?" Hannah asked the important question.

"I was, but I'm not right now. It's just that I want to keep my options open. I don't want to be tied down at this point in my life."

"Mmm," Hannah commented, keeping it neutral as she filled a plate with cookies. "Have a cookie and tell me what you think."

Michelle took a cookie and bit into it. She gave a little moan of delight and popped the remainder into her mouth. "I've got three words to describe them."

"And they are . . . ?"

"Mocha. Butter. Yum!"

"That's good enough for me," Hannah said, taking a cookie for herself. "So what are you going to do about Lonnie?"

"I don't know."

"Do you love him?"

Michelle took another cookie. "Yes, I love him. But he's demanding too much of me. Maybe next year, or the year after. But not right now. I'm still trying out my wings."

"I know," Hannah said, hoping those wings weren't flapping anywhere near Bradford Ramsey. One broken Swensen heart was enough.

"Men!" Michelle muttered around her third cookie. "You can't live with them, and you can't live without them."

"That's true, but it's okay."

"It is?" Michelle turned to stare at her.

"Sure it is . . . as long as the Mocha Nut Butterballs hold out."

MOCHA NUT BUTTERBALLS

Preheat oven to 325 degrees F., rack
in the middle position.

1 cup softened butter *(2 sticks, ½ pound)*
½ cup white *(granulated)* sugar
1 teaspoon vanilla extract
1 Tablespoon instant coffee powder *(I used espresso
  powder)****
¼ cup cocoa powder *(I used Hershey's)*
¼ teaspoon salt
1 and ¾ cups all-purpose flour *(no need to sift)*
1 and ½ cups finely chopped pecans ****

---

powdered sugar *(that's confectioner's sugar)* to coat
  the baked cookies

*** - *If the only instant coffee you can get comes in
granules or beads, crush them up into a powder with the
back of a spoon before you add them to the cookie dough.*

**** - *Mother likes these with chopped walnuts. An-
drea prefers pecans. I think they're best with hazelnuts.
Tracey adores these when I substitute flaked coconut for
the nuts and form the dough balls around a small piece of
milk chocolate.*

Soften the butter. Mix in the white sugar, vanilla extract, instant coffee powder, cocoa, and salt.

Add the flour in half-cup increments, mixing after each
addition. *(You don't have to be exact. It won't come out*

even anyway! Just make sure the flour is added in three parts.)

Stir in the nuts. Do your best to make sure that they're evenly distributed.

Form the dough into one-inch balls *(just pat them into shape with your fingers)* and place them on an ungreased baking sheet, 12 to a standard sheet. Press them down very slightly *(they're supposed to look like balls, but you don't want them to roll off on their way to the oven.)*

Bake the cookie balls at 325 degrees F. for 12 to 15 minutes, until they are set. *(Mine took 14 minutes.)*

Move the cookies from the cookie sheet to a wire rack. Let them cool on the rack completely.

When the cookies are completely cool, dip them in powdered sugar to coat them. *(If you roll them in powdered sugar while they're still warm, they have a tendency to break apart.)* Let them rest for several minutes on the wire rack and then store them in a cookie jar or a covered container.

Yield: Makes 3 to 4 dozen simply amazing cookies.

Hannah's 1st Note: After Michelle ate almost half a batch, she had a suggestion. She's going to try making them and rolling them in sweetened powdered chocolate instead of

powdered sugar. She thinks Ghirardelli makes a sweetened powdered chocolate that will work.

Hannah's 2nd Note: I think these cookies would be incredibly tasty dipped in melted chocolate. Too bad there aren't any left so that I can try it.

Chapter Seven

Hannah put on her sleep shirt, rested her head on the pillow, shut her eyes, and the alarm went off. At least that was the sequence as she perceived it. A little subtraction, not as simple as one might think this early in the morning, proved her wrong. She'd actually gotten a grand total of four and a half hours sleep. It wasn't enough. Her eyes still felt scratchy, and all of her muscles ached, not entirely because Moishe and Cuddles had tried to commandeer the entire mattress.

She forced her feet to cross the room and step into the tiled bathroom. Then she willed her hand to turn on the water in the shower. Seconds later, she was sputtering under the forceful spray, alive and awake enough to realize that she'd forgotten to turn on the knob for the hot water and she was still wearing her sleep shirt.

Hannah turned off the water, peeled herself out of the wet garment, and adjusted the temperature of the spray. After she'd taken her shower, she hung up her soggy sleep shirt on the showerhead to dry. Five minutes later, dressed in jeans and a blouse, she padded into the kitchen in her slippers only to realize that the coffee she'd set to go off automatically last night was half gone.

"Good morning, Hannah. Sit down. I'll get your coffee."

Hannah turned toward the voice. She blinked. Once, twice, and then she gave a half-hearted wave. Michelle was sitting at the kitchen table holding a mug of coffee, and she looked as fresh as a croissant that had just come out of the oven. Her eyes were clear, her hair was glossy, and she was dressed in a pair of white slacks and a crisp yellow blouse.

As she watched, Michelle jumped up and headed for the coffee pot. Hannah sat down on a chair and pondered an important question. It was obvious that Michelle had been up for a while. She'd curled her hair and put on makeup. How could anyone look so beautiful after so little sleep? Michele was lovely in the morning, and that made Hannah feel old and ugly in comparison.

"I made breakfast," Michelle said, carrying Hannah's coffee to the table and setting it down. "It's just scrambled eggs and cheese. Would you like some?"

Hannah nodded. She was incapable of speech. Michelle had gotten up so early she'd had time to make breakfast. Not only was she beautiful at this ridiculously early hour of the morning, she was also organized and energetic.

"Is something the matter?" Michelle asked.

"Why?"

"Because you're staring at me."

"I'm just envious."

"Of *me*?" Michelle looked shocked.

"Yes. It's only a few minutes past four-thirty in the morning and you went to bed the same time I did. I'm still dragging around, barely awake, and you're dressed with your hair done. Not only that, you've already cooked breakfast, and you look stunning. If you weren't my baby sister and I didn't love you so much, I'd probably hate you."

The day was busy, as all days at The Cookie Jar were, and Hannah was relieved when they locked the front door at five in the evening. No sooner had they thrown the lock when there was a knock at the back door, and Marge, Jack, Patsy, Herb, and Dillon came in. While they set up at the workstation in the kitchen, Hannah arranged the BLTs she'd made on a platter and carried them to the coffee shop. Then she called everyone in to eat, including Dillon who stretched out on the floor between Herb and Lisa and munched on the extra bacon that Hannah had made for him.

Once they'd finished eating, they went back to the kitchen to make turnovers. They'd worked steadily for what seemed like at least an hour when the phone rang. Lisa hurried to answer it and after listening to the caller for a moment, she motioned to Hannah. "It's for you," Lisa told her, holding out the receiver.

"Coming." Hannah dried her hands on a towel and glanced at the clock. The apple turnover assembly line had been working longer than she'd thought, because it was almost seven in the evening.

"I'll be right back," Hannah told Jack and Herb, who were operating the apple peeler to core, peel, and slice the apples, while she'd cut the apple slices into smaller pieces. Patsy was next in line, and she was mixing the apples with flour, sugar, and spices. When Patsy was through, she handed the bowl to her twin sister, Marge, who had rolled out puff pastry dough and cut it into squares. Marge spooned on the filling, folded the dough, sealed the edges with a fork, and then passed the cookie sheet to Lisa, who was responsible for brushing the tops with egg wash, cutting slits to let out the steam, and then ferrying the cookie sheets to the oven.

"Who is it?" Hannah asked Lisa, wondering who could be calling her at The Cookie Jar this late.

"I think it's Andrea," Lisa told her, covering the mouthpiece with her hand. "It's hard to tell, because whoever it is sounds really upset."

Uh-oh! Hannah's mind shouted a warning. *Bill took the job in Florida!* But thinking that way was borrowing trouble, something she tried very hard not to do, and she forced herself to think positively as she took the phone.

"Hello?" she said.

"Hannah! I . . . I tried you at home and you didn't answer, and I'm so glad I caught you at The Cookie Jar!"

Lisa was right. It was Andrea and she sounded on the verge of panic. "We're staying late baking apple turnovers," Hannah explained. "Is there something wrong?"

"Yes! Tachyon offered Bill more incentives and I think he's beginning to waver, Tracey needs a homemade snack for her bus trip to Alexandria tomorrow, and Grandma McCann is at a baby shower for a friend's daughter so I can't ask her for help. I'm stressed, Hannah. I'm really stressed!"

"I know you're stressed. I can hear it in your voice. Try to calm down, Andrea. I'm sure we can work everything out."

"Can you come over? Bill's working late, and Bethie's got a runny nose, and I can't find the listings I wrote up for the *Journal* yesterday, and . . . and I just can't cope anymore!"

That was unusual. Andrea could usually cope with anything . . . with the exception of cooking, of course. Andrea was the worst cook in all of Minnesota's eighty-seven counties.

"Will you come over, Hannah? Please?"

There was a desperate note in Andrea's voice that Hannah had never heard before. "Just hold on. I'll be there just as soon as we get our apple turnover count for the night," she promised.

"Go now," Lisa said, and everyone else nodded in agreement. "We can finish up here without you."

"But that's not really fair. I could . . ."

"Go," Marge said, and it was a command. "There's nothing more important than family. We've got the turnovers under control."

"I'll be there in a few minutes," Hannah said to her sister. "Tell me what kind of snack Tracey needs and I'll bring some ingredients with me."

"Anything she can eat on the bus without making too much of a mess. And she has to bring enough for two. The kids are going to team up in pairs, eat one snack on the way there and eat the other on the way back home."

Hannah thought fast. Sally made a snack at the Lake Eden Inn she called Imperial Cereal. She sent it along in the box lunches she packed when her guests went for walks around the lake. "How about some of Sally's Imperial Cereal?" she asked.

"That would be perfect. But do you have time to run all the way out to the Lake Eden Inn?"

"I don't have to run all the way out there. Sally gave me the recipe and I've got it in my book. Hold on a second." Hannah hurried to the book of recipes in sheet protectors that she kept in a three-ring notebook. She located Sally's snack and ran through the list of ingredients. "What kind of cereal do you have in the house?"

"I've got Multigrain Cheerios. They're Bill's favorites. And I picked up a box of Rice Chex for Bethie. She likes the way they crunch."

"Those will do just fine. How about frozen orange juice?"

"I've got some. I just made up a whole quart and it's in the refrigerator."

"I need some that's still frozen. You have extra, don't you?"

"There's another two cans in the freezer. Is that enough?"

"More than enough. All I need is a quarter cup. How about brown sugar?"

"Yes, but it's got big lumps. You'll have to pick them out before you can use it."

Hannah was surprised that Andrea knew about the lumps in her brown sugar. As far as she knew, Andrea didn't sprinkle it on anything and she certainly wouldn't have tried to use it in baking. "Did Grandma McCann tell you it had lumps?" she asked, latching on to the most likely scenario.

"No, Bill did. He complained about it yesterday morning when he tried to sprinkle it on his instant oatmeal. He asked me to buy fresh at the store, but I haven't done my shopping yet."

"Why don't you just keep molasses on hand? Then you could mix up your own brown sugar with white sugar and molasses."

"But then I'd have to mix it up every time Bill wanted it. It's easier to just keep brown sugar in the house."

"Whatever," Hannah said, restraining the urge to laugh. "How about your butter?"

"Butter doesn't get lumps!"

"I know that. I was just asking if you had some."

"We've got tons of butter. Grandma McCann won't let us buy anything else. She says butter is better for us than those artificial substitutes that don't taste like butter anyway."

"She's probably right. How about slivered almonds?"

"No, I don't have any of those."

"Then I'll bring them. Your oven works, doesn't it?"

"It did last night. Grandma McCann made a hamburger hotdish for dinner."

"Good. When you hang up, put on the coffee pot. I'll see you in about fifteen minutes."

"Hannah?"

The receiver was only inches from the cradle when Hannah heard her sister's far-away voice calling her. She stopped her forward motion and brought the receiver back up to her ear. "I'm here."

"I forgot to thank you. It's really nice of you to drop everything and come over here, just because I need you. You're the best big sister in the whole world."

"My program's over," Tracey announced, racing into the kitchen. "Hi, Aunt Hannah. I didn't know you were here!"

"Your mom said you were watching something for summer school, and I didn't want to interrupt you."

"It was a KCOW-TV special, and Mrs. Chambers wanted us to see it tonight. It was all about the Kensington Runestone, and we're going on the bus to see it tomorrow."

"What did you learn from the special?" Andrea asked, and Hannah could have applauded. Asking Tracey to talk about what she'd just seen would help to fix the details in her mind.

"They said the Kensington Runestone used to be out in the open, but it was moved to the Runestone Museum in nineteen fifty-eight."

"And you're going to the Runestone Museum?" Hannah asked.

"Oh, yes. Part of the program was about the museum and they've got lots of things to see. There's a Minnesota wildlife exhibit, and a place where you can learn about early pioneer life, and a hands-on children's exhibit. At least that's what they said. I don't think so, though."

"You don't think so about what?" Andrea asked her daughter.

"The hands-on children's exhibit. It never is, you know. The minute you start to touch things, somebody comes over and says to just look not touch, and to stay behind the ropes."

"So you're going to spend most of your time at the museum?" Hannah asked.

"Mrs. Chambers said we'll be there for about an hour. That'll give us time to see the log cabins, the one-room school, the doctor's office, and all the Indian stuff. And we're going to have fifteen minute to buy something in the museum gift shop." Tracey stopped speaking and turned to her mother. "Can I tell Aunt Hannah a secret?"

"Sure," Andrea gave her permission. "I'll just run up and check on Bethie."

Tracey waited until her mother was gone and then she stepped closer, almost as if she were afraid her mother was listening outside the kitchen door. "I'm going to buy Mom a Kensington Runestone coffee mug with the money Daddy gave me."

Hannah reached in her pocket and drew out some bills. She was sure the money Bill had given Tracey was for her to buy something for herself. Instead Tracey was spending it on Andrea, and that kind of generosity deserved to be rewarded.

"Here, Tracey," she said handing her the bills. "I want you to buy something for yourself."

A grin spread over Tracey's face. "Thanks, Aunt Hannah! I'm going to get a Viking helmet."

"A purple one with white horns?"

"No, Aunt Hannah!" Tracey giggled, and Hannah knew that she was delighted. "I'm going to buy a *real* Viking helmet, the kind they used in the thirteen hundreds to plunder and pillage. Big Ole wears one."

"Who's Big Ole?" Hannah asked, although she knew the answer.

"He's a twenty-eight foot high statue of a Viking."

Hannah put on her most innocent expression. "I didn't know they had statues of football players in Alexandria."

"No! He's a *real* Viking. They named the football team after the real ones, not the other way around."

"Right," Hannah said, smiling.

"Anyway . . . after we leave the Runestone Museum, we get back on the bus and go to Kensington Park. That's where Olaf Ohman's farm used to be. And *that's* where he found the Kensington Runestone in eighteen ninety-eight." Tracey took a step closer and lowered her voice. "They think it's a fake, but Mom doesn't know. And the scientists haven't made up their minds yet for sure, so I'm not going to tell her until they do."

"That seems wise."

There was the sound of footfalls coming down the hallway. A moment later, Andrea walked into the kitchen. "She's sleeping like an angel," she reported, and then she turned to Hannah. "I still don't know how you did it. She was so fussy with that runny nose. But somehow you managed to put her right to sleep."

"Mom?" Tracey spoke up. "It's not bedtime for me yet.

Can I sit here and watch while you and Aunt Hannah make what I'm taking on the bus for a snack?"

"No," Hannah said before Andrea could answer, and she laughed as both Andrea and Tracey stared at her in surprise. "You can't sit here and watch, Tracey. I want you to help us make it."

"You want *me* to help?" Tracey looked thrilled at the prospect.

"Absolutely. You can start by spraying that disposable roaster on the counter with Pam."

Tracey frowned. "All we have is the other stuff. Mrs. Evans was out of Pam when Grandma McCann took us to the Red Owl."

"That's okay. Any nonstick cooking spray will do."

Tracey went to the cupboard next to the stovetop and took down a can of spray. She carried it to the counter and sprayed the inside of the disposable roaster that Hannah had brought with her.

"Is this going to get heavy?" Tracey asked, returning the spray to the cupboard.

"Not too heavy, but it still might be a good idea to support the bottom by setting it on a cookie sheet." She turned to Andrea. "Do you have an old cookie sheet we can use?"

"I think so," Andrea said, but she didn't make a move to find one. Hannah got the feeling that her younger sister wasn't really sure where any cooking utensils or supplies were kept in her own kitchen.

"I'll get it," Tracey said, walking over to the oven and pulling out the drawer under it to reveal a stack of cookie sheets. "Do you want me to preheat the oven while I'm here?"

"Good idea. Set it for three hundred degrees," Hannah told her. "And once you slip the cookie sheet under the roaster, I want you to go wash your hands. It's summer cold season, so make sure you soap them for at least twenty seconds."

"Twenty seconds," Tracey repeated. "I know how to tell when twenty seconds are up without using a clock."

"You do?" Andrea sounded surprised at that revelation.

"Grandma McCann taught me. All you have to do is say, *one hundred one, one hundred two, one hundred three*, all the way up to one hundred twenty. It takes twenty seconds to say it that way."

"There's another way to do it, too," Hannah told her. "Janice Cox told me what she does down at Kiddie Korner. Some of her kids can't count as far as twenty, so she tells them to sing *Happy Birthday* all the way through twice."

"I'll have to tell Karen about that," Tracey said, naming her best friend. She washed her hands, mouthing the words to the birthday song, and then turned back to Hannah. "What next, Aunt Hannah?"

"Get out a one-cup measure, and put nine cups of cereal in the roaster. You can use some from each box."

Hannah and Andrea watched as Tracey carefully measured out the cereal. When she'd transferred nine cups to the roaster, she stepped back and turned to Hannah. "I'm ready for my next assignment."

"I want you to measure out one cup of slivered almonds. They're the nuts in that plastic bag on the counter. I think there's one cup in the bag, but you'd better check to make sure."

Tracey carefully measured out the almonds. "There's just a little over one cup, Aunt Hannah. Shall I put them all in the roaster?"

"Put them all in. More nuts will be fine. And then mix everything up with those clean hands of yours." Hannah waited until Tracey was busy and then she turned to Andrea. "What did they offer him this time?" she asked in a soft voice.

Andrea watched as Tracey dipped her hands in the roaster and began to mix up the cereal and nuts with her fingers. Then she replied, keeping her voice low. "Another ten thousand a year if he accepts by the end of the month. That's a lot of money on top of everything else they've offered."

"I'm done," Tracey said, stepping back from the roaster and turning to Hannah. "What should I do next?"

"Go find a quarter-cup measure." Hannah waited until Tracey had gone to search in the cabinet where Andrea had stored her measuring cups, and then she asked her sister another question. "You said there were other incentives?"

"I'll say! If he travels, he gets five hundred a day for meals and extras. That's a flat rate for every day he's on the road. He doesn't have to save receipts and invoice them when he gets back to the office."

"That's a real perk," Hannah said and then she stopped talking as Tracey came up with a quarter-cup measure.

"This is right, isn't it?" she asked.

"Absolutely. Now go find a glass measuring cup that'll hold a pint. That's two cups. If you can find one with a spout, that'll be perfect."

It was clear that Tracey was used to fetching bowls, measuring cups, and kitchen utensils for Grandma McCann, because she found the measuring cup that Hannah wanted right away. There wasn't even time to ask Andrea another question about the incentives that Tachyon had offered.

"I'm ready," Tracey said, waiting for her next task.

"Take a tube of frozen orange juice concentrate out of the freezer, open it, and measure out a quarter cup. Put the lid back on, seal it in a plastic freezer bag, and put the rest of the frozen orange juice back in the freezer. Then add the quarter cup of orange juice concentrate to the glass measuring cup."

Once Tracey was engaged in her task, Hannah slid her chair a little closer to Andrea. "Did they offer anything else?"

"They said they'd fly him down there first class to take a look at their headquarters. And they offered to pay for me to come along."

"What did he say to that?" Hannah asked, but before Andrea could answer, Tracey was back for more instructions.

"We need a quarter cup of brown sugar. Don't use the

sugar you have in the pantry. Take it from the bag I brought. It's on the counter."

After Tracey had found the bag and opened it, Hannah gave her further instructions. "Just dip the quarter cup measure in there and fill it up. Then pack it down until it can't hold any more, and level it off with your finger."

"Like this?" Tracey did as Hannah had told her. "Do I put it in the cup with the orange juice?"

"Yes. And then get out a stick of salted butter, cut it in half, unwrap the half, and add it to the glass measuring cup."

Once Tracey was occupied with the next instruction, Andrea answered Hannah's question. "He said he didn't think I'd be interested in coming and I really didn't want him to take the job. And when they asked him why, he explained that our families were here and we didn't really want to move."

"Mom?" Tracey called out. "Do you want me to add this leftover butter to the butter dish?"

"Yes, please." Andrea said, and Hannah noticed that she looked impressed with her daughter's ability to follow directions.

"But I thought you said you were afraid he was beginning to waver."

"I did. And I think he is. I found a piece of scrap paper in the wastebasket. He was figuring out how much more take-home pay he'd make every week if he took the job at Tachyon."

"But that doesn't mean he's planning to take it. Maybe he's just curious."

"Maybe, but . . ." Andrea stopped speaking as Tracey approached. "Is everything in the cup, honey?"

"Yes. What do I do with it now?"

"Heat the glass measuring cup in the microwave for one minute," Hannah answered her. "Take it out with an oven mitt, stir it all up together and if the butter has melted, pour it over the top of the cereal and almonds."

"How about the cranberries?" Tracey asked, pointing to

the bag of sweetened dried cranberries Hannah had brought with her. "Aren't we going to put those in?"

"Good question, but the cranberries go in after it bakes. Just stir everything up with a big mixing spoon, and then put the roaster in the oven. Close the door and set the timer for fifteen minutes."

Hannah waited until Tracey was busy, and then she turned back to her sister. "I really don't think you have to worry. Bill doesn't want to move to Florida, either. His parents, his relatives, and all of his friends are here in Lake Eden. He's Minnesota born and bred, and I really don't think he wants to leave. Tachyon might offer him the sun and the moon, but I'm almost positive he'll turn them down."

"I don't know . . ." Andrea looked worried. "It's a really good job, Hannah. And he'd be one of their top executives."

Tracey carried the roaster to the oven and placed it on a shelf. Then she closed the oven door and reached up to set the timer.

"You're forgetting one thing," Hannah said, giving her sister a smile.

"What's that?"

"Bill loves you."

Tracey turned around and came back to give her mother a big hug. "Aunt Hannah's right. Daddy knows you don't want to move to Florida, so he won't take that job."

Hannah and Andrea exchanged glances. They hadn't realized that Tracey was listening.

"Besides," Tracey continued, "he can't move to Florida."

"Why not?" Hannah and Andrea asked almost simultaneously.

"Because he likes the Vikings a whole lot more than he likes the Dolphins."

IMPERIAL CEREAL

Preheat oven to 300 degrees F., rack
in the middle position.

9 cups dry cereal *(any combination – I used Multi-grain Cheerios and Rice Chex)*
1 cup slivered almonds *(I've also used pecans and I like them better)*
¼ cup orange juice concentrate *(I used Minute Maid)*
¼ cup brown sugar *(pack it down when you measure it)*
¼ cup salted butter *(½ stick, 2 ounces, ⅛ pound)*
½ cup sweetened dried cranberries *(I used Craisins)*

Hannah's Note: The nice thing about this recipe is that you can use your choice of any dry cereal, any nuts, any frozen juice concentrate, and any dried fruit.

Place the cereal and slivered almonds in a large ovenproof bowl or a disposable roaster or steam table pan. Make sure to support the bottom with a cookie sheet if you use disposable vessels.

With your impeccably clean hands, mix the cereal and the almonds together until they're evenly distributed.

In either a 2-cup measuring cup or a microwave-safe bowl, combine the orange juice concentrate, brown sugar, and butter.

Heat the mixture in the microwave for one minute, or until the butter has melted. Stir thoroughly.

Pour the mixture over the cereal and almonds in the roaster. Mix it all together until the cereal is evenly coated.

Bake the mixture, uncovered, at 300 degrees F. for 15 minutes.

Take the roaster out of the oven and mix in the sweetened dried cranberries with a spoon.

Set the roaster on a cold burner or a wire rack until it has cooled to room temperature. Stir it again to make sure it's not stuck together in big pieces. Store Imperial Cereal in a tightly covered container at room temperature.

Sally sends little packages of Imperial Cereal along with guests when they go for boat rides, hike through the woods, or take walks around the lake. She also confesses that she's even eaten it for breakfast when she's in a hurry.

Sally calls this snack *Imperial Cereal* because it's fit for a king.

Yield: Approximately 10 cups of sweet, crunchy goodness that will be enjoyed by kids and adults alike.

Chapter
Eight

She had just turned over in bed and found a comfortable position midway between two lightly snoring felines when there was a soft knock on her door.

Must be the start of a dream, her tired mind said, reaching out to gather the warm soft blanket of semiconsciousness around her once again.

"Hannah?" a voice asked, and then there was a palpable change in the air, as if someone had entered her bedroom and was now sharing the prevailing oxygen with her.

The dream wasn't that interesting and Hannah wished she could change the channel. Unfortunately, dreams seldom responded to remotes. This one would go on, dull, flat, uninteresting, until . . .

"Hannah!"

The voice was louder, and despite her best intentions, Hannah opened her eyes. And there was Michelle standing close to her bed. "Huh?" she asked, surprised she could frame even that intelligent a question in the middle of the night.

But it wasn't the middle of the night! Hannah came to that realization with a jolt. The dawn was already breaking outside her window and that meant it was almost five in the morning!

"Wha . . . time?" Hannah asked, pleased that she'd regained at least some of her ability to verbalize.

"Ten minutes to five. I heard your alarm go off, but then it stopped. And you didn't get up. Don't you have to go to work?"

"Work. Yes." Hannah sat up and blinked several times. "Thanks, Michelle."

"There's coffee. Take a quick shower while I pour your coffee and dish up some pancakes for you. I made Sausage and Cheese Pancakes this time."

Michelle's pancakes were legendary. She'd run the gamut of additions to her excellent pancake batter, quite literally from fruit to nuts. Lately she'd been experimenting with meats and cheeses, and this morning's pancakes sounded like winners to Hannah. The thought of a tasty hot breakfast came close to making her actually *want* to get up and start her day.

Once Michelle had left the room, Hannah wasted no time getting out of bed. She was late to work and she'd have to hurry. One lightning-quick shower, a moment with both toothbrush and hairbrush, a jump into her clothes, and Hannah found herself sitting at the kitchen table clutching a life-giving mug of what one set of her grandparents had called *Swedish Plasma*.

"Here you go, Hannah." Michelle set a plate on the table in front of her older sister. "They've got breakfast sausage and sharp cheddar cheese."

"They look wonderful!" Hannah picked up her fork, preparing to dig into the fragrant dish.

"I'm all ready to go. Is there anything I can do for you while you're eating?"

"I don't think . . ." Hannah stopped as she remembered her promise to Lisa. "Yes, there is. I need Rose's recipe for Zucchini Cookies. Mother got it last Christmas at a cookie exchange."

"Mother baked cookies for a cookie exchange?!" Michelle looked completely shocked at the idea. As their mother so succinctly put it, she didn't bake. Since Hannah had left home, the interior of her mother's oven had seen the only two meals Delores ever made, Hawaiian Pot Roast and EZ Lasagna.

Dinner at the Swensen family home consisted of entrée A or entrée B served with a tossed green salad, packaged dinner rolls that could be reheated in the microwave, and ice cream with jarred toppings for dessert.

"No, Mother didn't bake cookies for a cookie exchange. *I* baked cookies for Mother so that she could take them to her cookie exchange. The recipe should be in a yellow folder on the second to the bottom shelf in the living room bookcase."

"Zucchini Cookies. I've heard of zucchini bread, but never cookies. I'll find it for you if I can have a copy."

"Of course," Hannah said, except that it didn't exactly sound that way since she was busy eating. Even so, Michelle must have understood the muffled assent because she gave a thumbs-up and went off to the living room bookcase to find the recipe.

By the time Hannah had finished her second helping, Michelle was back with the recipe. When she noticed that Hannah had refilled her plate, a smile spread over her face. "That must mean you like my pancakes," she said.

"I love them. I don't know why I never eat breakfast when I'm here alone. It's my favorite meal. And it's always wonderful when you make it for me."

"Thanks." Michelle looked proud as she sat down at the table and began to copy the recipe for herself. "What's on the docket for today? Mother said she could spare me if you need help with the turnovers."

"Thanks, but we should be okay. We've got double what we'll need for the talent show tonight and we'll reassess when it's over."

"Are you sure? Mother doesn't think there'll be much business today since everyone will be at the charity luncheon."

"She's going, isn't she?"

"Yes, but Luanne isn't. She's going to stay and work on the books. And Luanne said that since she's going to be there anyway, there's no reason for me to stay."

"Then come over to The Cookie Jar. You can always wait

on customers while Lisa and I get a head start on tomorrow's cookie dough."

"But aren't you going to the luncheon?" Michelle asked, looking puzzled. "Mother said she gave you one of her tickets."

Hannah groaned. She'd forgotten all about the luncheon ticket her mother had given her.

"You forgot?" Michelle guessed.

"Completely. I wonder if Mother would mind if I gave it to Lisa. Samantha Summerfield is the guest speaker and she's Lisa's favorite actress."

"I don't think Mother would mind. She likes Lisa and she'd probably enjoy having lunch with her. Besides, she knows you hate organized luncheons and you can hardly wait until they're over."

"You're right." Hannah finished her pancakes and stood up. "Are you ready to go? The only thing I have left to do is give the cats food and fresh water."

"And all I have to do is get an outfit for the luncheon."

"You're going, too?"

"No, but Lisa might need something and I think we're the same size. I'll take an outfit of mine along just in case."

Lisa's eyes began to sparkle and she gave a delighted laugh. "Your mother wants *me* to go with her?"

"That's what she said."

"But are you sure, Hannah? She bought the ticket for you."

"I'm sure." Hannah found herself enjoying Lisa's excitement about a thousand times more than she would have enjoyed the luncheon. She'd cleared the substitution with Delores, who had seemed very glad that Lisa, and not Hannah, would be attending the luncheon with her. "Mother told me she was looking forward to sitting next to you because if I went, I'd just fidget through the whole thing."

Lisa just stared at Hannah. "Would you really?"

"Probably. I don't like formal luncheons and I can't stand

guest speakers. They always go on and on until I'm bored stiff. I really didn't want to go, Lisa. You're doing me a big favor by taking my place."

"Oh, good! I've never been to a formal luncheon before. And I'll actually get to see and hear Samantha Summerfield. I'm so lucky I can hardly believe it!" Lisa stopped speaking and gave a little sigh. "What shall I wear? I've only got one party dress. It's the one you bought me two years ago. And it's way too warm for summer."

"Michelle's got that covered," Hannah told her, pointing to the garment bag hanging on one of the hooks by the back door. "She picked out something just in case you didn't want to run home and change. Go try it on."

Several minutes later, Lisa emerged from the miniscule bathroom and she was smiling. "We're the same size. How does it look? I couldn't get far enough away from the mirror in the bathroom to see."

"Gorgeous," Hannah pronounced as Lisa turned around. The floral print dress with cap sleeves and full skirt was perfect for a garden luncheon.

"I'd better go take it off before it gets chocolate or something just as bad on it."

"Just as bad?" Hannah teased. "Bite your tongue, Lisa. There's nothing bad about chocolate!"

Michelle had just come in to help Hannah handle the noon rush when Herb came in the front door. "Where's Lisa?" he asked.

"At the charity luncheon as Mother's guest," Hannah told him.

"Wow. That's nice of your mother to take her. She's crazy about Samantha Summerfield."

"Coffee?" Michelle asked, holding out a cup.

"Thanks." Herb took the coffee and turned back to Hannah. "I need to talk to you, Hannah. I've got a big problem, and you're the only one who can help me."

Hannah led the way to the kitchen, hoping that Herb's problem had to do with what to get Lisa for her birthday, or how to make dog biscuits at home. She could handle both of those. There was bound to be a recipe for dog biscuits online, and she knew the brand of perfume that Lisa loved. But from the frown on Herb's face, she sensed the problem was a bit more serious than that.

"Can Dillon come in?" Herb asked her. "He's out in the back in the car."

"Sure, as long as I can whistle for him this time. I want to see if I can do it."

Herb removed the dog whistle from his pocket and handed it to her. Then he went to open the back door. "Three whistles and a pause. And then two more whistles."

"Got it." Hannah put the whistle to her lips and blew on it three times. She waited a moment and then she blew twice more.

There was a thump as Dillon hit the pavement. A few seconds later he was through the open door and racing up to them. He skidded to a stop at Hannah's feet and looked up at her.

"He knows I blew the whistle?" she asked, incredulous.

"Yes, but that's because it's still in your hand. Give him a pat and tell him he's a good boy."

"Good boy, Dillon," Hannah said, patting the top of his head and rubbing his ears. "Hold on a second and I'll give Daddy a treat to give to you."

A few moments later, Herb was settled on a stool at the stainless steel workstation and Dillon was stretched out on the floor next to him, chewing his dog treat.

"Now tell me what's wrong," Hannah said, setting a plate of the Zucchini Cookies she'd just made in front of Herb.

"I need a favor. A big one." He delayed their dialogue by taking a bite of his cookie. "These are good," he said. "What are they?"

"Zucchini Cookies." Hannah realized that Herb wasn't

eager to go into details about that favor he needed. She was equally uneager to hear those details, but there was no time like the present. "What's the favor?"

"It's my cousin Mary Kate," Herb said. "She's got the flu and she can't be more than a couple of seconds away from the . . ." Herb stopped and cleared his throat. "Trust me. You don't want to hear the details."

"You're right. I don't. So what does Mary Kate have to do with this favor you need?"

"Mary Kate is Amazing Herb's assistant."

Hannah groaned. She couldn't help it. She'd promised herself she'd never agree to be Herb's magic show assistant again.

"I know you don't like helping me out with the act," Herb said, sighing deeply. "I can't blame you for that. It's not much fun getting into the Cabinet of Death. But Lisa can't do it. She's just too claustrophobic. And nobody else except Mary Kate knows the act. Could you be my assistant just once more, Hannah? I'm begging you. Otherwise I'll have to drop out of the talent show tonight."

Hannah took a deep breath and told herself to hold firm. And then she glanced at Herb. He looked unbelievably plaintive, so she switched her gaze to Dillon. Dear heavens! There were two of them! Two sets of begging puppy-dog eyes! Herb's entreating orbs reminded her of a basset hound pleading for a pat on the head. And Dillon's eyes were as sad as a grieving widow's, so desolate that Hannah could swear she saw tears glistening in their depths.

"Okay," she said, bowing to the inevitable.

"You mean . . . you'll do it?"

"Yes. If I don't help you out, your dog's going to cry. And if there's one thing I can't stand in this world, it's a crying puppy dog."

SAUSAGE AND CHEESE PANCAKES

Preheat oven to the lowest possible
setting, rack in the middle position.

1 large egg
1 cup unflavored yogurt
¼ cup cream
2 Tablespoons vegetable oil
2 teaspoons baking powder
½ teaspoon baking soda
¼ teaspoon salt
1 cup all-purpose flour *(pack it down in the cup
  when you measure it)*
½ cup ground *fried* breakfast sausage, broken up
  into small pieces
1 cup shredded sharp cheddar cheese
  (approximately 4 ounces)

Beat the egg with a wire whisk in a medium-sized bowl
until it's fluffy.

Whisk in the yogurt, cream, and the vegetable oil.

In a small bowl, combine the baking powder, baking soda,
and salt with the flour. Stir it around with a fork until it's
evenly distributed.

Add the dry ingredients to the wet ingredients and stir
well.

**Michelle's Note: At this point you can stop and refriger-
ate your pancake batter overnight. Then all you have to do
is give it a good stir in the morning, add your sausage and**

your cheese, and fry your pancakes. If you decide to do this, don't preheat your oven until you're ready to fry in the morning.

Add the fried sausage and shredded cheese to your batter, and stir in thoroughly.

If you're using an electric griddle, spray it with Pam or another nonstick cooking spray and preheat it to the pancake setting. If you're using a griddle on the stovetop or a large frying pan, spray it with Pam and heat it over medium-high heat. It's the perfect temperature when a few drops of water, sprinkled on the surface with your fingers, skitter around and then evaporate.

If you want to pour your pancakes onto the griddle, transfer the batter to a pitcher. If you'd prefer to dip a large spoon or a small cup into the bowl and transfer the batter to the griddle that way, that's fine, too. (*I use a quarter-cup plastic measure that has a little spout on the side – when I pour the batter onto the griddle, approximately 3 Tablespoons come out and 1 Tablespoon sticks to the sides, which is perfect!*)

Fry your pancakes until they're puffed and dry around the edges. If you look closely, little bubbles will form at the edges. If you're not sure they're done, lift one edge with a spatula and take a peek. It will be golden brown on the bottom when it's ready to flip.

Turn your pancakes and wait for the other side to fry. Again, you can test your pancake by lifting it slightly with a spatula and peeking to see if it's golden brown.

If you don't have a horde of people sitting at your table waiting to eat those pancakes and you want to keep them warm until everyone comes to the breakfast table, put them in a 9-inch by 13-inch cake pan, separated by paper towels, and slip them into a warm oven set at the lowest temperature until your sleepyheads arrive.

Hannah's Note: Mike likes these with maple syrup. Norman prefers them plain with a pat of butter on top. Mother likes them with a dollop of sour cream on top and Michelle and I just love to fry an egg sunny-side up with the yolk still runny and slip that on top of a stack of pancakes.

Yield: Approximately one dozen medium-sized pancakes.

Chapter Nine

The phone rang at precisely twelve-thirty, just as Hannah had made the rounds of the tables with the coffee carafe. Michelle answered and a moment later she motioned to Hannah. "It's Marge Beeseman," she said as Hannah took the receiver.

"Herb says you don't have your purple dress anymore," Marge stated, wasting no time on preliminaries.

"That's right. After I . . . um . . . *retired* as Herb's assistant, I didn't think I'd need it again."

"Can you get it back?" Marge got straight to the point.

"No." Hannah didn't bother to explain that she'd stuck it in a bag and given it to a group of Jordan High students who'd come to her door asking for used clothing and household items for their class rummage sale.

"Well, don't worry. Patsy will take over for me at the library this afternoon so Jack and I can go look for dresses at Helping Hands. That's where we got that lovely purple dress, you know."

"I know," Hannah said, and left it at that.

"We'll do things the same as we did the last time. We'll pick out several dresses in your size and bring them over to you around three this afternoon. You can try them on, choose the one you want, and we'll take the others back to the thrift shop."

"That's fine. Thank you, Marge. I really appreciate it."

"And I really appreciate how you're helping Herb. He was just beside himself when Mary Kate's mother called and said she had the flu."

Hannah said goodbye and hung up the phone. There was a smile on her face when she turned back to Michelle. "Marge and Jack are going shopping at Helping Hands for me."

"To pick out a magician's assistant dress?"

"That's right. I don't know what time Lisa will get back so can you stay until I try them on?"

"I can stay for the rest of the day if you need me."

"Great. I hope they can find something nice this time. That purple dress I wore at the fair was a horror."

"What happened to it?" Florence Evans asked. She was sitting at the counter waiting for the box of Cinnamon Crisps Michelle was packing for Florence's checkers at the Red Owl. It was clear that Florence had been listening to what they'd been saying. She wasn't the type to make a pretence of politely ignoring their conversation.

"That dress is history," Hannah told her. "I donated it to the Jordan High rummage sale."

"Was it really that bad?" Michelle asked.

"It was worse. Some redheads can wear purple and other redheads can't. I'm the kind of redhead that can't."

"Hannah's right," Bertie Straub said, leaning over to join their conversation. "You should have come down to the Cut 'n Curl before you went onstage with Herb. I've got a rinse that's guaranteed to tone down the color in your hair."

"That's good to know," Hannah said, wondering if it was the same rinse that gave several of Bertie's regular silver-haired customers blue hair. "Thanks for the offer, Bertie, but I won't have to worry about wearing that awful purple dress ever again!"

"Samantha Summerfield is a fascinating speaker," Lisa said, stepping quickly to the walk-in cooler with the bowl of

Molasses Cookie dough that she'd just mixed. "She told us all about a day in the life of a Hollywood star. It's not all glamour, you know. When she's shooting a movie or a television show, the car picks her up at five in the morning so she can get to the studio and be in makeup at six."

"That doesn't sound bad to someone who gets up at four-thirty and drives herself to work," Hannah said.

"You're right!" Lisa said, giggling a little. "I completely forgot that we do that every day!"

Hannah turned to smile at her young partner. Lisa had talked nonstop ever since she'd returned to The Cookie Jar. Hannah had heard all about the delicious luncheon, what a wonderful time she'd had talking to Delores, and the tidbits of information she'd learned about her favorite movie star.

"You really should have gone, Hannah. I just know you would have enjoyed yourself."

"Wrong. But I'm very glad you did. What time is it, Lisa?"

"Five minutes to three."

"Oh, good. Your dad and Marge should be here soon."

Lisa turned to Hannah in confusion. "Why are Dad and Marge coming here?"

"They're picking out a dress for me at Helping Hands."

"A dress," Lisa repeated, not looking in the least bit enlightened. "I thought you got all your dresses at Beau Monde because Claire gave you a discount."

"I do."

"Then why are Marge and Dad going dress shopping for you at the thrift store?"

"Because it seemed silly to pay good money for a dress I'm going to wear only once."

"Only once?"

Hannah stared at Lisa for a moment. Her partner looked thoroughly confused. "I thought Herb must have told you. Mary Kate got the flu and I'm filling in for her as his assistant at the talent show tonight."

"Oh! That's really nice of you, Hannah. I wonder why

Herb didn't call to tell me. I always carry my cell phone when I'm not here at the shop."

"Is it charged?" Hannah asked. It was a logical question, especially from someone who couldn't even count the number of times she'd forgotten to charge her cell phone.

"I know it was charged. I just took it out of the charger this morning."

"Is it turned on?" Hannah asked a second logical question, especially from someone who frequently forgot to turn on her cell phone.

"Yes, I always leave it on. I never know when I might get a call from Dad and . . . oh."

"*Oh*, what?"

"I just remembered. I turned off my cell phone when we got to the school. There was a sign up asking people not to answer their cell phones during the luncheon or the speech. I completely forgot to turn it back on and check for messages when I got back here."

There was a knock at the back door and Lisa went to open it. Marge and Jack were standing there, right on time. She gave both of them a hug and took the three plastic-covered bags her father was carrying. "Come in and try some of Hannah's Zucchini Cookies," she said. "They're really good."

Marge and Jack came in and took seats at the workstation. Lisa dished up some cookies, and Hannah filled two mugs with coffee from the kitchen pot.

"What kind of cookies did you say these were?" Marge asked, taking one from the plate.

"Zucchini Cookies," Hannah answered. "It's Rose's recipe from last year's Christmas cookie exchange."

"Vegetable cookies," Jack said, shaking his head. "What'll they think of next?"

"I used to make Carrot Cookie Bars for the kids when they were growing up," Marge said. "It was one way to get them to eat vegetables."

Jack took a bite of his cookie. "Here's another way. These are really good!"

Marge took a sip of her coffee and gave a little sigh. "We could only find three dresses in your size, Hannah."

"That's right," Jack said. "We looked through all the racks, but that was it. It must be a very popular size. They're nice dresses, though. I like the blue one the best, but the others are nice, too. Are you going to try them on . . . my dear?"

"Yes," Hannah answered, not reacting to the term of affection. Jack always called women *my dear* when he forgot their given names. Sometimes he came right out and asked her to tell him her name, which was fine with her, but today he turned to Marge.

"I hope you like the dresses, *Hannah*," Marge said quickly.

"So do I, *Hannah*," Jack said, latching on to the name that Marge had provided. "Why don't you try them on while we're eating our cookies?"

While Lisa took a few minutes to talk to her father and mother-in-law, Hannah retrieved the three bags from the hook by the back door and carried them into the small bathroom off the kitchen. There was barely room enough to turn around, but somehow she managed to remove the plastic covering and take the first dress from its hanger.

The dress was made of white lace with a full skirt, a fitted bodice with a scoop neckline, and long sleeves that ended in points at the wrist. Hannah couldn't quite decide whether it had been a wedding dress or a prom dress, but it was definitely the type of gown you'd wear to a formal event. She unzipped it, stepped into it, and pulled the dress up to zip it again.

It must have been a wedding dress, Hannah decided after one glance in the small mirror. She spotted three small pearl buttons in strategic spots on the back of the dress that had been sewn there for the purpose of attaching a train. Of course the buttons could be removed, but now that she examined the dress critically, she realized that it was all wrong for her. The scoop neck dipped too low, the sleeves were too tight, the lace ruffle below the waist made her hips look enormous, and the style was so outdated that even a non-fashion follower like her knew it. The overall impression was of a woman trying to make do with a dress she'd worn a decade earlier, and although it did fit in the waist, she really didn't want to have to worry about the low neckline every time she bent over to retrieve scarves, or flowers, or other paraphernalia from the low, square table that held The Amazing Herb's magic props.

The white dress went back on the hanger and Hannah slipped the plastic back in place. The dress wouldn't do at all. She went on to the second dress, took off the plastic, and removed it from the hanger. It was a gorgeous color, a cross between an ice blue and a light turquoise. She slipped it over her head, and it whispered down the length of her body, settling easily on her shoulders.

"Yes!" Hannah said, glancing in the mirror. The material gleamed with a satiny finish and the skirt spanned almost a full circle. The neckline was flattering, dipping down to just the right spot, and the darts in the bodice were perfectly placed. The three-quarter sleeves were less constraining than long sleeves, especially important when she handed The Amazing Herb his props, and the skirt ended just below the knees, ensuring that she wouldn't trip on it when she got into the Cabinet of Death. Jack was right. This was the perfect dress. All that remained was to zip it up to make sure it fit her properly.

Hannah reached behind her to grasp the tab of the zipper and pull it up. It slid easily to a point an inch or two below her waistline, but there it stopped. What was wrong? It simply wouldn't go up any farther, even though she tugged a little harder than was wise.

Imitating a contortionist in the tight confines of the bathroom was difficult, but Hannah managed to reach behind her with both hands, grasp the sides of the dress, and attempt to draw it closed. After two attempts, she realized that it was impossible. The dress was at least three inches too small in the waist. But how could that be? The label was still attached to the dress and the number it listed was her size. This was impossible. The dress should fit her perfectly.

It took only a moment to lower the zipper and step out of the dress. Hannah picked it up and turned it inside out to examine the seams. The mystery was solved. The owner of the dress must have lost weight, because the gown had been altered. There were deep darts that extended above and below the waistline, effectively reducing the number on the printed tag by at least two dress sizes.

There was only one dress left. Hannah found herself holding her breath as she returned the blue dress to the hanger and covered it with the plastic. This was her last chance, and her fingers were shaking slightly as she pulled off the plastic to reveal the dress inside.

One glance and the hanger dropped from her nerveless fingers. Fate was cruel. It had played a trick much too heinous to believe. It was the purple dress, the same purple dress she'd worn at the Tri-County Fair and had handed over to the Jordan High students to sell at their rummage sale!

Hannah shut her eyes. Surely she must be dreaming. This simply couldn't be happening to her. But when she opened her eyes again, the purple dress was still there, pooled in a heap of bilious color at her feet.

There was no benevolence. There was no kindness. There wasn't even a modicum of mercy. She had to wear the purple dress. There was simply no help for it.

Hannah stood there for a long moment before she picked up the dark lavender horror. And then her mouth opened and she whimpered like a condemned felon awaiting punishment from a cruel magistrate.

"It's back," she whimpered, staring down at the dress in total disgust. "I must have done something really awful to deserve this, because . . . it's baaack!"

ROSE'S ZUCCHINI COOKIES

Preheat oven to 350 degrees F., rack
in the middle position.

1 cup white *(granulated)* sugar
1 cup brown sugar *(pack it tightly in the cup when
   you measure it)*
1 cup softened butter *(2 sticks, 8 ounces, ½ pound)*
1 teaspoon baking soda
2 large eggs *(beaten)*
1 and ½ teaspoons vanilla
1 and ½ cups peeled and shredded zucchini *(that's
   about three 8-inch zucchini)*
1 cup chopped walnuts *(or pecans)*
6-ounce bag chocolate chips *(that's 1 cup)*
4 cups all-purpose flour *(don't sift—pack it down in
   the cup when you measure it)*

Measure out the white sugar and the brown sugar in a
large bowl. Add the softened butter and beat with a wooden
spoon until the mixture is nice and fluffy.

Mix in the baking soda and make sure it's evenly distributed.

Beat the two eggs in a glass with a fork and then add
them to your bowl. Add the vanilla extract and mix everything thoroughly.

Peel the zucchini. Shred them with a cheese grater *(I use
an old, four-sided box grater and shred with the second to
the largest grating side.)* You can also shred the zucchini

with the shredding blade in a food processor. Measure out one and a half cups, packing it down in the measuring cup, and then add it to your bowl.

Hannah's 1ˢᵗ Note: You don't really have to peel the zucchini, but if you don't you'll have little green dots in your cookies. Since green isn't the most appetizing color for cookies, I always peel mine.

Stir until the shredded zucchini is thoroughly incorporated.

Add the chopped nuts and the chocolate chips. Mix well.

Add the flour in one-cup increments, stirring after each addition. When all the flour has been added and stirred in, the resulting dough will be quite stiff.

Drop by teaspoonfuls onto a cookie sheet that has been sprayed with Pam (*or another nonstick cooking spray)* or lined with parchment paper.

This dough is soft. If you find it's too difficult to work with, chill it for 20 or 30 minutes in the refrigerator and then try again. I used a 2-teaspoon cookie scooper and dipped it in water every three scoops or so.

Bake the cookies at 350 degrees F. for 10 to 12 minutes or until lightly browned.

Cool the cookies on the cookie sheet for two minutes, and then remove them to a wire rack to cool completely.

Rose says that after these cookies are cool, you can store them in a covered container and they'll keep very well that way.

Hannah's 2nd Note: Tracey loves these cookies. She's trying to convince Andrea that they count as one daily serving of vegetables. Delores *(who's never been fond of vegetables)* **agrees. Bill and Andrea don't agree.**

Yield: Approximately 8 dozen tasty cookies.

Chapter Ten

"Ready?" Herb asked coming in the kitchen door at four o'clock in the afternoon.

"I'm ready." Hannah took her purse off the hook by the door and ducked into the coffee shop to tell Lisa and Michelle that she was leaving for an orientation meeting with the producer of the talent show.

"Sorry about this," Herb said, backing the cruiser out into the alley and heading for Jordan High. "I know you had work to do, but they said that if we didn't show up, they'd scratch us from the lineup."

"That's okay. From what you told me it shouldn't take long."

Hannah leaned back and shut her eyes as Herb drove the short blocks to the school. She was tired and she really needed to catch a nap. Unfortunately the commute wasn't long enough to do more than rest her eyes.

The front two rows of the auditorium were packed with contestants when they got inside. Hannah recognized the Langer Sisters, the Little Falls majorettes with their lighted batons, and Smokey Winslow clutching his banjo. "This looks like more than twenty acts to me," she said to Herb as they took seats in the unoccupied third row.

"They're up to twenty-six," Herb said, glancing at the program he'd taken from the stack in the lobby. "We're number twelve, right before Perry and Sherri's dance demonstration."

Hannah's breath caught in her throat as a tall, dark-haired man walked onstage and took up a position behind the podium. It was Bradford Ramsey and the very sight of him made her feel slightly queasy.

"There's the host of the show," Herb said, watching as he switched on the microphone. "He's a professor from Macalester. I'm pretty sure Michelle knows him."

"Right," Hannah said, wishing that weren't the case.

"Hi, Herb," someone tapped Herb on the shoulder and Hannah looked up to see Perry and Sherri Connors. "Is it okay if we sit next to you?"

"Sure." Herb turned to Hannah. "Do you know our local celebrities?"

"I certainly do! Sherri is one Regency Ginger Crisp with a glass of skim milk, and Perry is two Walnut Date Chews with a cup of Twining's Breakfast Tea."

Perry and Sherri laughed as they slipped into two seats next to Hannah and Herb. "Are you doing your magic act?" Sherri asked Herb.

"Yes, and Hannah's my assistant. My cousin usually goes on with me, but she's got a bad case of the flu."

"That could be what you have," Perry said, turning to look at his sister.

"But I feel okay now."

"I know, but it comes and goes." Perry turned to Herb. "She's not running a fever, but she can't keep anything down. Don't you always run a fever with the flu?"

"I don't know. Mary Kate's mother didn't say if she was running a fever or not." Herb gave a little shrug and deferred to Hannah. "Do you know, Hannah?"

Hannah shook her head. "It could be a mild case of food poisoning, I guess. I don't think you run a fever with that."

"That's probably it." Sherri seized Hannah's explanation eagerly. And then, when everyone turned to look at her, she gave a little laugh. "I don't *want* the flu. That can last for weeks. I'd much rather believe it's something I ate."

Bradford Ramsey tapped the microphone for attention, and then he began to speak. "I want to thank everyone for taking time out of their busy day and coming here for orientation," he said. "I promise not to keep you long. I just want to brief you on where things are and what procedure you should follow for the actual performance tonight."

Hannah listened as the man who used to hold a place of importance in her life told them about the cash prizes and how the winners were to be chosen. Then he said that they were to sit in designated rows in the audience, and he told them when to come backstage to the dressing rooms.

"If you're in act ten on the program, you won't leave your seat until act eight starts," he said. "That will give you the rest of act eight and all of act nine to get into your costume and get ready to go."

"How do we know when to come out of the dressing room?" one of the Langer sisters asked.

"There are slave speakers in the dressing rooms. They're hooked to the microphones on the stage and you'll be able to hear what the audience hears. When the applause at the end of the act begins, I want you to come to the wings at stage left or stage right and wait for me to introduce you."

"Stage left if our act is an even number?" one of the guys in the second row asked.

"That's right. Stage left if your act is an even number, and stage right if your act is an odd number on the program. It couldn't be simpler. Just remember that when you leave your seats in the audience, walk quietly up the side aisles, go straight down the hallway, and enter the backstage area through the green door."

"Will we get to rehearse it before the show?" one of the Little Falls majorettes asked.

"Yes. When we're through here, one of my student helpers will walk everyone through it. Just remember that when you pass through that green door, it will take you past the wings. That means you must be very quiet as you go to your respective dressing rooms to put on your costumes and your makeup."

There was a little sound next to her, and Hannah glanced over at Sherri. The young dancer was gripping the arms of her seat so tightly that her knuckles were white. "Are you okay?" she asked.

"I . . . I think I have to go to the ladies room. Can you let me out, please?"

Hannah stood up to let Sherri pass, and Herb did the same. She watched as Sherri hurried up the aisle and into the lobby, racing in the direction of the restrooms. Sherri's face had been pasty white and Hannah had noticed beads of sweat on her forehead. It was clear that Sherri was ill.

"Did she go to the ladies room?" Perry asked Hannah.

"Yes. I think she's really sick, Perry."

"So do I. She keeps telling me it's nothing, that she'll be fine in a day or two, but I'm getting worried. This has been going on for over a week."

"Has she seen a doctor?" Herb, who had been listening to their conversation, asked.

"Not yet. I offered to take her a couple days ago, but she said it wasn't necessary." Perry just shook his head. "I think it's because we don't have insurance."

"But I thought the Home carried medical insurance for all of you," Hannah said.

"They do, but we're not living at the Home anymore. Sherri and I graduated from Jordan High last May and both of us got full scholarships to the community college. We've been there for a year now and we're living in an apartment in that new building on campus."

Hannah raised her eyebrows. The upscale apartment complex was the community college's alternative to a dorm. The lovely building was only a year old, and Hannah had heard that it was quite expensive. It sported an indoor spa, a recreation room with all the latest in video games, wireless Internet connections in every apartment, and food service in an adjacent building that was more restaurant than cafeteria.

"I know," Perry gave a little smile, as if he knew what she was thinking. "It's really expensive to live there, but our place is the smallest unit and it comes with our scholarship. All we have to do is vacuum the hallways, clean the windows in the lobby and the spa, and replace burned out light bulbs. And the college placement service found us jobs. Sherri works all weekend as a student secretary at the English department, and I'm on the city grounds and maintenance crew. I work a half-day Friday and all day Saturday. Our tuition's paid and between the two of us, we earn enough for books and personal stuff."

"Sounds like a good deal to me," Herb said.

"It is. Not bad for two kids from the Home. And now we're the chief fundraisers. Right before we do our dance number, I have to get up to make a pitch for donations to the Home."

Hannah thought Perry sounded a little bitter, but she didn't comment. It couldn't have been easy growing up as an orphan in the Winnetka County Children's Home. Herb, however, wasn't that restrained.

"Sounds to me like it's payback time," Herb said. "The Home helped you out and now that you're successful, they expect you and Sherri to help them out."

"You're right," Perry replied, and a frown crossed his brow. "Sherri doesn't seem to mind doing it, but girls had it a lot easier at the Home. There were fights every night in the boys' wing, and most of the time they just left us alone to slug it out."

Hannah said nothing. She knew the Home was doing the best it could with overcrowded conditions and not enough staff.

"It wasn't all one big happy family, the way they try to

make you think it was," Perry continued. "There were rough times, especially for the boys. You have no idea how many times I had to fight just because I took dance lessons."

"I'm sure you did." Hannah did her best to smooth things over. "It must have been very difficult growing up without your parents."

"Not really. We never knew them."

Perry's face was hard and Hannah decided the hurt was too deep for platitudes. She glanced at her watch and said, "Do you want me to go check on Sherri? She's been gone for over five minutes."

"Would you?" Perry looked grateful. "Thanks, Hannah. I'd really appreciate it."

Herb stood up and Hannah exited the row. She walked up the aisle to the lobby and took the hallway to the ladies room. As she opened the door she heard the sound of someone being very sick. A moment later there was a flush, and Sherri came out of a stall.

"Are you okay?" Hannah asked her.

"I think so." Sherri headed for the sink and splashed some water on her face. She dried it with a paper towel, washed her hands and dried them, and then she turned to face Hannah. "Did Perry send you to check on me?"

"It was my idea, but Perry seemed glad that I offered."

"He worries too much. I'm really a lot better now. I can go back to my seat."

"Are you sure you don't want to see a doctor?" Hannah asked, reaching out to feel her forehead and hoping that she wouldn't take offense. "You don't feel hot. I don't think you're running a fever."

"I couldn't be running a fever. I've been taking aspirin every four hours for a week now."

"Maybe you'd better see Doc Knight and find out what's the matter. If it *is* the flu, he can give you something stronger than aspirin."

"I don't think I need a doctor. I should be okay now. I took some antacid for my stomach."

Hannah wasn't a great believer in over-the-counter remedies, but she decided not to say that. Instead she handed Sherri a tissue from the dispenser. "You'd better fix your makeup. Your lipstick's smeared."

"Thanks." Sherri turned to the mirror to wipe off her lipstick and apply new. "I think you're right, Hannah."

"About what?"

"Food poisoning. I made some tuna salad and I forgot and left it out on the kitchen counter. I stuck it in the refrigerator the next morning, and I ate it for dinner that night. Maybe it went bad. I heard you're not supposed to leave things made with mayonnaise out in hot weather."

Hannah shrugged. "I guess that could be it. How long ago did you eat the tuna?"

"I don't exactly remember. Maybe a week ago, or a little longer? I just bet that's it."

"It could be," Hannah said, but she doubted it. As far as she knew, a mild case of food poisoning didn't last a whole week. Or maybe it did. She'd studied literature, not medicine.

"We'd better go." Sherri turned from the mirror and slung her purse over her shoulder. "Perry gets nervous if I'm gone for too long. I think it's the twin thing. We were all we had for so long, and he looked out for me in the Home and everything. He forgets I'm grown up now and I can take care of myself."

There was a knock on the ladies room door and Hannah opened it to find Perry standing there. "Is everything okay?" he asked.

"I'm fine, Perry," Sherri said, giving him a big smile. "I just had a little stomach trouble, that's all."

"Okay. As long as you're sure you're all right." Perry waited for her to exit the ladies room, and then he took her arm.

"Are they ready to show us the wings and the dressing rooms?" Hannah asked, following the pair to the hallway.

"Yes. They're going to take us in groups of five. The first ten have left, so we'd better hurry." Perry turned to Sherri. "Ready?"

"You bet! I'm . . ." Sherri stopped and Hannah watched in horror as her face turned pasty white again. "I have to go back in. I'm so sorry. I'm sick again!"

Once the ladies room door had closed behind Sherri, Hannah turned to her twin. "Take her to the doctor," she said. "I think this is more serious than mild food poisoning or the flu."

"Me, too." Perry said, looking more than a little frightened. "I should have taken her earlier."

"It's not your fault. She didn't want to go. But you should take her now. And tell Doc Knight to put it on my bill."

"That's not necessary. You don't have to pay our bill. I know Doc'll let us pay him something every month until we can . . ."

"No," Hannah interrupted him, thinking fast. It was obvious that Perry wouldn't accept what he thought was charity. "I need a few things done at The Cookie Jar, and you can do them whenever you have a spare minute."

"Like what?" Perry looked a bit suspicious, like he wasn't quite sure if Hannah had real work for him or not.

"You can mix up concrete, can't you?"

"Sure."

"I need my back step repaired. It's got a crack and it's only going to get worse this coming winter. And then there's the pantry."

"What about the pantry?"

"We're reorganizing it and we've got heavy bags of flour and sugar, and great big containers of various supplies. I don't want to lift them, and Lisa shouldn't lift them either."

"How did they get in the pantry in the first place?"

"Most of our supplies are trucked in from a warehouse and the driver carries them into the pantry for us."

"Okay," Perry said, and he seemed to accept her explanation. "I can pour a new back step for you and help you move things around in the pantry. When does this have to be done?"

"The step should be finished by the end of September. The pantry can take longer, say by the beginning of November. We need to get everything set in place before our holiday rush." Perry began to look suspicious again and Hannah figured she'd better not be so generous with her timelines. "Of course I'd like everything done before then, but that's the longest I could wait."

I've got Wednesday afternoons free," Perry told her. "How about next Wednesday at one? I can do your back step then."

"That's just fine," Hannah said, even though it wasn't. There wasn't a thing wrong with her back step and she'd have to figure out some way to crack it so that Perry could repair it. "I'd better get back to Herb. It'll be our turn to go backstage pretty soon. Do you want me to tell someone that Sherri's sick and you took her to the doctor?"

Perry shook his head. "I know this stage like the back of my hand and so does Sherri. I can't even count the number of times we've danced here. If anybody asks, just say we'll see them tonight."

"Okay. Tell Sherri I hope she's better soon." Hannah gave a little wave and went back into the auditorium. As she walked toward her seat, she realized that now she'd have to take time out of her busy schedule to reorganize their perfectly organized pantry. It was time she really couldn't spare, especially since it was an unnecessary task.

There was a low whistle and Hannah turned to look. Herb was standing at the rear of a line that had formed in the center aisle. She'd been so deep in thought she hadn't even seen that the seats they'd occupied earlier were now vacant.

"Did Perry take her to the doctor?" Herb asked when Hannah had joined him in line.

"Yes. She was really sick."

"With the flu?"

"I don't know. I felt her forehead. I don't think she was running a fever, but she said she'd taken aspirin."

"How did you ever get her to agree to go to the doctor?"

"I didn't. I told Perry I thought he should take her, and he agreed. I promised to pay for it."

"Perry's touchy about taking charity. How did you get him to agree to that?"

"I told him I had a job for him at The Cookie Jar and he should consider it an advance on his salary."

"*Do* you have a job for him?"

"I do now."

Herb reached over to pat her on the back. "That was a really good deed, Hannah."

"Thanks." Hannah gave a fleeting thought to all the extra work she'd created for herself in her attempt to manufacture a job for Perry. And as the line moved forward, she muttered, "I should have known that no good deed goes unpunished."

Chapter Eleven

Hannah had barely had time to run home to feed Moishe and Cuddles before she had to drive back to Jordan High. She'd taken her designated seat at two minutes before the final call for contestants, and Herb, who'd looked a bit panicked at her late arrival, had given her a relieved smile.

Now, forty-five minutes after the curtain had risen, the talent show was running smoothly and everyone seemed to be having a wonderful time. Hannah was clapping right along with the rest of the audience to the beat of Kenny Kowalski's All-Girl Accordion Band when Herb tapped her on the shoulder.

"We'd better go," he said. "There's only one act after this, and then we're up. We're going to end the first half."

"But how about Perry and Sherri? I thought they were ending the first act with their dance number."

"Not anymore. I ran into Perry in the lobby and he said Sherri can't dance tonight. He's going to give his little talk for donations to the Children's Home right after intermission is over, and then he's going home to make sure Sherri's okay."

"Did he take her to see Doc Knight?"

"Doc gave her something to settle her stomach and said she should rest."

"Was it the flu?"

"Perry didn't say. I can tell he's worried about her, though. He looked really upset."

Hannah slid out of the row. She'd taken the seat on the aisle so that she wouldn't have to climb over people's knees and feet. She thought Herb was jumping the gun a bit. The Langer sisters were up next and they always sang two encores. He was probably nervous and wanted to take a little time to calm down after he'd donned the clothing and persona of his magician, The Amazing Herb.

Once they'd traversed the hallway and gone through the door that led backstage, Hannah let Herb lead the way. There were lots of obstacles and it was easier to follow than to lead. When they reached the rear of the backstage area, Herb turned right to enter the men's dressing room, and Hannah turned left.

She was only a few steps from the dressing room door when it opened and the Langer sisters emerged. They were talking about something among themselves, and although they smiled and acknowledged her with a wave, they didn't stop to chat.

Hannah entered the dressing room to find it deserted. That was fine with her. She didn't want to answer any questions about the ugly purple dress that she was about to don. She slipped out of her jeans and blouse, untied the plastic that covered the monstrosity, and unzipped it. Then she gritted her teeth as she pulled it on over her head, and zipped it back up.

The whole process of dressing in her magician's assistant costume took less than five minutes, especially since she didn't stop to put on makeup or primp in the wide horizontal mirror on the wall. It was illuminated by a line of lightbulbs running above the glass, but Hannah took pains to avoid her reflection for fear it would demoralize her. It had been bad enough when The Amazing Herb and his assistant had won first prize in the Tri-County Fair Talent Show. If they won again tonight, and she hoped they would for Herb's sake, Norman wouldn't be here to take their picture and use Photoshop to change the color of her bilious dress!

Thinking about Norman brought about a nervous little ping in the bottom of her stomach. She still couldn't shake the feeling that something was wrong. He hadn't sounded like himself on the phone, and she hadn't heard a peep from him since he'd left that short message on her answer machine. It simply wasn't like Norman to stay away an extra day, especially when he'd told her how much he missed Cuddles.

Hannah turned a chair away from the mirror and sat down to wait until it was time to go. She paged through a magazine that someone had left, but that only occupied her for the first two songs that the Langer sisters sang. The third song was one she knew and she mouthed the lyrics as they sang. Then she took time to brush her hair without benefit of mirror, and listened to the applause as they finished their act.

The applause went on for several minutes. It wasn't that the Langer sisters were that good, but they did have a lot of relatives in attendance to cheer them on. There was a silence and then, just as she'd predicted, they went into their first encore. It would be a while before they were through and there was no sense going out to wait in the wings early. She might run into Bradford Ramsey and he was the last person she wanted to see!

The sisters were singing the ever-popular *Danke Schoen* in German, a sure hit in a county that still had a large share of German speakers. Hannah listened for a moment and tried to interpret the words. She'd picked up a little German over the years, but most of the lyrics were beyond her. When the sisters switched to English to sing it all through again, Hannah's thoughts turned back to Norman.

In the message he'd left for her, he'd said that he wasn't coming home as planned because he had some things to take care of. Whatever they were, they must be important. Norman was a man who didn't do many spur-of-the-moment things.

He simply wasn't a spontaneous person. It wasn't normal for him to leave a message saying he'd changed his plans at the last minute and was staying away an extra day. And why hadn't he called The Cookie Jar to talk to her personally? Was he avoiding the questions he knew she was bound to ask?

Hannah told herself to stop worrying, that she'd find out soon enough, but of course that didn't work. She had two choices. She could sit here and worry about Norman, or she could stand in the wings to wait for Herb and take the chance of running into Bradford.

She came to a decision immediately. It was cowardly to sit here simply because she didn't want to deal with Bradford Ramsey. Thank goodness he didn't remember he'd dated her years ago! Even when Michelle had invited him to Hannah's condo for dessert this past Christmas Eve, Bradford had looked puzzled, as if he were still trying to place her. He hadn't remembered exactly who she was when he'd stopped in at The Cookie Jar to say hello to the Mayor and Stephanie and that was a good thing. With a little luck, he wouldn't remember her tonight either, and there would be no awkward conversation about the past with him.

The moment she decided, Hannah was up and moving. Their act was scheduled to enter stage left, and their guide had reminded everyone that stage left meant the entrance to the left as you faced the stage from the audience.

Hannah stepped out of the dressing room and crossed the backstage floor, careful to avoid the thick cables that snaked across the floor, the sandbags that held backdrops aloft, and the shadowy shapes of staircases that went up four steps to a landing and then right back down four steps to the floor. If these staircases were positioned correctly on the stage, it would look as if the actor were climbing up a flight of stairs and disappearing from view.

Hannah found a spot in the wings and glanced out at the lighted stage. The Langer Sisters had taken one curtain call and now they were beginning another encore, the crowd-pleasing Beatles hit, *I Want To Hold Your Hand.* The audience began to clap along with the beat, and Hannah was tapping her foot to the music when she heard a familiar and very unwelcome voice.

"Hello, Hannah."

She didn't need to turn around to know who was standing there. It was Bradford Ramsey. She sent up a little prayer that he still hadn't put two and two together and remembered what they'd been to each other, and then she turned with what she hoped was a polite but neutral expression on her face.

"I've missed you, Hannah," he said, standing much too close to suit Hannah. "I miss those days with you in my class . . . or maybe I should say I miss those *nights.* We had some fun back then, didn't we?"

He remembered her! The sword of Damocles had descended and the hair on the back of Hannah's neck bristled. "I don't miss anything about it," she said, brushing past him to wait for Herb in another spot, a spot as far away from the man she'd once thought she loved as she could get.

Hannah took a deep breath as the curtain went up. It was show time. She smiled as she handed The Amazing Herb doves in cages, colorful scarves, and collapsible flowers in full bloom. She may have seemed attentive to the audience, but only half of her mind was on their act. Bradford had mentioned their nights together. She didn't think he'd said anything about their former relationship to anyone else, but she expected that he would eventually. When he did, her name would be mud with her friends, her family, and the two men she was dating.

In what seemed like mere seconds to Hannah, they arrived at the finale of their act. Herb explained the feat he was about to perform and there were gasps of shock from the audience. Hannah felt a bit like gasping, too. She had to focus. The Cabinet of Death could be dangerous, possibly even lethal if she lost her concentration.

The audience was silent as Hannah stepped into the cabinet. Bradford had upset her so much, she was still shaking, but that actually worked in their favor, convincing everyone who watched that Hannah was truly afraid for her life. She stood there shaking, but smiling bravely as The Amazing Herb opened his case of wicked-looking knives with blades long enough to go all the way through the cabinet. Of course everyone knew it was an act, a trick of some sort. Their conscious minds knew that Hannah wouldn't actually be impaled alive, but Herb was an expert at building suspense and Hannah was willing to bet that more than a few audience members would avert their eyes when he closed the cabinet door and started to insert the long, sharp blades.

The moment that Herb shut the coffin-like door, Hannah got into the position clearly marked on the inside of the cabinet, the posture that would keep her safe.

Thunk! The first razor-sharp blade entered the cabinet at an angle, burying itself to the hilt. It missed her by a mile. It was followed by a second blade, and a third. Hannah moved and changed position in a preplanned choreography that was guaranteed to keep her safe and whole . . . as long as she didn't make a mistake.

It took some doing, but Hannah managed to focus on making the correct moves until Herb had thrust in the last long knife. She was perfectly silent as he removed the knives, one by one. Then he opened the door to the cabinet, and Hannah stepped out, unscathed, to thunderous applause. The audience had loved them. They were a hit despite the distraction of that snake Bradford Ramsey!

"That was great!" Herb said, patting her on the shoulder. "I'll meet you out front as soon as you change clothes."

"Thanks." Hannah stepped offstage with a smile on her face and ran straight into the arms of the man she'd been trying not to think of for the past fifteen minutes.

"I've been waiting for you," he said, tightening his arms

around her. "Where's that pretty little sister of yours? I haven't seen her in a while."

"Good!" Hannah said, and left it at that. She knew Herb was listening, but she was too angry to care.

"Don't be like that, Hannah. I've got a feeling she's a lot like you . . . and you were extra special. I really should get to know her better. . . . don't you think?"

"Leave Michelle alone!"

"That depends on you, Hannah. If *you* won't be nice to me, I'll just have to go younger."

Bradford smiled the smile that Hannah had once thought was sexy. Now it made her see red. She pulled back her arm to sock him, to hurt him, but then she remembered Herb and the questions that were bound to come from her partner's husband. "Just stay away from my sister!" she said, steel in her voice.

"And if I don't . . . ?"

There was that maddening smile again, and this time Hannah blew up. "If you hurt Michelle, you'll live to regret it!" she warned him. "Or better yet, you *won't* live to regret it!"

Hannah paced the dressing room floor for several minutes before she was calm enough to change into her street clothes. Her friends and relatives were waiting for her to join them, but she was so angry at Bradford, she couldn't seem to pull herself together. Thank goodness she had the luxury of time! The Amazing Herb had been the last act before a fifteen-minute intermission and everyone was milling around in the lobby of the Jordan High auditorium, drinking Silver Joe's coffee from the freshly-ground beans that Hannah's friend Pat had provided, and eating the apple turnovers that the assembly line at The Cookie Jar had made from Marge's recipe.

If she hurried, she'd be able to join her sisters and Delores in the lobby. There was only one more thing to do. Hannah made a knot in the bottom of the opaque plastic bag that covered the despised purple dress and carried it to the long pole that served as a temporary closet for costumes.

There were several items of clothing hanging on the pole. Hannah recognized the satin cape that the head majorette from the Little Falls Flyers had worn. Nestled next to it was a long pink scarf left there by a member of Kenny Kowalski's All-Girl Accordion Band. The last item was a red and white shawl and she hadn't seen any of tonight's performers wearing that. Hannah hung the purple dress on the very end of the pole, draped the shawl over it, and hoped that no one would discover it until The Amazing Herb had retired.

She had just gathered up the rest of her things and was ready to leave when she had a dreadful thought. What if Bradford was waiting for her outside the dressing room door? It wasn't that she was afraid of him. She knew how to defend herself. It was just that she wished to avoid any more confrontations with the man who'd made her last months at college a misery.

Hannah glanced up at the speakers mounted above the dressing room door. Right now the only sound they emitted was muted crowd noise from the lobby, but once intermission was over, she'd hear Bradford Ramsey welcome the audience back and introduce Perry, who would give a little talk about the Winnetka County Children's Home. All Hannah had to do was wait until she heard Bradford's voice and then hurry out of the dressing room while he was occupied onstage.

It seemed to take forever, but at last Hannah heard people begin to take their seats. Several more minutes passed, and she heard coughing, low murmuring, and rustling as those same people moved restlessly in their seats, impatient for the second half of the show to begin.

A few minutes more, and Hannah was just as impatient as the audience. Why wasn't the show beginning? There must be some sort of delay. It was silly for her to hide out in the dressing room, hoping to avoid Bradford.

Hannah picked up her things, pulled open the door, and

made her way past the obstacles backstage. She was about to turn toward the door that led to the hallway and the audience beyond, when she glanced onstage and saw Bradford Ramsey sitting in a tall director's chair.

The stage lights were dimmed for intermission and there was very little illumination onstage. Hannah took a tentative step toward the chair. Yes, it was definitely Bradford. He must have fallen asleep, because he'd dropped a half-eaten apple turnover on the stage floor.

"Wake up! They're waiting for you to start the show!" she ordered in her loudest whisper, but it had no effect on the sleeping professor. Hannah took a step closer and gave his shoulder a little shake. "Bradford? What's wrong with you?"

There was no answer and she gave him another shake, much harder than the first. How could he sleep when the audience was waiting? But instead of jumping to his feet as she expected, Bradford tumbled sideways and his head hit the floor with a solid thump.

Uh-oh! Hannah didn't need the little voice in her head to warn her that all was not well, and she fumbled in her purse for the little flashlight on her keychain. She flicked it on and aimed it directly at his face. Even accounting for the blue LED light that made everyone look ghastly, there was no doubt in Hannah's mind. She'd wished him ill, but not quite *this* ill. Bradford Ramsey was stone cold dead.

Chapter Twelve

"You can go home, Hannah." Mike walked over to the chair where she was sitting and patted her on the shoulder. "I'll come by later to take your statement."

"Thanks," Hannah said, pushing back her chair so that she could stand up. Except that she couldn't stand up. Her legs didn't seem to want to hold her upright.

"Take my arm," Mike said, and he lifted her to her feet. "You don't look good, Hannah."

Hannah pretended outrage. "That's something you should never say to a lady!"

"You're right. And I'm glad to see your mouth's all right, even if your legs are still shaky." Mike gave her a little hug. "All the same, I don't think you're in any condition to drive. Is Norman here?"

"No. Something came up and he's not coming back until tomorrow."

"Too bad. You could use some help. I'd better have someone take you home."

"Michelle can drive my truck if you can find her. She said she was coming to the show."

"She's here. I spotted her a couple of minutes ago. I'll have someone send her back here to you."

"Thanks."

"I want you to go home and rest. I'm going to be tied up here for at least two hours, probably three. We have to question all the members of the audience."

"To see if they noticed anyone who went backstage between the time the victim got his turnover and the time I discovered him?"

"That's right. It shouldn't take too long. I called in my whole squad to help. I'll stop by your place when I'm through to take your statement. Let's say around . . ." Mike glanced at his watch. "Is eleven-thirty too late?"

"No. I probably couldn't sleep anyway."

Mike gave her a sympathetic smile. "It's not easy finding murder victims. And you seem to do it an awful lot."

"That's what Mother always says."

"Okay, then. I'll see you . . ."

"Wait!" Hannah interrupted. "I almost forgot to ask you about the talent show. They're not going to do the second act, are they?"

"No. The stage is a crime scene. Since there were so many performers in and out of the area, it'll take the crime scene team the whole night to investigate. After that, the charity event can resume. Mrs. Bascomb is telling everyone to come back for the talent show on Saturday night. They're going to repeat both acts then."

"Do you mean . . ." Hannah cleared her throat. It was difficult to force out the words. "Do you mean that Herb has to do his magic act again?"

"That's right. Mrs. Bascomb didn't think it would be fair if the judges had a three-day lapse between the acts. They're going to do the whole show over again on Saturday."

Hannah felt her knees buckle and she sat back down. She told herself that it was the shock of finding Bradford dead that had made her a little light-headed, but she knew the real reason for her weak knees, her clammy palms, and her pounding heart. She'd thought it was over, that she could put it all behind her and dwell on more pleasant things. But how could life return to normal when she'd have to wear that awful purple dress again?

Of course they'd stopped to pet the cats who were snoozing on the back of the couch. Hannah buried her face in Moishe's soft fur and smiled as she heard him start to purr softly. It must be true that stroking a pet's fur can lower blood pressure and reduce stress. It certainly seemed to be working for her, because she felt much better than she had only moments before.

Michelle, who had been petting Cuddles, glanced over at her. "Do you want me to hang your purple dress in your closet?"

"No, I want you to hang my purple dress in *your* closet. I don't even want to look at it until I have to put it on again Saturday night."

While Michelle took care of the despised dress, Hannah went to the kitchen to put on the coffee. Then she went to the pantry to get out a bag of chocolate chips, a package of miniature marshmallows, and a box of unsweetened chocolate squares. She was standing at the counter, reading through the recipe she'd just taken from a drawer when Michelle came into the kitchen.

"I just can't believe he's dead! Why would someone . . . I mean, what reason did the killer have for . . ." Michelle stopped speaking as Hannah took a stack of mixing bowls out of the cupboard and reached for a baking pan. "What are you *doing?*"

"I'm baking."

"But you just found Bradford's body! You've got to be horribly upset!"

"I am."

"But you're going to *bake?*"

"That's right. Some people cry when they're upset. And

some people yell and punch holes in the wall with their fists. I bake."

"I think that's . . . that's good." Michelle drew a shuddering breath. "Can I bake with you?"

"It's *may I.*"

The corners of Michelle's mouth turned up just a smidgen. "*May* I?"

"Yes. Set the oven for three-fifty, will you? And go get an apron. I think we should make something with chocolate, don't you?"

"Chocolate would be good."

Hannah pointed to the handwritten recipe on the counter. "Jerry Meek, one of the contestants from the first Hartland Flour Bakeoff, gave me this recipe. He told me it was his favorite, and I've been meaning to try it. I think I've got everything I need on hand."

"Two kinds of chocolate?" Michelle surveyed the lineup on the counter.

"Yes. And marshmallows. And I know I've got cream cheese and chopped pecans."

"You can't go wrong with chocolate, and marshmallows, and cream cheese, and nuts," Michelle said, blinking hard several times. And then, even though she did her best to control her emotions, Hannah saw the tears begin to roll down her face.

"Don't you dare cry for him," Hannah admonished her. "He wasn't worth it."

Michelle wiped away her tears with the back of her hand and lifted her head to stare at her big sister. "How . . . how do you know *that?*"

"I found out the same way you did. We both misjudged him and made a bad mistake."

"You . . ." Michelle stopped and took a deep breath. "You knew him?"

"I knew him years ago, and he was a snake back then. He wasn't the type to change his ways."

Michelle grabbed an apron and tied it on, and when she looked up again, she seemed a bit more composed. "The other college he told me about . . . you were there?"

"I was there. He was an assistant professor in the poetry department and I was a very naïve graduate student." Hannah stopped speaking as the tears threatened her as well. She looked down at the recipe, and even though she tried to concentrate on the list of ingredients, the memories rushed back. "I think it was his eyes," she said. "He had the most wonderful eyes."

Michelle swallowed hard. "He *did* have wonderful eyes. They were so perceptive . . . or at least I thought they were. I really believed he knew what was in my heart."

"It was the poetry that convinced me. He read it so beautifully. He told me that I was his inspiration and we'd always be together."

Michelle just nodded. She didn't seem capable of speech.

"If I hadn't found the old hand-bound book when I was waiting for him in his office, I would have gone right on believing that he'd written that lovely poetry himself."

"He *didn't* write that poetry himself? The one about the angels and the faces in the clouds?"

"That poem and all the others were written by someone named Nathaniel Woodman. The book was dated eighteen-ninety."

A little sob escaped Michelle's throat. "He said I was his Elizabeth Barrett and he was my Robert Browning. I was so *stupid* to believe he loved me! And now I don't know if I should be sad, or . . . or glad, or . . . I don't know *how* I should feel!"

Hannah crossed the space between them to give her sister a hug. The whole Swensen family was restrained when it came to physical demonstrations of affection, but Hannah deemed a hug appropriate between two sisters who weren't sure whether to grieve or celebrate.

"He played both of us," Michelle said, blinking back bitter tears. "He must have felt pretty smug making two sisters fall in love with him."

Hannah took a deep breath and spoke the words that were so painful to her. "He didn't know we were sisters. He'd forgotten all about me. He didn't even recognize me when you brought him to the condo for Christmas Eve dinner. That's how important I was to him."

Michelle stared at Hannah in shock, and then she made a little sound of distress. She threw her arms around Hannah and hugged her so tightly that Hannah wondered if she'd have any ribs left intact.

"I'm sorry, Hannah," Michelle said when the hug had ended. "I'm so sorry. I . . . I didn't know."

"Of course you didn't." Hannah reached out to smooth back Michelle's hair, the way she'd done when her sister was a small child and had awakened with a nightmare.

"I wonder how many other women there were," Michelle said at last, and there was an undertone of bitterness in her voice.

"A lot," Hannah answered.

There was a moment, a long moment, when neither of them spoke. And then Michelle asked the question that weighed heavily on both of their minds. "Does anyone have to know?"

"No," Hannah said in her most definite, not-to-be-doubted tone. "No one has to know except the two of us."

"You're sure?"

"I'm sure. Just get some eggs, butter, and cream cheese out of the refrigerator. We're going to make Jerry's Chocolate Marshmallow Cookie Bars, and then we'll mix up some Aggression Cookies."

"Aggression Cookies?"

"They're Karen Moon's recipe, another one from last year's cookie exchange. Karen told Mother that when she has a bad day, she just mixes up a batch and punches out all her frustration on the dough."

"Do you think it'll work?"

"I don't know, but Mother said the cookies were excellent and it can't hurt to try it. Maybe it'll make you forget you ever even knew Bradford Ramsey."

Michelle smiled, but then she quickly sobered. "What if they question me? If Mike asks, I'll have to say I had a . . . a relationship with him!"

"Did anyone ever see you together in a situation that might suggest you were more than student and professor?"

"No. I was very careful about that. He was my faculty advisor at Macalester so nobody suspected anything when they saw us together on campus. Actually . . ." Michelle stopped and swallowed again and Hannah suspected she was choking back another sob. "Nothing ever happened at Macalester. It was only after he came here that . . ."

"I don't need to know the timeline," Hannah interrupted what was obviously a painful admission. "If Mike asks, just say that he was your faculty advisor."

"Okay." This time Michelle couldn't hold back a little hiccup of a sob. "I wish I could go back in time and do everything over!"

Hannah reached out to give her another hug. "So do I," she said.

CHOCOLATE MARSHMALLOW COOKIE BARS

Preheat oven to 350 degrees F., rack
in the middle position.

Bottom Layer:

½ cup butter *(1 stick, 4 ounces, ¼ pound)*

1-ounce square unsweetened chocolate *(I used Baker's)*

½ cup white *(granulated)* sugar

1 cup all-purpose flour *(pack it down in the cup when you measure it)*

1 teaspoon baking powder

1 cup chopped nuts *(I used pecans)*

1 teaspoon vanilla extract

2 eggs lightly beaten *(just whip them up in a glass with a fork)*

Cream Cheese Layer:

8-ounce package cream cheese, softened *(you'll use 6 ounces for this layer and the remaining 2 ounces for the frosting)*

¼ cup softened butter *(½ stick, 2 ounces, ⅛ pound)*

¼ cup white *(granulated)* sugar

2 Tablespoons all-purpose flour *(that's 1/8 cup)*

½ teaspoon vanilla extract

1 beaten egg *(just whip it up in a glass with a fork)*

½ cup chopped nuts *(I used pecans)*

1 cup semisweet chocolate chips *(I used Ghirardelli)*

2 cups miniature marshmallows *(I used Kraft's Jet-Puffed)*

Frosting:
  ¼ cup butter *(½ stick, 2 ounces, ⅛ pound)*
  1-ounce square unsweetened chocolate *(I used Baker's)*
  reserved 2 ounces cream cheese
  ¼ cup milk
  1 teaspoon vanilla extract
  1-pound box powdered sugar

Place butter and unsweetened chocolate in saucepan over low heat. Heat just until chocolate melts. *(You can do this in the microwave if you prefer.)* Stir in sugar.

Combine the flour, baking powder, and nuts. Add them to the chocolate mixture. Stir well.

Stir in the vanilla and the eggs.

Spread the batter into a greased and floured 9-inch by 13-inch cake pan. *(You can spray the inside with baking spray, if you'd rather.)*

Make the cream cheese filling.

Start with the cream cheese. Cut off 2 ounces and reserve it for the frosting. *(That's one-quarter of the package.)*

If your cream cheese isn't soft enough to stir, heat it in a microwave-safe bowl for 10 to 20 seconds until you can stir it. If your next ingredient, the butter, is still cold, you

can throw that in when you heat the cream cheese and do both together.

Combine the softened cream cheese with the butter, sugar, flour, and vanilla. Stir it until it's smooth.

Add the beaten egg and stir until well combined.

Mix in the chopped nuts.

Spread the cream cheese layer over the chocolate layer. Use a rubber spatula to smooth it out.

Sprinkle the chocolate chips over the top. Do this as evenly as you can.

Bake at 350 degrees F. for 20 to 25 minutes. *(Mine took 23 minutes.)*

Take the pan out of the oven, sprinkle the top with the miniature marshmallows, and put it back in the oven to bake an additional 2 minutes.

While the marshmallows are baking, start your frosting. Your pan will come out of the oven before you're through making the frosting, but that's okay.

Melt the butter in a two-quart saucepan over medium-low heat. *(You can also do this in a bowl in the microwave.)*

Break *(or cut with a knife)* the unsweetened chocolate square into two parts and stir them into the butter.

Stir in the softened cream cheese and the milk.

Heat the mixture until it can be stirred smooth. *(Again, you can do this in the microwave in 20-second increments, stopping to stir after each time period.)*

Remove the saucepan from the heat *(or the bowl from the microwave)* and beat in the vanilla.

Beat in approximately a cup of the powdered sugar. When that's incorporated, beat in another cup. When that's incorporated, beat in the rest of the box. *(Doing it this way keeps the powdered sugar in the bowl and not flying out like snow flurries all over your counter.)* Stir the frosting until it's smooth.

When the frosting is smooth, spread it over the hot Chocolate Marshmallow Cookie Bars, swirling it into the marshmallows. It'll be soft, but don't worry. It'll firm up as the bars cool.

Set the pan on a cold burner or a wire rack to cool. When you can handle it without using potholders, slip the pan into the refrigerator and let it chill for at least an hour. *(This makes the bars less crumbly and easier to cut.)*

To serve, cut the bars into 32 pieces. *(That's 8 rows and 4 rows crisscrossing them.)*

Hannah's Note: Chocolate Marshmallow Bars are very rich. (Mike's the only person I've ever known to eat four in

one sitting.) Make sure you have a full carafe of strong coffee right next to the plate with the bars. You should also have another pot all ready to go in the kitchen.

Yield: One recipe makes 32 incredibly chocolaty marshmallowy bars.

AGGRESSION COOKIES

Preheat oven to 350 degrees F., rack
in the middle position.

3 cups flour *(pack it down when you measure it)*
1 Tablespoon baking soda *(that's 3 teaspoons)*
3 cups brown sugar *(pack it down when you measure it)*
4 eggs, beaten *(just whip them up in a glass with a fork)*
3 cups salted butter, softened *(6 sticks, 24 ounces, 1 and ½ pounds)*
6 cups oatmeal *(I used Quaker Quick Oats)*
½ cup white *(granulated)* sugar for dipping the dough balls

Put the flour in a medium-sized bowl. Stir in the baking soda and mix until it's well combined. Wash your spoon and put it away. You won't be using it again today.

Go to your cupboard and find a large bowl, preferably one that's unbreakable. Dump the flour and baking soda mixture in the bottom.

Measure the brown sugar and dump that in on top of the flour mixture. Do not stir.

Whip up 4 eggs in a glass with a fork until they're frothy. Add them to your bowl.

Add all that softened butter. Just dump it in. Don't stir.

Dump in the oatmeal, too. Don't stir.

Think about something that really makes you mad. Now mash, knead, squeeze, pound, and pulverize all those ingredients in the bowl. Drum up every bit of aggression you can and take it out on your cookie dough. Don't stop until everything is mashed, and squeezed, and rounded up into a big ball.

Hannah's 1ˢᵗ Note: Karen says to use ungreased cookie sheets. I forgot and sprayed mine with Pam. Lisa says she used parchment paper. I think these cookies will turn out fine no matter what you do.

Put the ½ cup of white sugar in a small bowl.

Form the cookie dough into small balls about an inch in diameter. Roll the balls in the white sugar and place them on the cookie sheet, 12 to a standard-size sheet. They'll flatten out as they bake.

Bake your cookies at 350 F. for 10 to 12 minutes or until they're golden brown on top. Cool on the cookie sheets for 2 minutes and then remove them to a wire rack to cool completely.

Hannah's 2ⁿᵈ Note: Michelle and I added golden raisins to half of this batch, and chocolate chips to the other half. We thought the cookies were sweet enough without the added sugar on top, so we left that out. The dough balls flattened out by themselves as they baked. If you want to make several different types of oatmeal cookies, you can

divide the dough into several parts and knead something different into each part.

Michelle's Note: Mixing up these cookies is bound to relax you. I copied the recipe to use at Macalester for the times I study all night for a midterm and then find out that not one single thing I studied was on the test.

Yield: 12 dozen tasty cookies, depending on cookie size.

Hannah's 3rd Note: You can cut this recipe in half, if you wish. You can also make it in an electric mixer if you're not particularly mad at anyone.

Chapter Thirteen

The Chocolate Marshmallow Cookie Bars were cooling in the refrigerator and Hannah was just removing the last pan of Aggression Cookies from the oven when the doorbell rang. As Michelle went to answer the door, Hannah glanced at the clock on her kitchen wall. Only two hours had passed since they'd walked in the door. Mike was a lot earlier than she'd expected.

But it wasn't Mike. Hannah was in a position to see both cats sit up and stare at the doorway. Then Moishe's hair began to bristle, and he arched his back like the illustration of a Halloween cat. He gave a low growl, deep in his throat, and then there was a thump as Moishe, closely followed by Cuddles, jumped to the floor and made a beeline for her bedroom.

"Hello, Mother!" Hannah called out before Delores even stepped inside the door.

"Hello, dear." Delores followed Michelle to the kitchen. "How did you know it was me?"

"Just a lucky guess," Hannah answered, avoiding the cruel truth. It wouldn't be good for her mother's ego to know that Moishe disliked her so much, he'd taken his best kitty friend with him and they'd gone to hide under her bed.

"I came to see how you were," Delores explained, glancing pointedly at the coffee pot. "What smells so divine? Don't tell me that despite everything you've gone through tonight, you girls have been baking!"

"We've been baking," Hannah said.

"That's right." Michelle went straight to the coffee pot to pour her mother a cup. "It's like this, Mother. Some people cry when they're upset, and some people yell and throw things. Hannah and I bake."

"Well, that's certainly a lot more constructive." Delores sat down at the kitchen table and waited for Michelle to deliver her coffee. "But you still haven't answered my first question. What smells so divine?"

"I'm not sure. We made Chocolate Marshmallow Cookie Bars first, and then we made Aggression Cookies. And right now, we're mixing up a cake . . ." Hannah went to the refrigerator to take out the pan with the cookie bars. "Would you like a cookie bar, Mother?"

"Yes, thank you, dear. And I'll try the cookies, too. Bud and I met for dinner, but we were running late and we didn't want to take time for dessert."

"You went out with Bud Hauge on a dinner date?" Hannah asked, wondering if Andrea was right and their mother was showing an interest in dating again.

"I certainly wouldn't call it a dinner date, dear. We had patty melts at the cafe, and then we went over to the school for the talent show. Bud's niece plays with Kenny Kowalski's All-Girl Accordion Band."

Michelle delivered two cookies to their mother, one with chocolate chips and the other with golden raisins.

"Thank you, dear." Delores turned back to Hannah, who was cutting the cookie bars at the counter. "I just stopped by to see how you were faring in light of your . . . unfortunate discovery. I knew Norman wasn't back yet, and I was concerned. I'm very glad to see that you're coping so well." Delores stopped and took another sip of coffee. "You knew him, didn't you, dear?"

It was the question she'd been expecting ever since she'd

first seen her mother at the door. Although Delores didn't know for certain, she suspected that Bradford Ramsey had been the unnamed man Hannah had told her about, the man who'd broken her heart in college. Under any other circumstances, Hannah might have admitted it, but this was a murder investigation and she didn't want to put her mother in the position of having to lie to the authorities if she was questioned.

"We *all* knew him, Mother," Hannah said, settling for a partial truth. "Not only was he Michelle's faculty advisor, he was a guest right here in my condo for Christmas Eve dinner. But of course you were here too, so you already knew that."

"Yes. I just meant that . . . you seemed to be so upset when he bumped into you at Stewart Hall last winter when we were going to my small business class."

"Of course I was upset. He scattered the contents of my purse all over the floor."

"But you made some comment about how he wasn't a nice man."

"That's perfectly true. I thought his apology wasn't sincere. Anyone who was truly sorry would have gotten right down there on his knees and helped me pick up the contents of my purse, even though I said I didn't need help."

"Oh. Well . . . I suppose you're right. He did seem more interested in getting to his class on time than he was about helping to right the damage he'd caused."

"My point exactly. You remember what I said when you asked me about it, don't you?"

"Yes. You said you didn't want to talk about it."

"That's right. I was trying to calm down, and talking about it would have just made me angry at him again."

"Oh." Delores gave her a searching look. "Then I totally misinterpreted the reason you didn't want to discuss it?"

"Yes." Hannah found she couldn't quite meet her mother's eyes, so she busied herself by placing several cookie bars on a plate and carrying them to the table.

"These look lovely," Delores complimented her. "I'm glad you baked, dear."

"So am I. Baking is wonderful therapy." And then, because she just couldn't resist, Hannah added, "You really ought to try it sometime."

"*Moi*? Surely not, dear! Why would I even attempt to bake when you do it so well?"

Nicely said, Mother, Hannah thought, but she didn't say it. Instead she motioned toward the plate. "Please help yourself."

Delores selected one of the cookie bars and took a bite. A moment later, her face was wreathed in a smile. "Delicious!" she pronounced. "These are just wonderful, dear."

"I'm glad you like them. Will you excuse me for a couple of minutes? Michelle and I need to finish the Wacky Cake batter."

"The *what*, dear?"

"Wacky Cake. It's a one-pan cake. You mix it and bake it in the same pan. And it doesn't have any eggs."

"That's unusual for a cake?" Delores guessed.

"Very unusual," Hannah told her. "This is a cake that Suzy's grandmother used to make during the Second World War when there was rationing and sometimes people couldn't buy eggs."

"I remember your grandparents talking about that."

"There's a note on the recipe," Hannah told her, retrieving the folded piece of paper from the counter. It says, *From the time of World War Two when eggs could be scarce unless you kept chickens, there weren't fifteen different types of flour in the grocery store, and tap water was safe to drink.*"

Delores gave a little laugh. "I guess that says it all."

"I'll finish the cake," Michelle offered. "You can sit down and talk with Mother."

Hannah's eyes narrowed as she shot a look at her baby sister. The last thing she wanted to do right now was converse with her mother, and Michelle knew it. Delores would want to know the whole story of how she'd found Bradford dead on the stage, and she didn't feel like talking about it.

"Thanks a lot, Michelle," Hannah said, and Michelle winced slightly. It was clear she knew that Hannah meant just the opposite.

She was stuck and she knew it. Hannah poured herself a cup of coffee and carried it to the table. But before she could sit down across from Delores, the doorbell rang. She'd been saved by the bell, the doorbell to be specific. Mike must be here to take her statement.

"That's probably Mike," she said to her mother. "He said he'd drop by to interview me."

Delores looked pleased. "That's perfect, dear. I was planning to ask you all about it. If Mike takes your statement right here at the table, you won't have to tell your story twice."

Hannah said nothing, although she was fairly certain Mike would insist on taking her statement in private. Even though he was no longer a complete slave to police procedure, she doubted he'd bend the rules just to satisfy her mother's curiosity. She walked to the door and opened it, but it wasn't Mike who was standing there on the landing.

"Hi, Hannah," Andrea said, stepping into the condo. "I thought you might be upset, so I came over just as soon as I put Tracey to bed. Is that Mother's car in your extra space?"

"Yes. Come on in. We're in the kitchen, baking."

"Mother's *baking*?"

"Not Mother. Michelle and I are baking."

"But . . . isn't that a little inappropriate under the circumstances?"

"What's inappropriate about baking? I do it every day."

"I know that, but you just found another dead body. Aren't you upset?"

"Of course she's upset," Delores answered Andrea's question. "It's like this, dear . . . some people cry when they're upset. Other people yell and throw things. Hannah bakes. And Michelle bakes, too."

Andrea took a seat at the table and thought it over for a few seconds. "I guess that makes sense, in a way," she said.

"Is there any news about Bill's job offer, dear?" Delores asked.

"Yes. They called him again this afternoon. I told you that Tachyon wants to fly us both to Fort Lauderdale first class so that Bill can meet their top executives and take a look at their operation?"

"You told us that yesterday," Delores said.

"Well, Bill was pretty definite about refusing them yesterday. I heard every word he said."

"Did he know you were listening?" Michelle asked.

"Of course not. I didn't want him to think that I was eavesdropping."

"But you were, weren't you?" Michelle asked.

"No, I wasn't eavesdropping. I stopped by the sheriff's station to ask him what time he thought he'd be home. When I approached his office door, I heard him talking on the phone. The problem was, I wasn't sure whether it was a private conversation or not. I knew that if it was private, it would have been rude for me to go in, so I stood there politely to wait until Bill was through."

Hannah bit back a grin. If she ever needed a good spin doctor, Andrea would be her first choice.

"Anyway, I could tell Bill was talking to the man at Tachyon in Fort Lauderdale because he said it was really nice of them to offer to fly both of us there, but he really didn't think it was fair to leave me alone in a hotel room all day with nothing to do in a strange city while he toured their headquarters and met with their top executives."

"That was considerate," Delores commented.

"Yes, it was. And I only had to point it out to him once last night." Andrea stopped and shook her head. "They must want him really bad."

Badly, Hannah mentally corrected her sister, but she didn't say a peep. This was not the time for a grammar lesson.

"Anyway, he just listened for a few minutes and then he told them he'd think it over. And it turned out that it was really smart of him to say that about not wanting to leave me alone at the hotel."

"They offered him something else?" Hannah guessed.

"And how! They said they'd introduce me to one of the executives' wives my age and she'd show me around Fort Lauderdale. They said she'd take me to lunch at a wonderful restaurant where I could meet the other wives, and then the next morning a car would pick us up and we'd all spend the day at the most exclusive spa in town. They even mentioned a shopping spree to show me Fort Lauderdale's upscale boutiques. Can you believe it? It seems like the more Bill says no, the more they want him."

"I'm going to keep that in mind when I'm out there looking for jobs," Michelle said.

Andrea was silent for a moment, and then she gave a wry laugh. "I think that only works if they come to you. If I'd tried that with Al at the realty office, he would have told me to get lost. And then he would have turned right around and hired someone else."

WACKY CAKE

Preheat oven to 350 degrees, rack in
the middle position.

First set of ingredients:
  1 and ½ cups all-purpose flour *(don't sift—just
    scoop it up and level it off)*
  1 cup white *(granulated)* sugar
  ½ teaspoon salt
  1 teaspoon baking soda
  3 heaping Tablespoons cocoa powder *(about a
    quarter cup)*

Choose a pan. Suzy's cousin used a round cake pan about
2 inches high, her mother used a rectangular cake pan 8
inches by 12 inches, and her aunt used a square 9-inch by
9-inch cake pan that was two inches high. *(Suzy says that
opinions vary, but she doesn't think the cake cares.)*

**Hannah's Note: Suzy didn't say to spray the pan with
Pam or another nonstick cooking spray, but I figured it
couldn't hurt, so I did.**

Put the flour, sugar, salt, baking soda, and cocoa powder
into a bowl. Suzy says to sift all the ingredients together,
but Michelle and I just stirred them with a fork until everything was well blended.

Make three "pukas" *(Suzy says those are holes or wells)*
in the mixed dry ingredients, just as if you were making a
well in your scoop of mashed potatoes to hold the gravy.

Gather the second set of ingredients.

Second set of ingredients:
  6 Tablespoons vegetable oil
  1 teaspoon vanilla extract
  1 Tablespoon vinegar *(we used raspberry vinegar— it was good!)*
  1 cup cold water

Put the vegetable oil in the first puka, the vanilla extract in the second puka, and the vinegar in the third puka.

Pour the cup of cold water all over the top of the cake.

Mix everything up with a fork or a wooden spoon. Continue to beat *(or fork)* until the batter is smooth.

Bake at 350 degrees F. for 30 minutes.

Serve warm.

Suzy's cousin says you shouldn't remove the cake from the pan—just put the pan on the table and serve it that way. Suzy's aunt says you should serve it with sweetened whipped cream or ice cream. Suzy's mother frosts it in the pan. She sifts 2 cups of powdered sugar with a dash of salt in a bowl, and stirs in a teaspoon of vanilla extract and enough cream to bring it the right consistency.

Hannah's Note: This is a great dessert for a novice baker to make!

 # Chapter
Fourteen

They were all sitting in the living room, relaxing with another cup of coffee. A platter of cookies, bars, and frosted cake sat on the coffee table inviting everyone except the cats to indulge. Moishe had come out from under Hannah's bed and he was sitting on Michelle's lap. Cuddles, the sweet little cat that she was, had just left Andrea's lap and was crossing the middle of the couch toward Delores.

"Why, just look at this!" Delores remarked, clearly pleased as punch when Cuddles climbed onto her lap. "She *likes* me!"

Hannah watched as Cuddles started to purr and gazed adoringly up at her mother. Then she turned to look at Moishe, and was forced to cover her burst of laughter with a cough. Moishe's eyes had narrowed to slits, his hair was beginning to bristle, and his ears were flat against his head. Moishe was not at all pleased. He was staring at Cuddles as if her name were Benidicta Arnold, the biggest feline traitor ever to enter the Lake Eden city limits.

Delores had just said something about Joe Dietz and how he wanted her to come to his house to look at the silver he'd inherited from his sister, when there was a knock at the door. Hannah got up to answer it. This time it was bound to be Mike.

But she was wrong again and her eyes widened in surprise. "Norman?" she gasped.

Before Norman could answer, there was a gleeful yowl

from the direction of her mother's lap and a thud as Cuddles hit the rug running. Not to be outdone, Moishe jumped down with a heavier thud to run after her.

The spectacle of two cats racing toward him didn't seem to faze Norman in the slightest. He opened his arms to catch the two flying felines as they jumped up almost simultaneously, sending him back a foot or two on the landing.

"Good heavens!" Delores gasped. "That was quite a sight!"

"You should have seen it from here," Hannah told her. "I thought they were going to knock poor Norman over the rail."

Norman laughed and nuzzled the two purring cats. "Not a chance," he said, carrying them inside and placing them in their favorite spots on the back of the couch.

"Coffee?" Hannah asked him.

"Thanks, I could use some." Norman gave her a quick smile and then he turned to Delores. "Mother said to tell you she's going to bring you back some Venetian glass."

"Wonderful!" Delores looked very pleased.

"And then Earl said he was going to buy you some completely outrageous shoes."

Delores laughed. "I'm not sure I trust Earl's taste in shoes, not after those beaded boots he bought at the mall!"

"I can't say I blame you. Those eagles were pretty colorful."

"Well, I hope they have a simply wonderful time sightseeing, and shopping, and everything else. And how was your visit with your old friends in Minneapolis?"

"Just fine. I toured the clinic. It's ultramodern, and it's got everything a dentist could possibly want."

To Hannah's ears, Norman sounded a bit envious, but perhaps that was only her imagination. She knew Norman liked his own dental clinic and he'd refurbished it just the way he wanted.

"How long has it been since you've seen your friends?" Andrea asked, making conversation.

"I saw two of them at the dental convention I went to last year, but I haven't seen the other two for at least three years."

Hannah entered the living room with Norman's coffee and handed it to him. "I thought you weren't coming back until tomorrow." And then she asked the question that was uppermost in her mind. "What brought you back early?"

"I heard about the murder on the news. And I wanted to get back here as soon as I could. Do you need anything?"

"I don't think so, but I'm glad you're back," Hannah said. She smiled at him and fought back a rush of happy tears. Norman had thought she might need him and he'd come running. He really did love her.

"Besides, my friends all had plans for this evening. And it seemed silly for me to stay over just so I could drop by the clinic in the morning to say goodbye. I drove partway here, and then I stopped at The Moosehead for something to eat."

"I remember The Moosehead!" Delores exclaimed. "I'll never forget the night Carrie and I won their karaoke contest."

"Neither will we," Michelle remarked, exchanging meaningful glances with her sisters.

"That's where I heard about the murder," Norman went on. "I was eating a steak sandwich at the bar, and it was on the news."

Hannah's euphoria at Norman's return took a nosedive. He hadn't dropped everything to race back to her. He'd been coming home anyway.

"Try these, Norman," Delores said, pushing the platter closer to Norman and pointing to the Chocolate Marshmallow Cookie Bars. "Hannah and Michelle baked them, and they're divine."

"The Aggression Cookies are good too," Andrea offered. "And so is the Wacky Cake."

Norman shook his head. "Thanks, but I really can't eat any more. I had a hot fudge sundae before I left The Moosehead."

You betrayed me with dessert! Hannah's mind shouted. *You*

*know I always have something good to serve with coffee, but
you ordered dessert at The Moosehead anyway.*

It was difficult not to react when one's sensibilities had been
so badly injured, but Hannah did her very best. She knew it
was only a matter of time before the pleasant expression on
her face slipped.

"I'd better pack up Cuddles and get home," Norman said.
"Rose is booked for an early morning checkup before she
opens the cafe, and it'll be close to midnight before I get
home."

"But aren't you going to stay to say hello to Mike?" Delores asked. "He should be here any minute to take Hannah's
statement."

Norman turned to Hannah. "Do you need me to stay?" he
asked her.

"No, not really."

"Good. I've had two really late nights in a row, and all I
can think of is getting some sleep."

"I'll help you get Cuddles in her carrier," Michelle said,
jumping up from her seat on the couch.

Hannah said nothing. She was too surprised to speak. Not
only had Norman refused her baked goods, he'd chosen to
go home when he knew Mike was coming to see her.

"Something's wrong with Norman," Delores whispered,
mirroring Hannah's thoughts.

"I know."

"Aren't you going to find out what it is?" Andrea asked,
keeping her voice low.

"He's probably just tired," Hannah said, covering for Norman even though she agreed that he was behaving strangely.
"I'll see what he says when I walk him to the door."

"All ready," Michelle said brightly, coming into the living
room carrying a bag with all the things Norman had brought
for Cuddles. She was followed by Norman, who was carrying Cuddles in her carrier.

"Thanks, Hannah," Norman said. "I know she had a really good time."

Hannah jumped up and took the bag from Michelle. "Watch Moishe, will you? I'll see Norman and Cuddles out."

When Hannah stepped out the door with Norman, she took a deep gulp of the warm night air. The humidity was high and the air felt heavy, laden with the scent of lilacs from the hedge that bordered the back of the condo complex.

"I can take that," Norman said, holding out his hand for the bag.

"But can you handle that and the carrier, too?"

"Not a problem."

Norman took the bag and was about to leave when Hannah grabbed his arm. "Is there something wrong?"

"Other than murder, you mean?"

Hannah laughed. Perhaps it was a lame joke, but it was a joke nonetheless. "Yes, other than murder. It's just that you seem so . . . distant."

"I told you. I didn't get much sleep. Other than that, everything's fine."

"Okay. Goodnight then."

Hannah turned to go, but Norman pulled her back. He dropped the bag and wrapped his free arm around her waist. "Everything's going to be all right, Hannah. I promise." And then he kissed her.

The kiss was warm. Friendly. Nice. It lasted only a second or two, and then Norman picked up the bag and hurried down the stairs.

Hannah stood there for a moment, breathing in the scent of lilacs and blinking back tears. Something was definitely wrong. Norman's kiss had been the type of kiss you might give to an old friend.

Chapter
Fifteen

By the time Mike knocked on the door at twelve twenty-five, Delores and Andrea had left, and Michelle had gone off to bed. Hannah was sitting on the couch, feeling about as deserted as a woman can feel. Mike wanted her to marry Norman, Norman had kissed her like an old friend, and she hadn't heard from Ross in at least three months. The only bright note was that Bradford Ramsey was dead.

"Uh-oh," Mike said when she opened the door. He took in her baggy old gray cotton sweats with one glance, and his gaze lingered on the pair of red socks she was wearing with the hole in the toe. "Are we feeling a little sorry for ourselves?"

"I can't speak for you, but I am!"

A grin swept over Mike face. "Where's your entourage?"

"Moishe's sleeping with Michelle, Mother and Andrea left at eleven-thirty, and Norman took Cuddles home."

"Norman's back?"

"In a manner of speaking."

"What do you mean?"

"Nothing really. He didn't seem very glad to be back, but he was probably just tired."

"It could be the wedding, too."

"The wedding?"

"His mother just got married again. Maybe that made him

feel a little strange. It doesn't matter how old you are. If your mother gets married again, it's still an adjustment. It might even have made him miss his dad more . . . you know?"

"You're right! I didn't even think of that." Hannah felt a bit foolish for ignoring the obvious.

"Okay. Let's get this done." Mike took out his notebook while Hannah poured him a cup of coffee from the carafe on the table. He took a sip, ate one of the Chocolate Marshmallow Cookie Bars she served to him, and gave her a thumbs-up. "These are my new favorites," he declared, taking another sip of coffee and setting the mug down on the table. "Ready?"

"I'm ready."

"Tell me everything that happened from the time you left the ladies dressing room until you called me on your cell phone."

Hannah complied, telling the events in her own words. She recounted how she'd wondered why the curtain wasn't going up, how she'd glanced at the stage as she passed the wings, and how she'd seen Bradford sitting there in a chair. She told Mike how she'd attempted to wake him verbally from what she'd assumed was a nap. And then she stopped, shivering slightly.

"Good," Mike praised her. "Now tell me what happened next."

Hannah took another swallow of coffee in an attempt to clear the lump in her throat. She wasn't sure why it was so hard to talk about Bradford, but it was. "When shaking his shoulder the first time didn't work, I shook him harder. And then he toppled out of the chair and onto the floor and I . . . I saw he was . . . dead."

"Approximately how much time do you think elapsed between the point when you realized that Professor Ramsey was dead and the call you placed to me?"

"I don't know. Maybe two or three minutes? I stared at him for a while. It was just such a shock when he tumbled out of that chair. I remember noticing that he'd been eating one of our apple turnovers, because it was on the floor and half of it was gone."

"What made you suspect he was dead?"

"I knew that just falling to the floor from a chair shouldn't kill him. He hit his head, but not that hard. It was mostly as if he just crumpled, you know?"

"I know. Go on."

"Well . . . he wasn't moving and he didn't seem to be breathing, either. I knew something was wrong, so I got out my LED light on my keychain. It took a minute for me to find it in my purse. When I switched it on, I looked at him and I knew."

"How did you know?"

"I'm not sure, but I just knew. I didn't feel for a pulse. I really hate to do that with dead people, and I was pretty sure he was dead. And that was when I called you so you could come and take care of it."

"Thanks, Hannah." Mike made a final note in his book and put down the pen. "That was very good. You covered almost everything without being asked."

"That must be due to the practice I'm getting. How many dead bodies have I found anyway?"

"I think this makes it over a dozen, but who's counting?"

Hannah refilled their coffee mugs and passed the platter of goodies again. This time Mike took an Aggression Cookie. "How did he die? Do you know yet?" she asked, before he could take a bite.

"I'm sorry, but that information . . ." Mike stopped and shrugged. "I don't know why I'm bothering to give you the official party line. You'll find out anyway. Professor Ramsey was stabbed."

"Stabbed? But I didn't see a knife!"

"That's because the killer pulled it out and took it with him."

Hannah felt a sudden chill and she cupped her hands around her mug of coffee. How close had she come to surprising the killer and putting herself in mortal danger?

"What's the matter?" Mike asked.

"I was just wondering how close I came to . . ." Hannah stopped and swallowed hard.

"Interrupting the killer?" Mike waited until Hannah nodded and then he went on. "Did you see anyone backstage?"

"No. Not a soul."

"Did you hear footsteps? Breathing? Anything that might have indicated another human presence somewhere in the vicinity?"

Hannah thought about that for a moment, and then she shook her head. "No. I think I would have known if someone were there."

"How would you know if you didn't see or hear them?"

"This might sound a little crazy, but I would have gotten that creepy feeling I get when I'm supposed to be alone and I'm not."

"Okay. I'll buy that."

"You will?" Hannah was surprised. "It's not exactly scientific."

"Maybe not, but I get it, too. And it could be scientific."

"How?"

Mike grinned and Hannah thought he looked a little sheepish. "It's like a change in atmosphere, or in air pressure, or something like that."

"You mean . . . you can feel that there's another body in the space?"

"Yes. It's like there's a certain amount of air in the room. That's what you expect when you first walk in. But then you realize there's less air than you expected because somebody else who's not supposed to be there is breathing some of it."

"That's it!" Hannah stared at him in amazement. "That's exactly what I mean, but I never thought to say it that way."

There was a moment when both of them were silent, eyes locked together, minds merged as one. And then both of them broke the connection. Hannah's gaze dropped to her coffee mug, and Mike's to his notebook.

"Only a couple more questions and we're through," Mike told her. "Do you know anyone who might have wanted to kill Professor Ramsey?"

"Me," Hannah said, acting on instinct and jumping off into space like a cliff diver trusting that he'd hit the water just right and find the coins that the tourists had thrown for him.

It took Mike a moment to recover. Then he looked up from his notebook and stared at her. "*What* did you say?"

"Me," Hannah repeated. She knew she had to tell him the truth, or at least part of it. Herb had heard her fighting with Bradford, and she wasn't about to presume on their friendship by asking him to lie for her. She looked up at Mike, locked eyes with him again, and spoke in a completely steady voice. "I wanted to kill Bradford Ramsey," she said.

Another pot of coffee later, and Hannah had told as much of her history with Bradford Ramsey as she wanted to tell. Mike had listened to every word, making no comment throughout her long recital, until she arrived at the conclusion. "And that's why I wanted to kill him," she said.

"But you didn't."

"No. But I *wanted* to, especially after that crack he made about Michelle."

"Can't say as I blame you," Mike gave her a little smile. "As a matter of fact, it might be a good thing I'm *already* investigating his murder."

This time it was Hannah who smiled. Mike hadn't come right out and said he wanted to kill Bradford for what he'd done, but Hannah knew that's what he was implying.

"I hope you'll help me out on this one, Hannah," Mike said, turning to a fresh page in his notebook.

"I will if I can."

"I'm starting with a blank slate here. I didn't know the victim at all. Any background I get on him has got to come from computer searches or other people. I want you to think back, Hannah. Do you know anyone, from your time in college right up to the present, who might have had a reason to kill Professor Ramsey?"

"Try his ex-wife," Hannah suggested. "At least I *think* she's his ex-wife. He was married when I left college and there's no wife in the picture now."

Mike made a note in his book. "Anyone else?"

"You might want to check around at the community college. He started teaching there before Christmas, and he was the type to play around."

"With students?"

"Students, faculty, whoever," Hannah said with a shrug. "It's possible he left a trail of angry women behind him. And if any of those angry women are married, there could be angry husbands, too."

"I'll check on that. I'm almost positive this is a crime of passion and a jealous husband or wife would fit the M.O."

"How do you figure that?"

"The knife wounds were deep, and Doc Knight said the killer used a lot of force. Whoever did it really wanted Professor Ramsey dead. And although the first stab wound was lethal, the killer stabbed him four more times." Mike jotted another note to himself in his book and then he looked up. "Any other suggestions? You knew him a hundred percent better than I did."

"That's true, but it's been a while and it's not like we kept in touch. And I never knew that much about him personally. You could pull his personnel records from the college and explore his job history. And it wouldn't hurt to find out how he got along with his colleagues and his bosses. That might be important."

"How about Michelle?"

Hannah had all she could do not to gasp. "What about her?" she asked.

"She's been at Macalester for over two years. She might have heard some rumors about him."

"You're right." Hannah breathed a sigh of relief. Mike

wanted nothing more than background from Michelle. "I'll ask her in the morning and get back to you."

Mike snapped his notebook shut and stuck it back in his pocket. Then he reached out to pet Moishe, who had left Michelle's bed and come out to join them midway through the interview. "I guess that's it then."

"Aren't you going to ask if I'm going to nose around? And then warn me about interfering with an official investigation?"

"Are you going to nose around and interfere with an official investigation?"

"I wouldn't dream of it," Hannah said quite honestly. She never dreamed about things she was going to do.

"Gotta move, big guy," Mike said, gently unseating Moishe so that he could stand up. "Call me if you come up with anything, will you?"

"You'll be the first to know." Hannah followed Mike to the door.

"There's only one thing I don't get," Mike said, turning around to face her.

"What's that?"

"If you knew Professor Ramsey that well when you were in college, why did he pretend he didn't know you when he came here for Christmas Eve dinner?"

"He wasn't pretending."

"What?"

Hannah gave a little shrug, as if she didn't care. "Bradford didn't remember me," she said. "He knew my name because Michelle mentioned it, but he had no idea who I was."

Mike was silent for a moment and then he pulled her into his arms. He gave her a hug and then he kissed her. It was not the sort of kiss you'd give to an old friend, and Hannah felt her knees go weak.

"It's like I said before . . ." Mike reached out to touch her lips with his finger and then he opened the door and stepped out. "It's a good thing I'm *already* investigating his murder!"

Chapter Sixteen

It was just as her grandmother Ingrid had said. Old habits died hard. Hannah's eyes flew open on the dot of four twenty-nine and she reached out to shut off the alarm before it could ring. When her fingers touched the button that wasn't pulled out to activate the alarm, she remembered. This was the morning she could sleep in for an extra two hours. Lisa had promised to recruit Marge and Patsy to help her with the baking.

Two more hours in bed was a luxury. Hannah fell back against the soft pillows and gave a contented sigh. She reached out to pet the cat who was purring on the pillow next to hers, and let her eyes flutter closed. Two more hours of sleep was the best present in the world. She felt just like she had on Christmas morning, years ago, when she'd run down the stairs to find a shiny new bicycle under the tree!

The pillow was soft, the sheets were still warm, and sublime comfort was all around her, from the darkened room with the low glimmer of the bulb in the Tiffany lamp her mother had given her to the fluffy quilt kept ready at the foot of the bed, a precaution in case the morning hours brought the damp or the cold. This morning the air was perfect, both in temperature and in humidity. The slight breeze from the screened window was like a caress on her skin, and she was totally relaxed. She was tired, yes. But she wasn't sleepy. Not a bit. Not even a smidgen. And her mind was doing jumping jacks behind her closed eyelids, begging for its morning coffee.

Hannah mumbled a word she'd never use around her young nieces and sat up in bed. Since she couldn't go back to sleep, she might as well get up and start the day. Perhaps she'd have time for a nap in the afternoon. Just because she hadn't napped since she was three years old didn't mean it couldn't happen today.

Once she'd showered and dressed, Hannah hurried down the hallway, being careful to tread quietly as she passed the guest room. Michelle hadn't gotten much sleep either, and before Delores had left, she'd told Michelle to take the morning off and come in at noon.

As she approached the kitchen, Hannah began to frown. The bright lights were on. She must have been so tired last night that she'd forgotten to switch them off.

"Hannah!" Michelle gasped, so startled she came very close to knocking over the mug of coffee she was drinking at the kitchen table. "What are you doing up so early?"

"Woke up. Couldn't sleep," Hannah explained in the fewest words possible. This was not the time for an involved explanation that would take precious time, not when her throat felt parched and every cell in her body was screaming for caffeine.

Hannah poured herself a cup of coffee, carried it over to the table, and sat down in a chair. She took the first lifesaving sip, gave a sigh of utter contentment, and took another. The body was beginning to function again and the brain wasn't far behind. Another few sips and there should be a full lexicon of words at her disposal.

"I couldn't sleep, either," Michelle admitted. "I kept thinking about that last fight I had with him. I told him I hoped he'd choke on a mango and die!"

"It must run in the family."

"You told him you hoped he'd choke on a mango?" Michelle asked incredulously.

"I said a cantaloupe, but it's close enough. I assume he was still in the habit of eating fruit for breakfast?"

"Right." Michelle drew a deep breath. "And speaking of breakfast, I made some."

"I thought I smelled something good, and I didn't think it was leftover baking smells from last night."

"I baked Breakfast in a Muffin, and I think they're cool enough to eat. Do you want one?"

"Of course I want one. Is this another one of your creations?"

"Yes." Michelle went over to the counter and brought back two muffins on a plate. "It's for people on the go, like you and me. It's got bacon and egg and cheese on top. I tried one and they're good."

"It sounds good," Hannah said, breaking open a muffin, slathering it with butter, and taking a bite. She chewed, swallowed, and smiled. "It *is* good, and it's a great idea for the coffee shop. A lot of people feel guilty eating cookies for breakfast, but they'd gobble these right up."

Michelle was silent as Hannah ate her muffin. Her forehead was furrowed and Hannah could tell she was thinking about something that was bothering her deeply. "What's the matter, Michelle?" she asked.

"I've been thinking about that book you found in Bradford's office, the one with the poetry he said he wrote."

"Yes?" Hannah took another sip of her coffee.

"Well, I think there's a precedence for using someone else's work . . . in academia, I mean."

"What makes you think that?"

"Bradford used Tim Pearson's work."

Hannah got up to refill her coffee mug. "Who's Tim Pearson?" she asked as she carried it back to the table.

"He's Bradford's research assistant, and he brought me

home after the jazz concert on Sunday night. All the full professors have research assistants. Bradford brought Tim with him from Macalester because they were working on a project together."

"What kind of a project?" Hannah asked, even though she wasn't sure how important that was.

"Bradford said it was a study of seventeenth-century roots in eighteenth-century English poetry. He told me all about it. He said that it had turned into a really hot topic, and he had to publish fast before some other professor from another college beat him to it."

"Did he make it?"

"Yes, and it's a real coup for Macalester to have one of their professors lead the field on such an important topic. Bradford told me he was sure he'd be department head next year."

"Was it publish or perish?"

"I think so. But the thing is, I don't think Bradford wrote any of that paper. I'm pretty sure Tim wrote the whole thing."

"Did Tim get his name on it, too?"

"No. We talked about that when he brought me home on Sunday night. He told me he didn't expect any kind of credit."

"Why not?"

"Because it's almost never done. The professor takes full credit, and the research assistant just does his job."

Hannah bristled slightly. Inequity always disturbed her. Perhaps it was a good thing that she hadn't stayed in academia. "That really doesn't seem fair to me."

"I feel exactly the same way, but Tim told me it was a barter thing, that there was a job as an assistant professor at the community college and Bradford was going to recommend him for it. That was his payment for all the work he did on the project. Tim said the job was a sure thing and he was really looking forward to teaching in Lake Eden."

"So Bradford recommended him and Tim got the job?"

Michelle stared at Hannah for a moment, and then she

began to frown. "I don't know. I think Tim said the selection committee was supposed to meet yesterday morning."

Both sisters were quiet for a long, tense moment and then Michelle spoke. "Are you thinking what I'm thinking?"

"I'm almost certain I am. Do you know anybody at the college who'd know if Tim really did get the job?"

"Someone besides Tim, you mean?"

"Yes."

"Not really, unless . . ." Michelle paused, and then she smiled. "Let's ask Mother to ask her friend, Nancy."

"Good idea! Dr. Nancy might know, and if she doesn't, she can find out."

"I'll ask Mother to call her and get right back to you. But even if Tim didn't get the job, he's really not the kind to . . ." Michelle stopped speaking and gave a little sigh. "I keep forgetting."

"What?" Hannah asked her.

"I keep forgetting what you told me after you caught Larry Jaeger's killer. That almost everyone is capable of murder under just the right circumstances."

When Hannah and Michelle got to The Cookie Jar, they found Lisa hard at work with Marge and Patsy. The first baker's rack was already filled with baked cookies, and more were coming out of the ovens.

"You should have slept a lot later, Hannah," Lisa chided her. "We've got everything under control here."

"But I had to get here before you opened so I could tell you about finding the body, and you could embellish it to thrill our customers."

Lisa laughed as she handed Hannah a cup of coffee from the kitchen coffee pot. "I was going to make the whole thing up, but it's better if part of it's true. Herb wants to talk to you first, though. He's in the coffee shop having a cup of coffee. Just go on in and I'll join you in a couple of minutes."

Hannah took a deep breath and pushed through the

swinging door to the coffee shop. The first sight that met her eyes was a reflection of the eastern sky in the plate glass window of Lake Eden Realty across the street. The sky was a dim blue glow that was only slightly lighter than the darkness that framed the window. Hannah knew that the blue glow would soon lighten to violet, and then to pink. A few moments later it would take on a yellow tone, and finally it would graduate to a golden expanse of brilliance as the sun rose.

"Hannah?" a voice called her from the back table.

"Hello, Herb." Hannah carried her coffee cup to the table and sat down. "I hope you didn't have a bad night because of me."

"I sure wish I hadn't overheard that conversation," Herb said. "I just wanted you to know that I'm not going to say a word about it to anybody, and that includes Lisa and the authorities."

Hannah reached out to pat his hand. "Thanks, Herb. I already told Mike all about it, but I'd appreciate it if you didn't mention it to anyone else. It's . . . well . . . it's embarrassing."

"We've all got embarrassing things in our past," Herb said, giving her hand a little squeeze. "There are a couple of things that happened to me way back when that I'd rather Lisa wouldn't know about."

"I understand. I wouldn't want Michelle to know about that conversation I had with Bradford Ramsey, either."

"She won't hear it from me." Herb took a sip of his coffee, and then he chuckled. "Lisa's all excited about telling the story of how you found the professor. I think I married a frustrated actress."

"Who's a frustrated actress?" Lisa arrived at their table and plunked down her coffee cup. "I'm just glad you're here early, Hannah. Now you can give me some tidbits, and I can make up the rest."

Hannah smiled at her partner. She was surprised that the Lake Eden Players, their amateur theater group, hadn't waged an active campaign to recruit Lisa for their leading lady.

"I was still in the dressing room when I realized that it was time for the second act to start," Hannah told her. And then she proceeded to tell Lisa the details.

"Perfect!" Lisa exclaimed when Hannah was through. "Just hide out in the kitchen and I'll handle all the questions about the murder. We're going to sell a gazillion cookies today!"

"I'm sure you're right," Hannah said. And then she wondered how Bradford would have felt to know that he was worth at least five times his weight in cookies.

BREAKFAST IN A MUFFIN

Preheat oven to 400 degrees F., rack
in the middle position.

2 cups all-purpose flour *(no need to sift)*
1 heaping Tablespoon white *(granulated)* sugar
½ teaspoon salt
2 and ½ teaspoons baking powder
3 large eggs
1 cup whole milk or light cream *(I used milk)*
½ cup melted butter *(1 stick, 4 ounces, ¼ pound)*
12 strips of bacon, fully cooked
12 small or medium eggs
½ cup shredded cheddar, Swiss, or jack cheese *(I
used sharp cheddar)*

**Hannah's 1st Note: Before you start these muffins, you
must decide which type you want to make. You can use a
regular 12-cup muffin pan, or a jumbo pan that makes 6
muffins.**

In a large bowl, combine the flour, sugar, salt, and baking
powder. Stir them all up together with a fork until they're
evenly combined.

Break the 3 large eggs into a medium-sized bowl and
whip them up with a wire whisk.

Add the milk and whisk it in.

Add the melted butter and mix well.

Make a well in the bowl with the flour mixture. Dump the liquid mixture into the well and mix it all up with a spoon until everything is well moistened. *(This batter is supposed to be lumpy—don't stir it smooth.)*

Michelle's Note: I forgot once and mixed the shredded cheese into the batter. The muffins didn't look as nice, but they tasted every bit as good.

Grease (*or spray with Pam or another nonstick cooking spray*) a pan with 12 muffin cups, or a jumbo muffin pan with 6 cups.

Give the batter a final stir, and then put a spoonful of batter in the bottom of the cups, enough to cover the bottom.

Form one strip of cooked bacon into a circle that'll fit inside your muffin cup. Press it down in the batter like a little circular fence. Do the same for the other muffin cups.

Crack and separate a medium-size egg. Put the white into a bowl so that you can make Angel Kiss Cookies, Angel Pillow Cookies, or an egg white omelet later. Slide the yolk inside the little bacon corral you just made. *(If the yolk breaks, don't despair—it'll still taste good.)* Do the same for the other muffin cups.

Hannah's 2nd Note: If you're making jumbo muffins, use 2 strips of bacon and two egg yolks for each muffin.

Divide the remaining batter among the partially-filled muffin cups, just spooning it in on top. These muffins don't rise a lot, so they can be filled almost up to the top.

Sprinkle the grated cheese on the tops.

Place your muffin tin on a drip pan *(just in case)* and put it into the oven.

Bake the regular muffins at 400 degrees F. for 25 minutes. Bake the jumbo muffins at 375 degrees F. for the same amount of time, 25 minutes.

Yield: 12 regular or 6 jumbo muffins that look very pretty when you slice them in half.

Hannah's 3rd Note: These muffins can be reheated in the microwave and they're almost as good as they are right out of the oven.

Chapter Seventeen

Marge pushed through the swinging door to the coffee shop, and Hannah heard part of Lisa's rendition. Her partner was telling their customers the tale of how Hannah had found the professor's body.

"Professor Ramsey?" Hannah asked softly, but the only sounds she heard were the rustling of people fanning themselves with their programs, a low murmuring as they speculated on why intermission was lasting so long, and an occasional cough from the victim of a summer cold.

Lisa paused, and Hannah couldn't help but smile. Her young partner was a great storyteller.

"Wake up, Professor Ramsey" Lisa went on. *"It's time for the second act!"* Hannah's voice was a little louder, cutting through the noise behind the velvet curtain so that he could hear her. But again, he did not answer. She walked forward, right up to the chair where he was sitting and took hold of his shoulder with her fingers.

Hannah heard several gasps from the audience. They knew what was coming.

His shoulder was cold, but Hannah decided that was due to the powerful air-conditioning system they used on the stage to combat the heat from the white hot lights. She gave a little shake with her hand and leaned close to his ear. "Wake up! Everybody's waiting for you!"

He did not wake, and Hannah shook his shoulder again, a bit harder. And then harder still until . . . to her horror . . . he toppled from the chair like a rag doll, arms and legs flopping helplessly to land on the stage in a tangled heap.

"Poor Hannah!" someone exclaimed. Hannah was almost positive it was Bertie Straub.

"Shhh!" someone else warned. "Go on, Lisa."

Hannah's hands flew to her mouth to muffle her startled gasp. What was wrong with Professor Ramsey? Could he possibly be drunk? But there was no smell of strong spirits emanating from his open mouth as he lay there perfectly still, perfectly unmoving, perfectly silent. Hannah glanced down at him, horrified. And then she knew . . .

The door swung closed behind Marge and Lisa's recital was cut short. Hannah chuckled so hard, she had to sit down at a stool at the workstation. Between the murder mysteries Lisa had been reading on the nights Herb worked late, and her natural flair for the dramatic, they really ought to sell tickets instead of cookies.

She'd just taken the last sheet of cookies from the oven when there was a knock on the back door. Hannah slid the cookies onto the baker's rack, wiped her hands on a towel, and went to the back door to open it.

"Hannah." It was Mike and he looked a bit contrite. "I know you're working, but I really need to talk to you for a minute."

Hannah smiled and ushered him to a seat at the workstation. "Coffee?" she asked.

"Only if you have time."

"I've got plenty of time. Lisa's out there performing a solo play called, *Hannah Finds the Professor's Body*, Marge is dishing up cookies by the dozen, Jack is going around with the coffee carafe, and Patsy's running the cash register."

Mike laughed and shook his head, but he sobered when Hannah brought him a mug of coffee and two cookies.

"What are these?" he asked, indicating the cookies. "They've got little holes all over them."

"They're Sesame Seed Tea Cookies. I got the recipe from Sally when she packed those lunches for the film crew."

Mike took a bite. "They're good, and they're different. I like that. And they go really well with coffee."

Hannah took a stool across from Mike and waited until he'd finished one cookie. Then she asked, "What can I do for you?"

"I just finished interviewing the victim's ex-wife. Did you know her?"

"I met her at an English department party, and I saw her around campus, but I really didn't know her. We said hello when we saw each other and that was about it."

"Would you say they had a good marriage?"

"I have absolutely no idea." Hannah looked up at Mike and sighed. "I told you all about it, how he said we'd always be together, and all the time he was engaged to her. It was painful for me when I saw them together. I avoided them the best I could, but the campus still wasn't big enough for the three of us."

"Do you think he told her about you?"

"I'm almost sure he didn't. I'm basing that assumption on the fact that he didn't tell me about her. She certainly didn't act as if she knew. Stacey was always quite friendly when we met."

"Stacey?"

"Yes. Her name was Stacey."

"You're absolutely sure?"

"Of course I'm sure. As far as I was concerned, she was the other woman!"

"When did they get married?"

"Let me see . . ." Hannah thought back to that unhappy time in her life. "It was a little over four years ago, I think."

"Uh-oh," Mike said, rubbing his eyes. "The woman I interviewed wasn't Stacey. Her name was Marilyn Ramsey."

"But that's impossible unless . . . Marilyn must be another ex-wife."

"You're probably right." Mike flipped through his notebook. "I didn't ask her when they were married. Turns out I should have. I'll do a search for Stacey Ramsey and interview her, too. Two ex-wives in four years . . . the professor sure got around, didn't he?"

"I guess he did," Hannah admitted.

"You knew that about him?"

Hannah shook her head. "I trusted him completely."

"You *did*?"

"Yes. Isn't that what people in love are supposed to do?"

Mike thought that over for a long moment and then he got up, walked around the workstation, and leaned over to kiss her on the cheek.

"Yes. And that's probably why I love you so much," he said.

There was a buzzing in her ears like a thousand mosquitoes had descended on her arm. Hannah adjusted her cheek on the hard surface and decided that she was too tired to wave them away. After all, mosquitoes had to eat, too.

The buzzing continued, but her arm felt fine. It wasn't itching, or swelling, or feeling any other way than normal. Perhaps the mosquitoes didn't like her blood. That was the reason Norman always gave for the fact that mosquitoes didn't seem to bite him.

There was a breeze as a door opened. Hannah felt it, but she didn't open her eyes. And then she felt eyes staring at her. A giant mosquito who'd come to feast on her and leave her drained dry like an empty husk? The chorus of mosquitoes was still buzzing. Were they, perhaps, paying homage to their leader?

"Hannah? You're going to get a stiff neck sleeping like that," a voice said very close to her ear. "And your stove timer's ringing. Do you want me to take something out of the oven for you?"

Marge. It was Marge's voice. The giant mosquito sounded exactly like Marge. Hannah lifted her head from the stainless steel work surface and blinked groggily. It *was* Marge.

"Is there something in the oven?" Marge asked.

"Cookies," Hannah just barely managed to say.

"Just sit there. I'll get them. And then I'll pour you a cup of coffee so you can wake up. Norman's out front and he wants to see you."

"Norman," Hannah mumbled. The stainless steel surface of the workstation was beckoning. Who would dream that stainless steel could be so comfortable. But Norman was here and she had to wake up.

"Drink this," Marge said, much too soon to suit Hannah, as she plunked a mug of coffee down next to Hannah's head. "Wake up and smell the caffeine."

One sniff and Hannah felt almost alive. Another sniff and she sat up to reach for the mug. She took a sip of the scalding hot brew and gave a grateful sigh. "Coffee. Good," she said.

"You sound like Frankenstein's monster," Marge said, chuckling at her own joke. "You'd better have more coffee before I send Norman back here to see you."

Hannah took another sip. And then she took another. With each swallow, the curtain of sleep lifted slowly from her eyes. By the time she'd drained the coffee mug, she felt almost like her old self again.

"Ready?" Marge asked her.

"Ready. I didn't burn any cookies, did I?"

"No. Do you feel better after your sleep?"

Hannah made a quick assessment. She felt more alert than she had all day, and other than the soreness in her neck, she seemed to be just fine. "I'm a lot better now. It's amazing how refreshing a ten-minute nap can be."

Marge laughed. "It wasn't ten minutes," she said. "It was

more like an hour and a half. I looked in twice through the window on the door and you were sleeping like a baby."

"I don't understand. I distinctly remember setting the timer for ten minutes. If I really did sleep for an hour and a half, the cookies would be incinerated."

"That's true," Marge said, and then she turned around to point to the sheets of unbaked cookies on the baker's rack. "But you forgot to put them in the oven!"

"Hi, Hannah." Norman walked into the kitchen. "I had an hour between appointments, and I thought I'd drop in to see you."

"That's nice. Do you have time for cookies and coffee?"

"Yes, thanks."

"Which kind of cookie would you like?"

"Whatever you have handy will be fine. All of your cookies are great."

Hannah went to the coffee pot to pour Norman a cup. They were being unbearably polite. It was almost as if they were strangers, and that was about as far from the truth as you could get.

"How's Cuddles?" Hannah asked as she handed Norman his coffee mug and went to the baker's rack to fill a small plate with cookies.

"She's fine. I think she was happy to get home, but I'm pretty sure she misses Moishe. When we went to bed, it took her a while to get comfortable. And maybe I'm imagining things, but I thought she looked a little lonely. I figured that was because both cats slept with you and she missed the company."

Hannah smiled as she delivered the plate of cookies. "You're right. They both slept in my bed and there was barely room for me. I was absolutely amazed how much space two cats can take up when they're all stretched out."

"It's pretty amazing, all right. I'll bet you slept better last night."

"I was so tired last night, I went to sleep the minute my head hit the pillow. But I did notice that Moishe seemed a little restless. Maybe it was a dream, but I thought he kept going back and forth into the living room."

"That's what Cuddles did!"

"Do you think she was looking for Moishe?"

"Maybe. And maybe Moishe was looking for Cuddles." Norman gave a little chuckle. "We might have to arrange sleepovers for the cats. On Monday, Wednesday, Friday, and alternate Sundays, I get Moishe. And on Tuesday, Thursday, Saturday, and alternate Sundays, you get Cuddles."

"Do we need Howie Levine to draw us up an order for joint custody?" Hannah joked. And she was rewarded with a big laugh from Norman. Hearing him laugh made her feel better immediately. He seemed almost like his old self again.

"You're going to investigate, aren't you?" Norman asked, biting into a cookie. "I like these, Hannah. They're not too sweet and they crunch. They'd be really good with a dish of ice cream."

"Thank you. They're Sesame Seed Tea Cookies. And yes, I'm going to investigate."

"Is there anything I can do?"

"I'm sure there is, but I don't know what it is yet." Hannah stopped and thought for a moment. "You could help me put together my suspect list. You're good at things like that."

"I'd be glad to help."

"Good. Maybe we can do it at dinner before we go to the school."

"The school?"

"You know. For Casino Night. I've never been to a fundraiser like that, but everyone says it's lots of fun. You got the advance tickets, didn't you?"

"Oh. Sure I did."

"If you don't mind, let's not go all the way out to the inn for dinner. I really should help out for an hour on the apple turnover assembly line. If you pick me up at six-thirty, we'll still have time to grab a hamburger at the cafe and get over to the school by seven-thirty."

"Fine." Norman said, finishing his cookies and standing up. "I'll see you at six-thirty then."

Hannah watched as he carried his mug to the sink. He gave a little wave as he went out through the swinging door to the coffee shop and she smiled and waved back. But the moment the door had swung closed behind him, her smile disappeared like one of Herb's multicolored scarves. She supposed it was possible that she was mistaken, but she was almost positive that Norman had forgotten all about the plans they'd made for dinner and Casino Night before he'd left Lake Eden.

SESAME SEED TEA COOKIES

Preheat oven to 375 degrees F., rack
in the middle position.

3 cups all-purpose flour *(pack it down in the cup
    when you measure it)*
¾ cup white *(granulated)* sugar
2 teaspoons baking powder
⅛ teaspoon salt
½ cup butter, softened *(1 stick, 4 ounces, ¼ pound)*
2 large eggs, beaten *(just whip them up in a glass
    with a fork)*
¼ cup whole milk
2 teaspoons vanilla extract
¼ cup whole milk in a bowl *(not a misprint—you
    need ½ cup total)*
¾ cup sesame seeds

Grease your cookie sheets or spray them with Pam or
another nonstick cooking spray. You can also use parchment paper, if you prefer.

In a large bowl, stir together the flour, sugar, baking powder, and salt. Mix them up until they're well blended.

Cut the butter into pieces and add them to the bowl.
Blend them in with a pastry blender, or a fork, or two knives
until the mixture resembles coarse cornmeal.

**Hannah's 1st Note: You can do the above in a food
processor with the steel blade by putting in the flour, cut-**

ting COLD butter into 8 pieces and adding them, and then covering the butter with the sugar, baking powder, and salt. All you have to do is process with an on-and-off motion until the mixture resembles coarse cornmeal. Then transfer the mixture to a large mixing bowl and complete the recipe by hand.

Make a well in the center of the flour mixture and add the beaten eggs, ¼ cup milk, and the vanilla extract. Mix with a spoon until a soft dough forms.

Divide the dough into 4 pieces. *(Just eyeball it—this doesn't have to be perfect.)*

With your hands, roll each dough piece out into a long roll *(resembling a snake)* that's approximately ½ inch in diameter. The rolls should be about 24 inches long.

Cut the rolls into 2-inch pieces with a sharp knife.

Put the sesame seeds in a shallow bowl. Dip each piece into the bowl of milk, and then roll it in the seeds. *(The milk will make the seeds stick to the cookie dough.)*

Place the sesame-covered pieces one inch apart on greased or Pammed cookie sheets. *(Parchment paper or baking paper works well also.)*

Bake the cookies at 375 degrees F. for 20 to 25 minutes, or until they're golden brown.

Let the cookies sit on the cookie sheets for one or two minutes, and then remove them to a wire rack to cool completely.

Yield: Approximately 4 dozen, depending on cookie size.

Hannah's 2nd Note: These cookies are light, crispy, and not too sweet. Mother loves them with strawberry ice cream, and Carrie likes them with sweetened herbal tea.

# Chapter
Eighteen

"So you knew him?" Norman asked, picking up his last French fry.

"He was an assistant professor when I was going for my masters," Hannah said, hoping that would be enough of an explanation to satisfy Norman.

"That's funny. He didn't act as if he knew you on Christmas Eve."

"It was pretty clear he didn't remember me. And I wasn't about to embarrass a guest by reminding him we'd known each other years ago."

"Right." Norman nodded. "What do you know about him?"

"I don't know anything about his recent life, but there were rumors about him on campus. He had more than one girlfriend and it turned out that he was engaged at the time."

"Then he's got a wife or an ex-wife?"

"He's got one ex-wife that Mike interviewed, and that's not the same woman he married while I was on campus."

"Two ex-wives then. How about now? Is he married again?"

Hannah shrugged. "I'm not sure. I don't think we have to worry about the wives, though. Mike's checking into those. He does seem to think it's a crime of passion since the first stab wound was lethal and he was stabbed four more times."

"Revenge?"

"That's certainly possible. Revenge, jealousy, hatred . . . it could be any strong emotion, I guess."

"He sounds like a guy that really played the field," Norman said. "I wonder if any of that playing took place here in Lake Eden."

"I'd be willing to bet it did. The only problem is identifying his playmates."

"Delores?" Norman suggested. And at almost the same time Hannah said, "Mother?"

They looked at each other and laughed. "I'll ask her," Hannah promised. "It's too bad your mother isn't here. She'd enjoy helping."

"I know. She loves to nose around for information. But what we really need is a spy on campus."

"Michelle." Both of them spoke at once again, and they even nodded in tandem.

"We did it again," Hannah commented. "It's like we're twins or something. And that reminds me . . . You know the Connors twins, don't you?"

"Sure. I whitened their teeth before their last big competition. I figured it was the least I could do for Lake Eden's most famous couple."

"Better not let Mayor Bascomb and Stephanie hear you say that!"

"You're right. Now what about the twins?"

"They're living on the campus now, and Sherri's a secretary at the English department office. We could ask her if she's heard the other secretaries talking about Bradford's romances."

"Good idea." Norman waited until Hannah had jotted it down in the new steno pad she'd brought with her. "I wonder where Professor Ramsey lived."

"Andrea could find out for us. If he lived on campus, there'll be a vacancy and Lake Eden Realty handles all the college apartment leases. And if he lived off campus, there'll be a house for rent and Lake Eden Realty will handle that, too."

"We can talk to her tonight at the school. She's going to Casino Night, isn't she?"

"Yes. She called me this afternoon and said they'd be there. As sheriff, Bill's expected to attend these big charity events."

Norman glanced down at the steno pad and pointed to an entry Hannah had made earlier. "Who's Tim Pearson?"

"Bradford's research assistant. Tim wrote a paper for Bradford that gave him a rung up the academic ladder at Macalester. In payment, Bradford assured Tim that the assistant professor spot here at Lake Eden Community College would be his."

"But those things are decided by committee, aren't they?"

"Yes, they are. But Bradford knew everyone on the hiring committee, and he assured Tim that they'd take his recommendation."

"I see. If Tim didn't get that job, it's a motive for murder. And that's why you wrote down his name as a suspect?"

"Right."

They both fell silent as Rose approached their booth with the coffee carafe. "More coffee?" she asked.

"Yes, thanks," Hannah said, and Rose filled her cup. "How about you, Dr. Rhodes?"

"I could use another cup," Norman said.

"Now how about dessert?" Rose asked, once she'd cleared their table, rather efficiently Hannah thought, by moving their dirty dishes to another unoccupied booth. "I've got two pieces of Peachy Keen Cake left."

Hannah sighed. There was no way she could resist Rose's Peachy Keen Cake.

"Was that sigh a yes?" Rose asked her.

"Yes." Hannah looked over at Norman. "Have you ever tried it?"

"No," Norman said, looking interested.

"Well, then you're in for a treat." Hannah looked up at Rose with a smile. "We'll each have a piece with a scoop of vanilla ice cream, please."

Rose delivered their cake within a minute or two, and for

almost a quarter-hour, there was no sound in Hannah and Norman's booth any louder than the occasional soft moan of pleasure. But all good things must come to an end, and once they'd finished their cake and their dessert dishes had been cleared, Hannah turned back to her suspect list.

"Back to work," Hannah said, staring down at the blank lines on the pad.

"How about students he flunked?" Norman suggested.

"Would that be a motive for murder?"

"It could be. Let's say Professor Ramsey's failing grade was the straw that broke the camel's back. Because the student flunked his class, he flunked out of college. And because he flunked out of college, he . . . I don't know. Lost his girlfriend? Got disowned by his family? Whatever. It's got to be some dire consequence."

"Or at least some consequence that the student thinks is dire."

"Right."

"It's a great idea, Norman. But how can we get access to the community college grades?"

"I can probably find a way. Just write down *failing student* and leave the rest up to me."

Hannah was more than happy to do that, and as she wrote it down, she thought of something else. "We should probably check into his finances to see if he was living above his means."

"What will that prove?"

"College professors don't make that much money, and he had two ex-wives. He might have had alimony and maybe even child support."

"If he was strapped for money, he might have turned to some illegal way to get it?"

"Exactly." Hannah gave him a smile. Norman always caught on fast. "There's dealing drugs, blackmail, gambling, all sorts of things."

"So we need to find out his salary. And then we need to find out what he was spending to see if he had any extra."

Hannah glanced at her watch. "We'd better go. Casino Night starts in less than ten minutes."

"Okay. I'm ready. I hope they have all the casino games. I feel lucky tonight."

"So do I," Hannah said, and it was perfectly true. Perhaps Mike had been right and Norman had been upset over Carrie's marriage. Or perhaps he'd been exhausted from late nights with his dental school friends. It could even be that he envied their fancy new dental clinic and felt less successful practicing run-of-the-mill dentistry here in Lake Eden. It didn't really matter what the problem had been, now that it appeared to be solved. She was just happy to have the old Norman, the comfortable sweet Norman she loved, back with her again.

ROSE'S PEACHY KEEN CAKE

Preheat oven to 350 degrees F., rack
in the middle position.

4 egg whites *(save the yolks to add to scrambled
eggs in the morning)*
¼ teaspoon cream of tartar
¾ cup softened butter *(1 and ½ sticks, 6 ounces)*
1 package *(8 ounces)* softened cream cheese *(the
brick kind, not the whipped kind)*
2 cups white *(granulated)* sugar
3 teaspoons baking powder
½ teaspoon salt
2 beaten eggs *(just whip them up in a glass with a
fork)*
½ teaspoon almond extract
½ teaspoon vanilla extract
1 and ½ cups mashed peaches ***
2 and ½ cups all-purpose flour *(don't sift—just fill
the measuring cup and level it off with a knife)*
1 cup finely chopped blanched almonds

**** - You can use fresh and peel and slice your own, or
you can buy them already sliced and prepared in the
ready-to-eat section at your produce counter, or you can
use canned peaches.*

**Hannah's 1ˢᵗ Note: This is a lot easier with an electric
mixer.**

Beat the egg whites with the cream of tartar until they form soft peaks. Set them aside in a bowl on the counter while you mix up the rest of the cake.

In another bowl, beat the softened butter, softened cream cheese and sugar together until they're nice and fluffy.

Add the baking powder and salt. Mix them in thoroughly.

Add the beaten eggs, the almond extract, and the vanilla extract. Mix until they're well incorporated.

Peel and slice the peaches *(or drain them and pat them dry if you've used prepared peaches or canned peaches.)* Mash them in a food processor with the steel blade, or zoop them up in a blender, or squash them with a potato masher until they're pureed. Measure out 1 and ½ cups of mashed peaches and add them to the bowl with the butter, sugar, eggs, and flavorings. Mix everything thoroughly.

Gradually add the flour to the peach mixture, beating at low speed until everything is incorporated. If you're doing this by hand, add the flour in half-cup increments, stirring it in after each addition.

Mix in the chopped almonds by hand.

Gently fold in the beaten egg whites, trying to keep as much air in the batter as possible. It's okay if there are a few white spots from the egg white that hasn't been thoroughly incorporated.

Spray the inside of 3 round layer pans, one 9-inch by 13-inch cake pan, or one Bundt pan *(don't forget to spray the middle part)* with Pam or another nonstick cooking spray, and then dust it lightly with flour. You can also use "baking spray," the type with flour added.

Pour the cake batter into the pan or pans you've chosen.

Bake at 350 degrees F. for approximately 15 minutes for the layers, and 40 minutes for a 9-inch by 13-inch pan. A Bundt pan will take 50 to 60 minutes. Test for doneness by using a cake tester or a long toothpick inserted one inch from the center. When it comes out dry and not sticky, your cake is done.

Let the cake cool in the pans on a wire rack. If you used a Bundt pan, cool it on a wire rack for 15 minutes and then gently pull the edges of the cake away from the sides of the pan. Do the same for the fluted column in the middle of the pan. Then invert the cake onto another wire rack, lift off the pan, and allow it to cool completely.

Yield: One deliciously peachy cake.

Hannah's 2nd Note: Rose says that when she makes this cake in layers, she uses peach jam between the layers and frosts it with Peachy Keen Frosting. When she makes this cake in a Bundt pan, she either dusts it with powdered sugar to "pretty it up," or drizzles the top with Peachy Kean Glaze for Bundt Cakes. Sometimes she puts a few

canned peach slices in the bottom of her Bundt Pan so that they're on top when she turns out her cake.

Hannah's 3rd Note: If you want to make cupcakes, pour the batter into greased and floured (or cupcake papered) muffin tins and bake at 375 degrees F. for 20 minutes or until a toothpick inserted in the center comes out clean. (Mini cupcakes should bake for 10 to 12 minutes or until slightly golden on top.)

PEACHY KEEN FROSTING

¾ cup peach jam *(I used Knott's)*
1 egg white *(add the yolk to the 4 others you've saved to add to scrambled eggs)*

Hannah's 1ˢᵗ Note: If you can find peach jelly, (it's clear with no pieces of peach in it) by all means use it. It will eliminate one step in making this frosting. I've never seen peach jelly in any store, so I use the jam.

Hannah's 2ⁿᵈ Note: You can do this with a portable electric mixer or even an old-fashioned crank-type egg-beater. You might be able to do it with a wire whisk, but it'll take some muscle.

Puree the peach jam in a food processor with the steel blade or in a blender. Once it has no lumps and is perfectly smooth, measure out 1/2 cup to use for the frosting. *(If there's any left over, just stir it into the jam left in your jar and put it back in the refrigerator.)*

Put some tap water in the bottom of a double boiler and heat it until it simmers. *(Make sure you don't use too much water – it shouldn't touch the bottom of the pan on top.)* Off the heat, beat the egg white with the peach jam in the top of the double boiler. When it's thoroughly blended . . .

Set the top of the double boiler over the simmering water and continue to beat until the jam has melted. You can tell because it will get thinner, almost like juice *(3 minutes or so.)*

Shut off the heat, lift the top of the double boiler off the bottom, and place it on a cold burner, or a towel on your kitchen counter. Continue to beat the frosting until it will stand up in peaks. *(To test this, just turn off your beaters and lift them from the pan—if they leave peaks on the frosting, it's ready to use.)*

Yield: Enough Peachy Keen Frosting to cover a 9-inch by 13-inch loaf cake or 12 cupcakes.

Hannah's 3ʳᵈ Note: If you've used layer pans for this cake, Rose says to double the recipe because there's nothing worse than trying to make frosting stretch. If you just make double in the first place, you'll have plenty.

PEACHY KEEN GLAZE FOR BUNDT CAKES

½ cup peach jam
½ cup powdered sugar

Hannah's Note: Rose says to tell you that making this glaze is almost as easy as dusting the cake with powdered sugar. You can do it in the microwave and it takes only 2 minutes.

Scoop the jam into a microwave-safe bowl with a pour spout or a 2-cup glass measuring cup.

Heat the jam on HIGH for 20 seconds. Stir. If it's melted, you're done. If it's not, give it another 20 seconds.

Stir the powdered sugar into the hot melted jam by spoonfuls. Continue to add and stir smooth until your glaze is the right consistency to pour on top of your Bundt cake. You'll want it thin enough so it'll drip down the sides of the cake, and thick enough so it won't all just run down in a flood and pool at the bottom of your cake plate.

Drizzle the glaze on top of your cake and let it drip artistically down the sides. Let the glaze cool and then refrigerate your cake until you're ready to serve it.

Chapter Nineteen

Bright flashing lights, the sound of laughter, and excited voices spilled out of the open double doors to the Jordan High auditorium. Hannah and Norman handed their tickets to a student at the door and entered the transformed space.

Vegas couldn't have done better. The seats had been removed from the floor of the auditorium and replaced with bistro-style tables and chairs. The area that had housed the last five rows of seats had been turned into four colorful booths. The outer two booths sold tokens to use at the game tables, and there was a line in front of both of them. One of the inner booths featured their apple turnovers for sale, and the other sold Silver Joe's coffee made in the thirty-gallon coffee pots that the company had donated to the cause. Hannah had expected all that, but the central area between the turnover and coffee booths was a total surprise. It was called "Make Wishes Come True," and it featured a decorative fountain with a ledge where people could sit. The fountain was a smaller rendition of the famous fountain in Rome, and it was a working fountain with real water jetting up into the air and cascading down to the pool below.

"That's really something!" Norman exclaimed, spotting the fountain.

"It certainly is," Hannah said, noticing that the pool was already filled with glittering coins.

"Watch the woman in pink," Norman said, and Hannah turned to see a woman leave the token booth and toss some coins in the fountain. "She's the third person to leave that booth and drop her change in the fountain," Norman commented.

"That figures. It's in the perfect spot."

While Norman got in line to get their tokens, Hannah checked in at the apple turnover booth, accepted a small cup of coffee to go, and went back to sit on the ledge of the fountain to wait. Within a minute or two, five people had tossed in their loose change. It made perfect sense to Hannah. Tossing coins in the fountain was a lot easier than opening your purse, finding the right pocket for coins, and dropping them inside. She had no doubt that the fountain would be drained and relieved of its riches the moment Casino Night was over. When it came to raising money, Stephanie Bascomb didn't miss a trick.

Once Norman had purchased their stack of tokens, they walked up the steps to the stage. The curtains and backdrops that had defined the stage area last night at the talent show had been pulled up to the ceiling to expose the whole basketball court. The wooden floor, itself, had been completely covered with carpeting. A sign hanging over the first row of gaming tables read *Lake Eden Casino* in flashing neon lights, and Hannah suspected it had been a charitable donation that would be auctioned off to enhance someone's basement recreation room on the final night of the charity event.

"What do you want to play first?" Norman asked her. "Roulette? Poker? Blackjack?"

"I don't know. I'm not very good at any of them. What do you suggest?"

"Roulette. It's a game of pure chance, no skill required." Norman took her arm and they began to walk toward the Roulette table. "All you have to do is choose red or black. Or odd or even. Those are all even money bets. Or you can pick a series of numbers like one through eighteen, or eighteen through thirty-six. Those are all even money bets."

"Okay," Hannah said, but it was a bit too much information to process. "I'll choose . . ."

"Wait. There's more," Norman interrupted her. "I haven't
covered the two-to-one bets. You can choose dozens."

"There are dozens of two-to-one bets?" Hannah asked,
knowing she'd never keep all this straight.

"No. The bet is called *dozens*. If you pick the first dozen, it
means you're betting the ball will fall somewhere in the first
twelve numbers. There's also the second dozen, and the third
dozen, so you've got a choice. And then there are the columns.
You can bet on any column of three on the grid and that'll
pay two-to-one if you're right. Dozens and columns are outside bets."

"Great. Thanks for explaining it to me. I'll choose . . ."

"Not quite yet," Norman interrupted her again. "I still have
to cover the inside bets. You can bet a single number, a street,
a split, a corner, a five-number, or a double street. Most people
say that the five-number bet is the worst bet on the table."

"Then I won't choose that." Hannah gave a little laugh.
"I'll choose red since that's my favorite color."

"Okay. but it's an even money bet. If you win, the payoff's
not as big."

"Not as big as what?"

"Not as big as if you choose an inside bet."

"Okay," Hannah said. It was pretty obvious that Norman
wanted her to make an inside bet, but things like corners, and
streets sounded complicated. The easiest seemed to be the single number bet, but which number should she choose?

"Sit here, Hannah." Norman pulled out a chair for her
and took one himself.

"It looks complicated." Hannah gazed down at the wheel,
the grid, and the boxes. "Can't I just watch?"

"If you're sitting here, you have to play," Norman explained. "Non-players have to stand."

Hannah didn't think it over for long. She was tired and she
wanted to sit down. "I'll play," she said.

"Then place your bet."

Unbidden, an image popped into Hannah's mind. It was from a James Bond movie and he had just bet a bundle on seventeen. If that number was good enough for such an important fictional character, it was good enough for her! She reached out and placed her bet on number seventeen.

"They used to use an ivory ball," Norman explained, gesturing to the wheel. "Now they're usually plastic."

Hannah stared at the wheel. It had thirty-eight numbered slots, each with the same colored background as the number on the table layout. She watched as the dealer spun the wheel in one direction and then rolled the ball in the opposite direction on a track that ran around the bowl that held the wheel. When the speed of the ball decreased, it fell off the track and onto the wheel itself. There it bounced around wildly until it settled in a numbered slot.

"Seventeen!" Hannah gasped. "That's my number! Does that mean I won?"

"Yes it does, Little Lady," the dealer said, smiling at her.

Under any other circumstances, Hannah would have bristled at the term *Little Lady*, but she was willing to be magnanimous, especially when the dealer pushed a big pile of chips across the table to her.

"Pick them up, Hannah," Norman said, nudging her.

"But why? They're okay there, aren't they? There isn't very much room in front of me and . . ."

Hannah was so excited, she didn't even notice that the wheel was spinning again. The ball in the track slowed and the dealer called out, "No more bets."

"But I didn't get a chance to bet," Hannah complained to Norman.

"Yes, you did. You bet that whole stack of chips you didn't pick up."

"Uh-oh!" Hannah groaned, mentally kicking herself for not listening to Norman's advice. "Now I'm going to lose it all."

"You're only out one chip. The rest was house money. And don't forget it's all for charity."

"Right," Hannah said, but she continued to kick herself as the ball began to slow and settle in the numbered slot . . .

"Seventeen again!" Hannah couldn't believe her eyes. "I won twice in a row!"

"Makes me wish we were betting real cash," Norman said.

Hannah shook her head. "Then I wouldn't have won. Tell me what to pick up . . . quick!"

They stayed and played for another few minutes, Norman instructing and Hannah listening carefully. There really was no skill required. All she did was choose a number, place her bet, and either pick it up herself or see it swept away by the dealer.

"Ready for some coffee?" Norman asked, not a moment too soon to suit Hannah.

"Yes. And then let's walk around to see who's here."

Ten minutes, four wishes at the fountain, and two cups of coffee later, Hannah spotted Delores at a Blackjack table seated next to Doc Knight. "Let's go say hello," she suggested.

"Perfect timing," Norman said as they approached. The dealer, who was using a shoe, had decided to replace the decks. That meant he had to break out, display, and shuffle four decks while the players waited. The process would take a few minutes, and that meant Hannah and Norman had time to talk to Delores and Doc Knight.

"Hello, dear," Delores said when Hannah tapped her on the shoulder. And then she turned to Norman. "I'm glad you're back at work, Norman. Luanne had a toothache this afternoon. She comes in at nine tomorrow. Do you have any time to see her in the morning?"

"Hold on. Let me check." Norman pulled out his cell phone and pressed a few buttons. From where Hannah was standing, she saw a display with times and dates. "Send her down at ten."

"Thank you, Norman. After you're through, tell her it's covered under the Granny's Attic employee dental plan."

"Which dental plan do you have?"

"The Delores Swensen checkbook plan. But I don't want you to mention that. I'll pay and she'll think that our insurance covered it."

"Must run in the family," Doc said, who up to that point had taken no part in their conversation.

"Nonexistent dental plans?" Hannah asked him.

"No, paying medical bills for people who can't afford them. And you know what I'm talking about, Hannah."

"Oh, that." Hannah dismissed it with a wave of her hand.

"You paid someone's medical bill?" Delores asked her.

"Yes. Sherri Connors was really sick yesterday afternoon at the talent show orientation and I told Perry I'd pay if he took her to Doc Knight's clinic." Hannah turned to Doc. "Perry said it wasn't serious."

Doc nodded. "She's a sweet girl and it's a real pity, but she'll be feeling better in a week or so."

"Mother?" Hannah considered the best way to ask about Tim Pearson and whether Nancy had found out anything.

"Yes, dear." Delores responded, and then she smiled. "I'll bet you're wondering why Nancy's not here."

"Right." Hannah mentally complimented her mother for being such a good recipient of daughterly radar.

"She invited a few of the faculty over for cocktails and canapés this evening, a little gathering of department heads, now that she's chairman of the psychology department. She said she'd give me a call later, when I got home."

"Wonderful."

Doc Knight turned to look at Hannah, and then he turned back to Delores. "Why do I get the feeling I'm listening to Julia Child?" he asked.

"Julia Child?" Hannah repeated, wondering what on earth the celebrated French chef had to do with it.

"She was a spy in the Second World War, and it sounds to

me like you and your mother are passing secret messages right under my nose. What's going on?"

"We're passing messages under your nose," Delores said, perfectly deadpan, and Doc Knight laughed so hard, he almost upset his stack of chips.

"Is this about the professor's murder?" he asked, when he'd stopped laughing.

"Yes," Hannah answered him.

"Well, I could take a guess on who did it, but I won't," Doc said, turning to Delores. "Unless your mother worms it out of me. She's good at things like that."

"Oh, *you*!" Delores said playfully. And out of the corner of her eye, she gave Hannah a clear daughter-motherly radar signal to get lost.

They'd been wandering around for about an hour, stopping to play at various games, when Norman's cell phone rang. He took it out of his pocket, glanced at the display, and said "I'd better get this."

"Okay," Hannah said, waiting for him to press the right button and speak to his caller. But instead of answering the call, Norman slipped the phone back into his pocket.

"I'll go outside to take it," he said. "It's pretty noisy in here. Why don't you go play Keno until I get back? They've got chairs set up, and all you have to do is mark numbers on a card."

It was pretty obvious that Norman didn't want her to go outside with him. Hannah smiled and nodded, and then she headed back to the Keno area. She sat in a chair, reached down to rub her aching feet, and was surprised when someone tapped her on the shoulder.

"Hi, Hannah."

Hannah turned to look and found herself staring straight into the eyes of her sister Andrea. "Hey!" she exclaimed. "I've been looking for you."

"I've been hiding out here while Bill does the obligatory

glad-hand thing," Andrea explained. "I just couldn't say another, *Oh my, how wonderful it is to see you again!*"

"But you're so good at that."

"Not tonight. I'm too worried about Bill's latest offer."

"From Tachyon?"

"Who else? It's a brand new luxury car and it's free. He can use it for work *and* for personal driving. They're going to give him a gas card and pick up all expenses, including parking."

"You were right. They really do want him."

"I know. I'm just scared to death he'll accept. The kids and I will have to move and . . . and . . ." Andrea stopped, struggling to blink back tears. "I'll be down there in Fort Lauderdale with the bugs and the crocodiles . . . and you'll have to deal with Mother all by yourself!"

"Alligators," Hannah corrected her automatically. "And what do you mean, *I'll have to deal with Mother?*"

"I mean you'll have to . . ." Andrea stopped and stared at Hannah. "You didn't see her?" she asked.

"I saw her. She was playing Blackjack with Doc Knight."

"Well, they weren't playing when I saw them." Andrea stopped and frowned. "Or maybe they *were* playing. It all depends on how you look at it. All I know is they were sharing one of your apple turnovers the same way Lady shared that strand of spaghetti with the Tramp!"

Hannah's eyes widened. "You mean they were actually holding it in their mouths and eating it from opposite corners?"

"No. I was just using a meta . . . what do you call that?"

"Metaphor?"

"Yes. I was just using a metaphor. They didn't have it in their mouths, but they were eating bites of it with their forks. Mother was forking from one corner, and Doc was forking from the other. I . . . well . . . I didn't stick around to see what happened when they got to the middle."

Hannah couldn't help it. She laughed. And that earned her a scowl from Andrea.

"I don't think this is one bit funny," Andrea said.

"I do." Hannah knew she had to come up with an explanation that Andrea would accept, and she glommed onto her sister's reference to the Disney movie. "I was thinking about Lady and the Tramp," she explained. "I just love that scene with the spaghetti. It's funny, but it's so sweet . . . you know?"

Andrea smiled. "I *do* know. I feel the same way. It's my favorite part of the movie, even better than the ending with the baby and the puppies. Tracey loves it, too." Hannah watched as Andrea stopped speaking and began to look worried again. "What do you think we should do about Mother?"

"Nothing."

"Nothing?"

"Nothing yet. Carrie's wedding seems to have inspired all the eligible men in Lake Eden, and Mother's simply enjoying all the attention."

"Then you don't think she's serious about Doc?"

"I don't think so, not when I happen to know that she had dinner with Bud Hauge last night."

"Really?"

"That's what she said. And then they went to the talent show together." Hannah gave her sister a reassuring smile. "I really don't think we have to worry about Mother unless she dates the same man a couple times in a row."

"*Dates?*" Andrea picked up on Hannah's word choice. "Then you think Mother's *dating?*"

From the horrified expression on Andrea's face, Hannah knew she had to backtrack fast. "Not dating exactly," she said. "It's more like renewing old acquaintances with everyone she knew years ago when she went to Jordan High."

"Oh." Andrea looked relieved. "Well . . . I guess that's all right then. It's good to keep in touch with old friends." Andrea stopped speaking and nudged Hannah. "Here comes Norman and he looks upset."

Hannah looked up. Norman was still half a basketball court away, but he did look upset. "He went outside to take a phone call. I hope it wasn't bad news."

Both sisters watched Norman bob and weave around stationary people. He was making good progress even though the auditorium was crowded with human obstacles. When he arrived at their sides, he gave a sigh of relief. "Why do people always stop in the middle of the aisle to talk? They do it in grocery stores, too."

"I don't know," Andrea said.

"Me either," Hannah concurred. "Just one of the peculiarities of human behavior, I guess."

"I'm sorry that took so long," Norman said to Hannah. And then he turned to Andrea. "I ran into Bill when I was outside. He was just leaving, and he asked me to find you and tell you he got called in."

"Wonderful," Andrea said in a tone that clearly said it wasn't.

"Anyway," Norman turned back to Hannah. "I'm afraid I have to leave. Something's come up. Do you want me to give you a ride to The Cookie Jar to get your truck?"

Hannah shook her head. "No, I'll stay here with Andrea for a while."

"Okay then. Thanks for a fun evening and . . . I'll probably see you tomorrow."

Both Hannah and Andrea watched as Norman turned and headed for the exit. Once they lost sight of him in the crowd, Andrea turned to Hannah. "What was all *that* about?"

"I haven't the foggiest idea. Something's been bothering Norman ever since he came back from the Cities and he hasn't told me what it is."

Andrea looked concerned. "Do you think he'll tell you?"

"I'm sure he will . . . eventually. But in the meantime, both of us are here without partners . . . right?"

"That's right."

"Good. Does Lake Eden Realty still handle rentals on that new apartment complex at the community college?"

"Yes. I rented a unit just the other day."

"Is there a master key that will let you into all of the apartments?"

"Yes, but . . ." Andrea stopped and stared at Hannah in disbelief. "You want me to let you into Bradford Ramsey's apartment?!"

"Bingo," Hannah said. And smiled.

Chapter
Twenty

"I shouldn't be doing this," Andrea whispered as the elevator doors opened and they stepped in.

"Would you rather wait in the truck?" Hannah asked.

"No. Bill told me he was a real ladies' man. Is that true?"

"That's what I heard," Hannah replied, hoping Andrea didn't ask her for details.

"Well, I want to see if he's got one of those bachelor pads you read about in magazines, the ones with the round beds, and the mirrors on the ceiling, and fur bedspreads."

Hannah was about to laugh when she remembered Bradford's old apartment. There *had* been a fake fur bedspread.

The hallway was deserted, and the two sisters walked quickly to Bradford's door. Andrea used the master key and pushed the door open. "Flashlights?" she asked, once they'd both stepped inside.

"Yes," Hannah said, after one glace at the living room window. It faced a wooded area, but there was a patio with tables and chairs next to the building. Any resident who stepped out on the patio could see the lights and they'd wonder why someone was in Bradford's apartment on the night after his death. "Let me close the drapes before we turn them on."

The moon shining in the large window made hulking shapes of the furniture. Hannah made her way cautiously past a large leather armchair and stepped around the corner of a massive wooden coffee table. It would be worse than embarrassing if she broke her ankle by stumbling over furniture in a place they weren't authorized to enter. She'd tried to think of some excuse in case someone happened to catch them, but nothing seemed plausible. No one would believe that the sheriff's wife was showing her older sister the apartment because Hannah thought she knew someone who might want to rent it.

After a close encounter with a leather-covered hassock, Hannah made it to the window and drew the drapes. "Okay," she whispered. "You can turn on your flashlight."

There was an audible click in the stillness and Andrea's flashlight sent out a beam of yellow light. A split second later, Hannah's did the same.

"Where shall we start?" Andrea asked. "And what are we looking for, anyway?"

"I'll know it when I see it. Just point out anything that looks out of place."

They started in the kitchen, a room so small Hannah would have called it a kitchenette. "If you were listing this place, what would you say about the kitchen?" she asked Andrea.

"I'd call it a cozy dream of a kitchen," Andrea said.

"In real-estate-speak, *cozy* means *small*?"

"That's right. And *spacious* means *medium-sized*."

Andrea started with the refrigerator while Hannah checked the cupboards. It was quickly evident that Bradford Ramsey hadn't done much cooking since food supplies were almost nonexistent. Hannah found a box of crackers, several cans of soup, two boxes of natural grain, heart-healthy cereal, and a jar of instant coffee. "Anything?" she asked, turning to her sister.

"Not really." Andrea shut the refrigerator door. "A dozen eggs, milk with an expired date, and some dried-out cheddar cheese."

The living room was next, and it yielded equally unsatisfying results. There was nothing but dust under the cushions of the couch and chair, and only books on the bookshelf. It was surprising how little evidence there was to indicate that a living, breathing, human being had called this home.

Hannah left Andrea to go through the second bookcase and went ahead to the bathroom. There wasn't much to look at in the shower besides a bar of soap and a razor. The medicine cabinet didn't yield much either, only a bottle of Pepto Bismol and a half-empty tin of throat lozenges. If Bradford had been dealing illicit drugs for extra cash, he certainly hadn't stashed any in his medicine cabinet!

After the obligatory peek into the watery depths of the toilet tank simply because she'd once seen it in a movie, Hannah emerged from the room frowning. There was a matching frown on Andrea's face. So far their search had been fruitless.

"The bedroom?" Andrea whispered.

"Yes. I'll go in first and check out the windows."

When Hannah entered the bedroom, she saw that the curtains were already drawn. She parted them enough to look out and realized the reason they'd been closed. The window looked out on an ivy-covered brick wall that formed the side of the hallway leading to the indoor spa and swimming pool. The only view was of the wall, and although Bradford had probably kept the curtains open during the day for the sunlight that would shine in, it made sense to close them at night rather than look out at the darkness.

"If you shut the door, you can turn on the lights in here," Hannah said, motioning Andrea into the room. This window faces a blank wall."

Andrea flicked the wall switch and a large lamp on the dresser turned on. Hannah walked over to turn on the other two lamps, one on either side of the bed, and then she turned to find Andrea just staring at the room.

"What's the matter?" Hannah asked her.

"It's just a bedroom."

"You sound disappointed."

"I am. I thought it would be more . . . exciting."

Hannah was amused, but she didn't dare show it. There

were times when Andrea wasn't very worldly, but that could be because she'd married Bill right out of high school and she'd never left Lake Eden for any length of time.

"Let's see what we can find," Hannah directed. "Why don't you start with his dresser drawers."

"Ooh! I love to go through people's drawers. You never know what secrets you'll find."

Hannah laughed. Perhaps Andrea would find something. People did hide things in dresser drawers. "Have fun. While you're doing that, I'll check the closet."

It was an eerie feeling going through a dead man's clothing, especially a dead man you'd known. Hannah checked the upper shelf, but nothing was there. And the only thing on the floor was a large shoe tree with pairs of shoes neatly arranged on its tubular holders. The clothes were neatly hung on hangers, and there was nothing of interest that she could see.

"Hannah?" Andrea called her softly from the bedroom.

"Yes?"

"Come out here quick! I think I found something!"

Hannah hurried out of the closet. She found Andrea sitting on the edge of Bradford's bed holding something that glittered brightly in her hand. "What is it?"

"An earring. I think it's sapphire with diamonds all around it. It's not costume jewelry. I know the real thing when I see it."

Hannah looked down at the earring that rested on her sister's palm. "Where was it?" she asked.

"On the floor behind the headboard. I got down on the rug to look under the bed and I spotted it. Have you ever seen anything like it before?"

Hannah drew a deep breath and let it out slowly. "Yes," she said. "I have."

"Who do you think . . . what's that?!" Andrea grabbed Hannah's arm and pointed toward the living room.

There was a swishing sound as the outside door opened, and a click as it shut again. Someone had come into Bradford's apartment!

"Quick! Under the bed!" Andrea whispered, but Hannah grabbed her arm and pulled her the other way.

"The closet," she whispered, opening the door and shoving Andrea inside. A second later, she joined her sister in the walk-in closet and not a moment too soon, for they heard footfalls on the carpet coming toward the bedroom.

"The earring," Andrea breathed, passing it to Hannah in a rush, almost like they'd done in the games of *Hot Potato* they used to play with their grandparents. The only difference was that this time there wasn't any music . . . only the sound of someone walking into the bedroom and stopping by the bed.

The door to the closet was louvered and Hannah moved to a better position. She could barely make out a woman bent over at the waist, peering under the bed. She might not have known who it was if she hadn't seen that outfit earlier.

"Can you see who it is?" Andrea whispered, close to Hannah's ear.

"Stephanie Bascomb. Take a deep breath and stay right here. I'm going out to confront the first lady of Lake Eden."

There was an audible gasp from Andrea, but Hannah didn't worry about that. As Stephanie straightened up and whirled to face the closet, Hannah pushed the door open and stepped out, shutting it behind her so that Andrea would remain hidden.

"Hannah!" Stephanie exclaimed, her hand fluttering toward her throat. "What are you doing here?"

Hannah didn't bother to answer. She just crossed the floor to Stephanie and held out her hand. Then she opened it so Stephanie could see the earring. "Looking for this?" she asked.

"Yes! But it's not what you think. I lost it on Monday afternoon when Bradford and I met to discuss the talent show."

Hannah raised her eyebrows. "Really?"

"We had to work out the order of the contestants, and how long he should speak, and things like that."

Hannah had the urge to ask Stephanie how her earring

had gotten into the bedroom if all they'd done was discuss the talent show, but she didn't. It really wasn't any business of hers.

"So . . ." Stephanie stopped and swallowed with difficulty. "Could I please have my earring now?"

"Of course." Hannah waited until she visibly relaxed before she threw in the condition she'd decided should be invoked. "But first you have to tell me where you were between the time the curtain went down after the first act on Wednesday night and the time the police went backstage."

Stephanie's mouth dropped open. "Surely you don't think that I would ever . . ."

"No, I don't think you did," Hannah interrupted her. "But I still need to know exactly where you were during intermission."

Stephanie thought for a second. "I left my seat with Richard and we walked back to the lobby. We stood in line for coffee and turnovers, and then we joined Stan and Lolly Kramer, and Al and Sally Percy. They're some of our biggest supporters, you know."

"Were you with them until the gong sounded to signal the end of intermission?"

"Heavens, no! Richard and I made the rounds. We talked to your mother and Bud Hauge." Stephanie paused and frowned slightly. "She's not really interested in him . . . is she?"

"Bud's an old friend, I think."

"That's what I thought, since I saw her with Doc Knight at the Blackjack table tonight. He's a much better catch."

"I don't think Mother is looking to catch anything other than a good night's sleep. Let's get back to Wednesday night. Did you talk to anyone after you left Mother and Bud?"

"Hal and Rose MacDermott. And after we left them, we talked to Howie and Kitty Levine. Then we went on to George and Pam Baxter, Eleanor and Otis Cox, and Lorna Kusak."

"Who else?"

"That was it. The gong rang and we went back in to sit down."

"And you sat there with Mayor Bascomb until the authorities came?"

"That's right. I never left my seat." Stephanie gave an exasperated sigh. "Could I please have my earring back now?"

"Certainly." Hannah held out her hand and Stephanie snatched up the earring. "By the way . . . how did you get into Bradford's apartment tonight?"

"I still had his key."

"You still had his key?"

The color fled from Stephanie's face. She knew she'd incriminated herself, and Hannah could almost see the wheels turning in her mind, looking for the perfect excuse. "That's right. He gave me his *extra* key," she said. "I told him I thought I'd lost my earring in his apartment, and he told me to drive out and get it after the talent show was over. He said he was going out with friends and he wouldn't be back until late."

Quick thinking, Hannah thought. *I almost believe you.* But all she said was, "I see."

"Well . . . if there's nothing else . . ." Stephanie took two steps toward the door, but then she turned. "I hope you won't mention this to anyone."

"I won't," Hannah said. And then when Stephanie had made a quick exit from the bedroom, she added under her breath, "Not if your alibi checks out."

"I was so scared, I could barely breathe," Andrea confided as they walked down the hallway and took the elevator to the ground floor. "I thought for sure she'd seen me."

"When I came out of the closet, she was too shocked to look for anyone else. And I blocked the doorway with my body until I'd shut the door."

"Thanks!"

"You're welcome. I didn't think the sheriff's wife should be seen skulking around in a murder victim's apartment."

"You're right. Especially by the mayor's wife!" Andrea began to frown. "I wonder why she didn't ask why you were there."

"She was so busy trying to cover her you-know-what, she probably didn't even think of it."

They walked out the door in silence and hurried to the parking lot, where Hannah had parked her cookie truck. Once they'd climbed in, Andrea turned to her sister. "That was a little too close for comfort. My heart's beating a hundred miles a minute."

"Hold on a second." Hannah got out of the truck and went around the back. When she came back, she was carrying a paper plate filled with cookies.

"For me?" Andrea asked when Hannah handed them to her.

"For you. I was going to give them to Norman as a thank you for taking me to Casino Night, but then he got that phone call and he left so fast, I forgot."

"Norman's loss, my gain." Andrea glanced down at the cookies and smiled. "What kind are they?"

"They're Sun Moon Cookies. Have you ever heard anyone call the sun a big orange ball in the sky?"

"Yes, I have."

"These are orange-flavored sugar cookies. That's to remind you of the sun. After they're baked, half of each cookie is dipped in chocolate."

"So it's dark like it is when the moon shines at night?"

"Exactly right. Try one and see how you like them."

Hannah started the truck and drove down the hill from the college as Andrea peeled off the plastic wrap covering the cookie plate. She took a cookie and held it up. "I suppose I should start with the sun part," she said.

"Whatever. It's your cookie."

Andrea took a bite of the white part of the cookie and

made a little sound of enjoyment. "I love the way your sugar cookies crunch," she said. "And the orange is wonderful. It's very refreshing."

"Try the chocolate part next," Hannah urged her.

Andrea turned the cookie around and took a bite. She chewed and gave a little groan of enjoyment that was louder than the preceding one. "The moon part is just great!" she exclaimed. "These are wonderful cookies, Hannah!"

"Thanks." Hannah turned at the base of the hill to follow the access road that led to the highway. "Do you think we should sell these at The Cookie Jar?"

"Definitely! I think they're one of your best cookies."

"We'll have to charge the same as we do for frosted cookies."

"People won't mind that once they taste them. I'll think I'll try the sunset next."

"The sunset?"

Andrea chuckled. "That's what I'm calling the part of the cookie that's halfway between the moon and the sun. I'm going to take a bite right where the chocolate part meets the white part."

"Okay . . ." Hannah said, hiding a grin. It was pretty clear that the chocolate had put her sister in a playful mood, or perhaps it was just relief at getting out of a potentially damaging situation. If she had to choose, Hannah would bet on the chocolate.

"Perfect!" Andrea exclaimed once she'd taken a bite and swallowed. "Sunset is very tasty."

"How about sunrise?" Hannah asked, deciding to get into the spirit of things.

Andrea laughed. "I'll just have to find out, won't I?"

There was a crunch as Andrea took a huge bite on the other side of the cookie. "I'd say sunrise is equal in goodness to sunset."

"Glad to hear it," Hannah said, stepping on the gas as she merged onto the highway.

"Bill's just going to love these." Andrea glanced down at the cookies on her lap. "And so will Tracey, and Bethie, and Grandma McCann." She reached down to open the plastic wrap again and took out another cookie. "If there's any left by the time I get home, that is."

SUN MOON COOKIES

DO NOT preheat oven. Dough must
chill before baking.

2 cups melted butter *(4 sticks, one pound)*
2 cups powdered sugar *(not sifted)*
1 cup white *(granulated)* sugar
2 eggs
2 teaspoons orange extract
1 teaspoon orange zest
1 teaspoon baking soda
1 teaspoon cream of tartar *(critical!)*
1 teaspoon salt
4¼ cups flour *(not sifted—just scoop it up and level
  it off with a knife.)*
½ cup white sugar in a small bowl *(for later)*

Melt the butter in a microwave-safe bowl in the microwave for 3 minutes on HIGH.

Add the sugars to the melted butter and mix. Let the
mixture cool to room temperature on the counter.

When it's not so hot it'll cook the eggs, mix them in, one
at a time, stirring well after each addition.

Add the orange extract, orange zest, baking soda, cream
of tartar, and salt. Mix well.

Add the flour in half-cup increments, mixing after each
addition. *(You don't have to be exact about measuring—
just guesstimate—it won't come out even anyway.)*

Chill the dough for at least one hour. *(Overnight is fine.)*

Preheat your oven to 325 degrees F. and place the rack in the middle of the oven.

Use your hands to roll the dough in one-inch balls. Roll the dough balls in a bowl containing the last half-cup of white sugar.

Place the dough balls on a greased cookie sheet, 12 to a standard-size sheet. Flatten the dough balls with a greased spatula *(or the palm of your impeccably clean hand)*.

Bake at 325 degrees F. for 10 to 15 minutes. *(They should have a tinge of gold on the top.)* Cool on the cookie sheet for 2 minutes, then remove them to a rack to finish cooling.

When the cookies are completely cool, prepare them for dipping by laying out sheets of waxed paper on your counter, enough to hold all the cookies you baked.

Make the Chocolate Dip.

Chocolate Dip:
2 cups chocolate chips *(12 ounces)*
1 stick butter *(½ cup, ¼ pound)*

Melt the chips and the butter in a microwave-safe bowl on HIGH for 90 seconds. Stir to make sure the chips are melted. If they're not, heat in 20-second increments until you can stir them smooth.

Dip the cookies, one by one, so that half of the cookie is chocolate coated. *(The half you hold will not be chocolate coated, naturally!)* Place them back on the wax paper to dry.

Yield: Approximately 10 dozen *(depending on cookie size)* pretty and tasty cookies. Yum!

Chapter
Twenty-One

It was almost ten by the time Hannah and Andrea got back from the college. "Back to Casino Night?" Hannah asked. "Or would you rather go home?"

Andrea glanced down at the cookies in her lap. "Home," she said. "I've got four cookies left and that's just enough for the family."

Hannah bit back a startled burst of laughter. There had been a dozen cookies on the plate when she'd handed it to Andrea, and her sister had eaten two-thirds of them.

Andrea and Bill lived only a few blocks from the school, and after Hannah had dropped off her sister, she took a run past the school parking lot. She drove up and down the rows, but Doc Knight's vehicle was gone. She also kept a sharp eye out for her mother's sedan, since Delores could have met Doc Knight at the school, but that wasn't parked in any of the spots, either.

Should she call her mother, or shouldn't she? That was the question. Hannah debated it for all of ten seconds before she decided to drive past her mother's house to assess the situation.

There weren't that many variables. It had been years since she'd taken a logic class, but Hannah was fairly confident that she could come up with all the possibilities. If Doc Knight's vehicle was parked outside on the street, it meant one of two things . . . either he was inside with Delores after driving her home from Casino Night, or he had parked there earlier and they had taken her mother's sedan. One glance in the window of the garage would tell her if this was the case. And if her mother's car was gone, Hannah would know that Delores had driven somewhere with Doc and no one was home.

Not bad, the logical part of her mind praised her. *Now what if Doc Knight's vehicle is gone and your mother's car is in the garage?*

"I'll go in because she's there alone . . . unless, of course, the lights are off," Hannah answered aloud, feeling a bit silly to be talking to herself. "That means she went to bed and I wouldn't want to wake her."

Very good! the logical part of her mind said. *And what will you do then?*

"I'll drive home and call her in the morning. I can wait a few hours to find out what Nancy knows about the assistant professorship at the college English department."

The logic problem had occupied her through most of the trip. Hannah turned the corner and drove down her mother's street. It was deserted. Doc Knight's vehicle wasn't there, but the lights were on.

Check the garage, Hannah's logical mind insisted. *It's possible she left the lights on and they went somewhere else together after they left the school.*

"I understand. But since Doc's car isn't there, I can just ring the doorbell," Hannah argued. "If nobody's home, nobody will answer."

True, but you're going to be really embarrassed if Doc Knight didn't use his car at all. Say your mother picked him up at the hospital and she hasn't taken him back yet. They could be in there engaging in activities that you don't really want to . . .

"I don't want to hear it!" Hannah yelled, getting out of the truck and into the muggy heat of the summer night. The mosquitoes found her almost immediately, descending like a hungry cloud on her bare arm. Why hadn't she worn mosquito repellent?

Several slaps and two brushes with the palm of her hand, and she arrived at the door. Her finger was poised to ring the bell, when her logical mind spoke again.

You're not thinking this through, Hannah. Doc could be there with your mother. What if they're on the couch, and . . .

"Shut up!" Hannah yelled. But before she could press the doorbell, the porch light went on, and the door opened.

"Hannah?' Delores stared at her daughter in complete confusion. "Who are you talking to?"

"No one, Mother."

"But I heard you tell someone to be quiet."

Hannah smiled. Delores wouldn't use the phrase *shut up* even to repeat what her daughter had actually said. There was no way she wanted to tell her mother that she'd been having an argument with herself, so she settled for the first excuse that popped into her mind. "I was just talking on my cell phone."

"And you told the person on the other end of the line to . . . to be quiet?"

"Yes. It was a telemarketer. Is it okay if I come in for a couple of minutes?"

"Of course." Delores stepped back so Hannah could enter, and then she led her into the living room. "Would you like coffee?" she asked.

"Only if it's made."

"It is. Doc just left a few minutes ago and I still have half a pot. Just sit for a minute and I'll get it."

Hannah sat. And then she had a completely silent, no-holds-barred conversation with her logical mind. By the time Delores came in with a tray from the kitchen, Hannah had thoroughly cowed the logical part of her brain and elicited a promise never to interfere in her life again . . . unless she called on it, of course.

"Have a cookie, dear," Delores said, serving Hannah's coffee and cookie. "Florence is carrying a new brand at the Red Owl and I think they're better than the cookies I used to buy."

"They look good," Hannah said, looking down at the perfectly round, perfectly baked cookie. "Oatmeal-cranberry?"

"Yes, but with coconut. They're nice and moist, and chewy. You don't make anything like that, do you, dear?"

"No." Hannah took a sip of her coffee. It was time to address the reason she'd come to her mother's house. "Did Nancy call you?"

"Yes, and I'm afraid it's bad news for poor Mr. Pearson."

"He didn't get the job?"

"No, dear. Nancy talked to John Sidwell. He's the head of the English department. He was quite forthcoming when she asked him about the meeting of the selection committee."

Hannah took another sip of her coffee. It wasn't very good and she made a mental note to get her mother some from the Cookie Jar. "What did Professor Sidwell tell Nancy about it?"

"He said he was upset at the way things had gone, because the other four members of the committee were swayed by Professor Ramsey's recommendation."

"But I thought he was recommending Tim Pearson."

"That's what John thought, but Professor Ramsey changed his mind at the last minute. He told the committee that he'd found a much better candidate and that he thought they should hire his other research assistant, Tiffany Barkley."

Let me guess, Hannah thought. *Tiffany Barkley is young, gorgeous, and willing to get personal with her boss.* "So they hired Tiffany instead of Tim?" Hannah asked.

"That's right. Professor Sidwell was the only one to vote for Mr. Pearson. Nancy said he was really upset. He told her that he thought the committee had been swayed entirely by Professor Ramsey's recommendation, and he didn't think that recommendation was based entirely on academic qualifications."

"I understand," Hannah said. It was clear to her that Professor Sidwell had known Bradford quite well.

"Try the cookie, dear. Tell me what you think."

Hannah took another swallow of coffee and bit into the cookie. It wasn't wonderful, but she did admire the texture. The oatmeal cranberry cookies they baked at The Cookie Jar were crisp and they didn't have coconut. This cookie was soft. Perhaps their customers would like a cookie with a texture like this.

"I like the texture a lot," she said. "I think I'll try to make something that's as soft and chewy as this."

"Wonderful! I'll be happy to taste test them for you. Will you try to bake them tonight?"

"Perhaps," Hannah said. She'd gotten very little sleep, but she wasn't all that tired.

"Nancy told me that the results of the selection committee were made public late Wednesday afternoon," Delores said, answering the question Hannah had been about to ask. "Professor Sidwell told Nancy that he called Mr. Pearson personally to give him the news and tell him that he didn't agree with the decision of the committee."

"Did he tell Tim that Professor Ramsey had changed his mind and recommended Tiffany Barkley for the job?"

"Yes. Nancy mentioned that specifically." Delores took a sip of coffee and looked at Hannah over the rim of the cup. "Does this help, dear?"

"Very much, Mother."

"Does this mean that Mr. Pearson is a suspect in Professor Ramsey's murder?"

"Oh, yes." Hannah took her steno pad out of her purse and retrieved a pen from the outside pocket. She made a note, and then she looked up at her mother. "Is it all right if I call Nancy to see if she has any other information?"

"Of course, dear. I suggested that myself. Nancy's perfectly willing to speak to you about anything at all."

"I have only one other question, Mother. It's important."

"Ask away, dear."

"Did you see Stephanie Bascomb during the intermission of the talent show?"

Delores looked a bit startled at the question. "Why yes, I did. She came over to talk to us for a minute or two. She was very interested in the grave art that Bud just installed on the outside of the Henderson tomb. As a matter of fact, she asked him if he could make a metal sculpture of an open book for her."

"You mean for her family's mausoleum?"

"No, for the community library. She thought it would make a nice decoration."

"Did you happen to notice if she stayed in the lobby for the entire intermission?"

"Yes, I did. Her outfit was so striking, I couldn't help but glance at her every few minutes. It was a white lace suit and she looked marvelous. I asked her about it, and she said it was entirely handmade. I'm sure it must have cost a fortune!"

"Thank you, Mother," Hannah said, now convinced that Stephanie had told them the truth. There was no way a clotheshorse like Stephanie Bascomb would stab Bradford while she was wearing an expensive white lace suit!

"Why did you want to know about Stephanie, dear?"

"I just needed to check her alibi."

"Her . . . alibi? Then you must think she had some reason to kill Professor Ramsey! And the only reason I can think of that would make her do something like this is . . ." Delores gave a little chuckle. "Never mind, dear. I get the picture. Ricky-Ticky's had his share of flirtations and I can't say I blame Stephanie one bit."

It was almost eleven by the time Hannah unlocked the door to her condo. Even though it was late, Moishe hurtled into her arms and she nuzzled him as she carried him in to the couch and gave him a salmon-shaped treat.

"Oh, good. You're home," Michelle said, coming out of the kitchen. "Do you want some coffee?"

"Not really. I just had some at Mother's."

"That can turn you off coffee for life!" Michelle laughed, and then she must have realized what Hannah said because she asked, "What were you doing at Mother's?"

"Finding out about your friend Tim Pearson. He didn't get the job."

"Oh, no! Does he know?"

"Professor Sidwell from the English department called to tell him on Wednesday afternoon. Bradford didn't keep his promise about the recommendation."

"That's just awful, Hannah! Tim really wanted that job. He was going to get married this fall and Judy was already looking for a job here. I just don't understand why Bradford didn't recommend Tim when he said he would."

"Professor Sidwell said he changed his mind and recommended Tiffany Barkley instead."

Michelle looked dazed. "That's ridiculous! Tiffany doesn't have even half the qualifications that Tim does. I'll bet Tim was steaming when he heard that, especially after he did all that work. He probably wanted to strangle Bradford."

Hannah watched as Michelle's mind replayed her own words, and their effect was reflected on her face. "No! I refuse to believe it!" she said. "He might have wanted to and I can't blame him, but there's no way Tim would actually kill Bradford!"

Hannah just sat there, waiting for Michelle to calm down. It took a minute or two before her breathing returned to normal and she leaned back in her chair again.

"You need to know where he was on Wednesday night . . . right?" Michelle asked.

"That would be helpful."

"Okay, I'll find out. But I'm almost certain that Tim didn't have anything to do with it."

Hannah took the steno pad that she used as a murder book out of her purse and flipped to the suspect page. "I'll write your initials next to Tim's name," she said. "That means you're going to investigate his alibi if he has one."

"Right." Michelle leaned closer as Hannah wrote the name of another suspect on her list. "Stephanie Bascomb?" she asked.

"Yes." Hannah added her own initials next to Stephanie's name. And then she crossed Stephanie off her list.

"Why did you cross her off?" Michelle asked.

"Her alibi checks out. Mother saw her in the lobby during the talent show intermission."

"But . . . why did you write her down in the first place if you were going to just cross her out?"

"So I could feel as if I accomplished something tonight."

Michelle gave a little laugh. "I must be tired, because that makes perfect sense to me."

Chapter Twenty-Two

Hannah had just said goodnight to Michelle and was heading down the hall toward her bedroom when the phone rang. She glanced at her watch. It was ten past eleven. No one who knew her schedule would call her this late. That meant it was an emergency, a telemarketer working much too late, or a wrong number. She thought about letting the answer machine get it, but her curiosity won out. It could be important. Maybe.

She leaned over the back of the couch to reach the phone and plucked it from its cradle. "Hello?" she said, petting Moishe with her free hand.

"I didn't wake you, did I, Hannah?"

It was Norman and Hannah had half a notion to hang up. He'd left her high and dry at Casino Night. But perhaps his cell phone summons had been a dental emergency. Right now, as she sprawled over the back of the couch holding the phone with the cord that was far too short and petting a cat who was purring louder than an outboard motor, some Lake Edenite with a numbed mouth had been relieved of his pain from a tooth that had broken off in an auto accident. "It's okay. I'm still up," she said.

"Good. I wasn't sure if I should call, but I decided that I could leave the information on the answer machine if you didn't pick up."

"What information?"

"The name of the student that Professor Ramsey flunked. There was only one, and it was spectacular. A second-year student named Kyle Williamson flunked out of his Introduction to Poetry class."

"Hold on," Hannah said, setting the phone back down on the end table and walking around the couch to sit down and pick it up again. "What made this student's failure so spectacular?"

"He got three percent correct on the midterm, and two percent on the final. His poetry project was late, and it received a "U" for "unsatisfactory." There was also a note in his file that said he cut over three-quarters of the class sessions."

"That *is* spectacular," Hannah agreed. "Is this student still in school?"

"Yes. He's got a three-point eight grade average. Professor Ramsey's course is the only one he hasn't completely aced."

"But why? I mean . . . was there some sort of personal issue?"

"I don't know, but I think we ought to find out. Do you want me to go out to the college tomorrow and talk to him?"

"That would be great. Do you think you can get him to tell you where he was on Wednesday night?"

"I'll try. I'm really curious about him, especially since this sort of thing didn't happen in any of his other classes. I want to find out what Professor Ramsey did or said to turn him off so completely."

"Do you want me to go with you?"

There was a long silence before Norman spoke again. "I think I might do better alone. From what I've read of his academic records and college application, he sounds like a loner. I can identify with that. You don't mind if I go by myself, do you?"

"No. Of course not," Hannah said. "Good luck tomorrow, and let me know what you find out."

"You'll be the first to know." There was another long silence, and then Norman cleared his throat. When he spoke again, his voice was husky. "Goodnight, Hannah. I *do* love you, you know."

"I know," Hannah said And then she hung up the phone. But she didn't know, not really.

"Norman?" Michelle asked, coming into the living room in her robe and slippers.

"Yes. He's going to go out and interview a student who flunked out of Bradford's Introduction to Poetry class."

"But Bradford never flunked anyone." Michelle looked puzzled. "He was very proud of that fact. He said that poetry should be accessible to everyone and it was a reflection on him if any of his students didn't develop an appreciation for the genre by the end of his introductory course."

"Well, this student flunked," Hannah said. "Norman looked up his grades on the computer."

"What's his name?"

"Kyle Williamson."

Michelle sat down on the couch next to Hannah. "Kyle Williamson. That's vaguely familiar, but I'm not sure why."

"Norman's going out to talk to him tomorrow. Maybe he'll come back with something that'll jog your mem . . ." Hannah stopped speaking as the phone rang again.

"Do you want me to get it?" Michelle asked.

"I'm closer," Hannah said, reaching out for the receiver. "Hello?"

"Hi, Hannah."

It was Mike. Hannah gave a fleeting thought to other women and how they seemed to receive calls at normal hours of the day and night. Someday, when she had a few minutes, she'd have to figure out why her boyfriends always called her in the hour before and the hour after the witching hour. "Hi, Mike," she said, deciding not to address the issue right now.

"Will you be up for another forty-five minutes or so? I'm

driving back from Fergus Falls, and I should be there by midnight. I just met with Professor Ramsey's first wife and I wanted to run a couple of things past you."

"I'll put the coffee on," Hannah said, not even considering the option of refusal. For the first time since they'd met, over two years ago, they were fairly close to working together. She wasn't about to throw a wrench into the works.

"Let me guess," Michelle said, after Hannah had hung up the phone. "Mike's coming over."

"Right. You can go to bed if you want to. I had a nap at the shop today, so I'm fine."

"So am I. I had sleep instead of food during my lunch hour. Mother's got a great four-poster up on the second floor and it's very comfortable. I just hope she doesn't sell it before we catch Bradford's killer."

"We're narrowing the field," Hannah told her. "When Mother cleared Stephanie Bascomb, she cleared the mayor, too. They were together all through intermission, and they sat together when they went back inside the auditorium."

"I didn't know the mayor was a suspect!"

"Of course he was. Even though Stephanie insisted her relationship with Bradford was all business, the mayor must have noticed that his wife was spending quite a bit of time at the college."

"But maybe he assumed it was payback time, and he was okay with that."

Hannah shook her head. "Not a chance! The mayor's very territorial. What's good for the gander is definitely *not* good for the goose."

"That's not exactly fair," Michelle pointed out.

"Who said life was fair?"

"No one, I guess." Michelle looked thoughtful. "If you suspected the mayor, why didn't you write his name on your suspect list?"

"Because I'm saving him for tomorrow. That way I can get up in the morning and write him down when I have my first cup of coffee. And then I can cross him out before I leave for work. That means I've accomplished something before I even leave the house."

"Neat trick," Michelle complimented her. "The next time I make out a *To Do* list, I'm going to write down something I've already done so I can cross it out and feel good."

"That's my girl!" Hannah said.

Michelle laughed and got up, heading down the hall toward the guest room. But before she got there, she turned back.

"Don't bother setting your alarm," she told Hannah. "Lisa said you should sleep in tomorrow morning. Herb's got an early meeting with Mayor Bascomb, and she's going to work early with Marge and Patsy. They're going to take care of everything so that you can concentrate on the murder case."

"That is *so* sweet," Hannah said, and she meant every word of it. "Just when I think there aren't enough hours in the day, Lisa takes over the work and I've got more time for other things. Do you know anything about Herb's meeting with the mayor?"

"Yes. Lisa and I talked about it and had a good laugh. You know about Lover's Lane, don't you?"

"Yes, if you're talking about the gravel road by the apple orchard just outside the city limits."

"That's it. Well, ever since Mayor Bascomb asked Herb to start patrolling there, the high school students have stopped using it as a parking spot. Herb found out that they're all going to Spring Brook Cemetery now and parking on that winding road that divides the old cemetery from the new cemetery. The mayor figures it's only a matter of time before they start getting out of their cars and spreading out blankets by the brook, and . . . well, you know. So Herb and the mayor are working out a schedule for him to patrol there."

"They're teenagers who want to be alone. If Herb patrols their new spot, they'll just go somewhere else."

"You know that, I know that, Lisa knows that, and Herb knows that. But Mayor Bascomb seems to have forgotten."

Hannah bit her tongue. She knew the mayor occasionally frequented the Blue Moon Motel outside of town and no longer needed the dubious comfort of a blanket and a warm night, or the darkened interior of a second-hand car. "I'd better heat the oven," she said.

"You're going to bake?"

"Yes, but not cookies. Mike probably didn't have time to stop for anything to eat and I'll put in a Too Easy Hotdish."

"A what?"

"Too Easy Hotdish. My friend, Mary Blain, used to make it in college. It's the kind of thing you can throw together with whatever you have in the refrigerator."

"I'll turn on the oven." Michelle walked into the kitchen, with Hannah following close behind. "What temperature do you want?"

"I need a hot oven. Make it four hundred."

Michelle turned on the oven and set the temperature. "I'll help you get it in the oven before I go to bed. What do you want me to do"

"Spray my cake pan with Pam. Then look in the freezer and see if I have a package of Tater Tots. If I don't, any kind of frozen potato will do."

While Michelle prepared the pan and checked the freezer, Hannah went to the pantry and took out a can of cream of mushroom soup and one of cream of celery soup. She carried them to the counter where Michelle had placed the package of potato nuggets. "Is there any meat in the refrigerator?" she asked. "I could probably make this with canned tuna or canned chicken, but I think fresh meat would be better."

"Here's a pound of hamburger," Michelle said, her voice muffled since her head was in the refrigerator. "And I've got some sausage left from those pancakes I made."

"That'll be perfect. I need about a pound and a half. Did you have any leftover shredded cheese?"

"Right here. I'll bring it."

The two sisters worked quickly, layering everything evenly

in the cake pan. Less than five minutes had passed when Hannah slipped the pan into the oven.

"How long does it bake?" Michelle asked her.

"Thirty-five to forty minutes, just until the potatoes are crisp."

"I can see why your friend called it Too Easy Hotdish."

"We finished just in time. There's Mike," Hannah said, reacting to Moishe's sudden dash toward the front door.

"How can you tell? The doorbell didn't ring."

"It's my early cat warning," Hannah explained. "The doorbell should ring right about . . ." But she didn't get a chance to finish her sentence because she was interrupted by the peal of the doorbell.

"I'll go let him in," Michelle said, heading for the door. "You get his coffee. I'm just going to say hello, and then I'm going straight to bed."

TOO EASY HOTDISH

Preheat oven to 400 degrees F., rack
in the middle position.

1 and ½ pounds lean ground meat *(you can use
hamburger, pork, chicken, turkey, lean sausage,
or venison—any ground meat will do—or you
can use any leftover meat cut up in bite-size
pieces)*

2 cans *(12-ounce)* condensed cream of almost anything soup *(I usually use cream of celery, or
mushroom, or chicken, or any combination—I'm
not sure I'd use asparagus, but it might be good)*

1-pound package frozen potato nuggets *(I used
Tater Tots)*

1 cup shredded cheese *(I used cheddar, but other
cheeses are also good)*

Hannah's 1st Note: You can put in a thin layer of chopped
onions, or a thin layer of vegetables cut in small pieces.
Just don't add too many things or the potatoes and cheese
on top will burn before the inside gets done.

Spray a 9-inch by 13-inch cake pan with Pam or another nonstick cooking spray.

Put the ground meat in the bottom of the pan, spreading
it out as evenly as you can. Press it down with your impeccably clean hands, or use the back of a metal spatula. *(The
fat does not drain out of this hotdish and that's why you
should use lean ground meat.)*

Spoon the 2 cans of cream-of-whatever soup on top of the meat. Using a rubber spatula, spread the condensed soup over the meat as evenly as possible.

Put the frozen potato nuggets on top of the soup in a single layer. *(I've substituted hash browns or potatoes O'Brien when I didn't have Tater Tots in my freezer.)* Spread them out as evenly as you can.

Sprinkle on the shredded cheese to top the potatoes.

Hannah's 2nd Note: Mary's recipe is so easy, it's almost impossible to get it wrong unless you use too much cheese. It's a case of twice as much cheese is NOT twice as good. Too much melted cheese may act as an insulator, just like the insulation in your attic to keep out the cold Minnesota air in the winter. In this case, it could have the opposite effect. The cheese, when it melts, will spread out like insulation on top of the potatoes and keep the heat of the oven away from your Too Easy Hotdish. *(I know. I made that mistake.)*

DO NOT COVER your hotdish with anything. Just slip the pan in the oven at 400 degrees F. and bake it for 35 to 40 minutes, or until the potatoes on top are browned and crispy. *(If you used a glass cake pan, it may bake a little faster.)*

Hannah's 3rd Note: You may have noticed that this hotdish uses no additional seasonings. Mary says some mem-

bers of her family like to sprinkle it with Worcestershire sauce, but most people love it just as it is.

Yield: Mary says that accompanied by hot rolls and a tossed green salad, a pan of Too Easy Hotdish will serve 4 teenage boys, or 6 normal adults. *(Unless, of course, you invite Mike for a late supper—he must have been really hungry because he ate almost half the pan!)*

Chapter
Twenty-Three

"Thanks for dinner, Hannah," Mike said, finishing his last forkful of Too Easy Hotdish. "It was great! Sometimes I feel like a freeloader because you always feed me. I'm going to have to take you out to dinner more often so I can pay you back."

"It's not about paybacks," Hannah said, although she certainly wouldn't mind going out to dinner more often. She reached out to refill Mike's coffee cup from the carafe on the table and passed the plate of cookies left from the previous night.

Mike ate one cookie, took another to put down on a napkin, and pulled his notebook from his pocket. "I just finished meeting with Stacey Ramsey, Professor's Ramsey's first ex-wife. It turns out she had a very good reason to murder him."

Hannah could barely believe her ears. She remembered Stacey as a tall, sylph-like girl with long brown hair, far too quiet and shy to ever commit murder. "What's that?" she asked.

"Her parents were so impressed with Bradford, they wrote him into their will. He was to get half their estate, and Stacey would get the other half."

"They *must* have been impressed!"

"It gets worse. Stacey's parents were killed in an auto accident on Tuesday morning, and they never got around to changing their will after Bradford and Stacey divorced."

"You're telling me that Bradford was still in his first ex-in-law's will?"

"That's right. Bradford was all set to inherit half of Stacey's parents' assets. And according to the family lawyer, that amounted to several million dollars."

"Several million which should have been Stacey's alone."

"Exactly."

"Did Bradford know that Stacey's parents had left him half of everything?"

"Yes. The family lawyer spoke to him on the phone Tuesday night. Bradford was supposed to drive to Fergus Falls on Thursday to sign all the documents."

"But he was dead on Wednesday night, so the documents were never signed?"

"Right. You're quick, Hannah."

"Thank you. So what happens to the house and the land now?"

"Everything goes to Stacey since Professor Ramsey is dead. There was a provision in the will stating that if, at the time the will was formally read, either of the two beneficiaries had preceded the other in death, the living beneficiary would inherit the entire estate."

"Do you think Stacey killed Bradford so that she could keep everything for herself?"

"That would be the logical conclusion, but it didn't happen. Stacey has an iron clad alibi. She was riding in the backseat when her parents were killed, and she broke her shoulder. She didn't get out of the hospital until this morning."

"How about a new husband, or a boyfriend, or someone who wanted Bradford out of the picture?"

"Good thought, but there isn't anybody." Mike picked up his other cookie and took a bite. "How about you? Did you get anywhere?"

"Yes, and no. We discovered that Stephanie and Mayor Bascomb were suspects, but we cleared both of them."

"Who's *we*?"

"I don't think you want to know that."

Mike looked as if he might object, but then he shrugged. "Okay. Tell me why Mayor Bascomb and his wife were suspects."

"Well . . . it's like . . ." Hannah stopped and threw up her hands. "Actually, it's better if you don't know that, either."

"But they both have alibis?"

"Oh yes," Hannah said, happy that she could answer at least one of Mike's questions. "Mother saw both of them in the lobby during intermission at the talent show. They were there for the whole time, and then they went back to their seats together."

"Okay. How about any other suspects?"

"Norman's checking into any students that Bradford flunked."

"That's really unlikely as a motive. Anything else?"

"Nothing important. Michelle knows one of Bradford's research assistants, so she's going to talk to him to see if he knows anything. How about you?"

"I talked to a couple of people who'd been at the luncheon on Wednesday afternoon. One of them said she saw Professor Ramsey getting into Samantha Summerfield's car right after the luncheon was over."

"Really?"

"I checked it out and her driver said he took them to Professor Ramsey's apartment building. Then he waited in the parking lot for them to come out."

Hannah didn't ask. She just stared at Mike knowingly.

"Ten minutes," Mike answered her unspoken question.

"Ten *minutes*?"

"That's right. And when Miss Summerfield got back to the car, she wasn't happy."

"The driver could tell?"

"Anyone in the vicinity could tell. When Professor Ramsey turned to leave, Miss Summerfield rolled down her window and yelled, "Just stuff it, Brad! And if you even think about upstaging me tonight, I'll bury you!"

"Do you think she was angry enough to kill him?"

"Possibly, but she didn't have the opportunity. The driver said he waited for her at the back of the auditorium, and the moment the curtain came down on the first act, they hurried back out to the car. It wasn't quite fast enough, because there were dozens of fans waiting for her. She got into the car, rolled down the window, and signed autographs for at least twenty minutes. I checked that out, and it's true. And then the driver took Miss Summerfield back to Minneapolis."

"I guess that clears her."

Mike gave her a knowing grin. "But you still want to know what Professor Ramsey did to make her so mad, don't you?"

"Yes," Hannah admitted.

"Well, so did I, so I called and asked her."

"You didn't!"

"I did."

"What did she say?"

"She said she thought they were going to talk about the talent show, but Professor Ramsey told her he'd admired her from afar ever since he'd first seen her on television, and he'd written a poem for her. He read it aloud, and then he . . . well . . . you can probably guess what he tried to do."

"I can guess."

"She told me that it might have worked on a naïve college freshman, but she wasn't impressed with his line. She told him to get lost and marched right out of there."

"Good for her!" Hannah said, wishing she'd done the same. But this was no time to indulge in regrets and recriminations. "Do you have any other suspects?"

"No, but I'm heading to Macalester in the morning to

check out things there. Stella Parks is going to meet me on campus."

Hannah remembered the Minneapolis detective with fondness. "Tell her hello from me," she said.

"I will. Anything else I should know?"

"I don't think so. If I think of anything, I'll call."

Mike stood up and headed to the door with Hannah following close behind. When he got there, he turned and asked, "How's Norman?"

Hannah was ready to give her standard *just fine* answer, but Mike was Norman's friend and she could tell he really wanted to know. "I'm not sure," she said honestly. "Sometimes he seems just fine, but other times I know there's something bothering him." She stopped and took a deep breath. "I wish he could tell me what it was."

"Me, too," Mike said. "Then maybe we could do something to help."

They stood there quietly, looking at each other, until Hannah dropped her eyes. "Goodnight, Mike," she said.

"Goodnight, Hannah." Mike pulled open the door, but he didn't step out immediately. First he touched her cheek very gently, with the tip of his finger. "Take care," he said, giving her a smile. And then he turned and walked down the stairs.

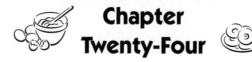

Chapter
Twenty-Four

Hannah awoke to a rough tongue licking her nose and sunlight streaming in her bedroom window. "What time is it?" she asked her feline bedfellow.

"Rrowww!" Moishe answered, assuming a sphinx-like posture on the pillow next to hers.

Since she didn't speak cat and had no interpreter, Hannah turned to look at the clock. It was seven-thirty, and she'd gotten over six and a half hours of sleep. This hadn't happened since . . . Hannah's mind balked at going that far back in time. It certainly hadn't happened since she'd opened The Cookie Jar.

She threw back the light cotton coverlet she used during the summer months and smiled. This morning there was time for a luxurious cat stretch that imitated Moishe's ritual stretch. Hannah rolled over on her stomach and extended her arms and legs in random order until they were spread out in opposite directions. When that was concluded, she tucked arms and legs back in and rolled to one side, then the other side, and ended up on her back. And then came the best stretch of all, with all four paws, or in Hannah's case limbs, pointing straight up to the heavens. After that there was a flip to the side, another stretch extending toward the doorway, and Hannah sat up on the edge of the bed feeling better than she had in months. Obviously sleep was the key. If only there were some way to get more of it! Leaving her roommate to take quite literally a spit bath, Hannah headed off to the shower.

Twelve minutes later, cat and mistress left their bedroom and padded down the hall. Moishe was wearing his orange and white fur suit, and Hannah was dressed in jeans and a short-sleeved buttercup yellow blouse. Hannah was still wearing her fur-lined slippers and Moishe was doing the same.

"Oh, my!" Hannah said as a welcome aroma drifted out from the kitchen. She'd forgotten to set the timer for the coffee last night, but Michelle had made a pot.

"Good morning, Hannah," Michelle greeted her. "I'm falling down on the job. All I made for breakfast this morning is coffee."

"Coffee's perfect. It's exactly what I need. Can you think of a better way to start the day?"

Michelle didn't waste any time thinking. "You're right. Sit down and I'll get yours. And I'll have another cup with you."

"You know, it's just amazing how alert I feel. And I haven't even had my first cup of coffee."

"Sleep will do that to you. You should really try it more often." Michelle handed Hannah her coffee cup and sat down at the table with her.

The two sisters sipped in companionable silence for several minutes, and then Hannah spoke. "What are your plans for the day?"

"Mother doesn't need me, so I thought I'd run out to the college and talk to Tim Pearson if I can borrow your truck."

"Ride in to work with me and you can have it. Just make sure you're back before the Donkey Baseball Game."

"When is that?"

"It starts at three and lasts until six. Then there's a barbecue and pizza feed in the big tent on the football field."

"And after that is the auction . . . right?"

"Right. I know Mother was resisting. Did Stephanie end up talking her into donating something?"

"Yes, she did. Mother gave her a carved umbrella stand. It's ebony and Luanne got it at an estate sale in Edina."

"Sounds nice."

"It isn't. The carving is well done, but there are grotesque-looking rodents all over it. Mother's never been able to sell it, so she decided to give it to Stephanie and take the write-off."

"Smart move," Hannah said, downing the last of her coffee and standing up. "Let's get ready to go. I want to take a look at that umbrella stand for myself. I might just bid on it for Moishe."

Lisa looked shocked as Hannah came in the back door of the shop. "It's only nine o'clock. You didn't have to come in this early."

"Yes, I did. I wanted you to see how alert I am before I get tired again."

Lisa laughed. "Marge baked her Cottage Cheese Cookies this morning. I'll bring you a couple."

Hannah poured herself a cup of coffee from the kitchen pot and sat down at the stainless steel workstation. Lisa brought her two cookies on a napkin and sat down across from her.

"Very good," Hannah said after one bite. "How did Herb's meeting with the mayor go?"

"Just fine. He's going to start patrolling the cemetery this afternoon. He's going to do a drive-through every two hours in the afternoon and increase it to once every hour when it gets dark out."

"He's not going to patrol all night, is he?" Hannah asked, hoping Mayor Bascomb wasn't expecting his town marshal to go without sleep.

"Just for the first two nights. And that's because Friday and Saturday nights are popular date nights. The mayor figures the news will spread pretty quickly and parking in the cemetery will lose its appeal."

"But how can the mayor possibly expect Herb to go two nights without sleep?"

Lisa laughed. "I guess I forgot to tell you. Mayor Bascomb relieved Herb of all his other duties until the city maintenance crew can put up motion lights. They promised him the lights would be up and working by Sunday afternoon. They're sending a man out there this morning to take photos and measurements. They did the same thing with the road past the apple orchard. They put up motion lights."

"I wonder where the kids will move next?" Hannah mused. "And I also wonder if Mayor Bascomb owns stock in any motion light company."

The next two hours passed quickly while Hannah baked. She was about to mix up a batch of Mystery Cookies when Lisa came in from the coffee shop.

"Norman's here to see you," she said. "Shall I tell him to come back here to the kitchen?"

"Yes, please," Hannah said, wondering why Norman hadn't simply parked in her spot and come in the kitchen door.

It appeared that Norman had been waiting very close to the door for Lisa's summons, because Lisa left and only a second or two later, he pushed through the door.

"Hi, Norman. Coffee?"

"I'd love some. Thanks. Is it okay if I sit here?"

Hannah nodded when Norman pointed to a stool at the workstation. It was the same stool where he usually sat. Either Norman had suffered some unfortunate memory loss that had erased all recollection of their former relationship, or he was withdrawing again.

"Here you go," Hannah said, setting his coffee in front of him. "How about a cookie?"

"That would be nice. Whatever you've got is fine."

Hannah placed a Molasses Crackle and a Black and White on a napkin and handed them to Norman. And then, because she was frustrated with what she thought of as a subterfuge, she asked, "What's wrong, Norman?"

"What do you mean?"

Since he'd dropped his eyes, Hannah could tell he knew exactly what she meant, but she decided to spell it out for him. "Sometimes you're warm and loving, just like you were before the wedding. But other times, like now, you're cold and distant. You're perfectly polite, but you're treating me like a stranger."

"Fair enough." Norman signed deeply. "I'm sorry, Hannah. It's a personal problem I'm trying to work out. It has nothing to do with you."

"But it affects me."

"Yes. It does." He was silent for a moment and then he gave her a little smile. "Just try to be patient with me. I'll work it out eventually."

"And then things will return to normal?"

"I hope so. Just give me a little time, Hannah. That's all I ask. Will you do that for me"

"Of course," Hannah said. What else could she say? But she was left with a vague and unsatisfactory answer to what was obviously a big problem. Rather than dwell on it and make both of them miserable, she smiled brightly and asked, "What did you learn from Kyle Williamson? I've been on pins and needles, waiting to hear."

"I learned a lot." Norman returned her smile. "I like him and I think the feeling's mutual. At least he really opened up to me. He reminds me of me at that age. A little nerdy, a little bit too non-athletic to be very popular with the girls, and a little too eager to speak up in class when he knows the answer."

"He sounds like a kid I might like," Hannah ventured.

"You would. And he's not really a kid. He's got a degree in music from Juilliard, but it's like he says, there's not much work for a concert pianist who came in fourth in the important competitions and didn't quite make the concert circuit. You know what I mean?"

"I *do* know. I thought for a while that I wanted to write poetry. I cared so much and I tried so hard. I put my heart on the page, but I just wasn't good enough."

"Do you still have any of your poetry?"

"It's probably kicking around somewhere in the guest room closet."

"If you're willing, I'd like to read it sometime."

"Maybe sometime," Hannah said, wondering if that would ever come to pass. She couldn't help but doubt the depth of their relationship. Right now, at this moment, Norman was his old self. But he could change in an instant to that distant stranger.

"I painted," Norman said. And then he was silent. Hannah wondered if he were wishing he hadn't revealed that about himself.

"What did you paint?" she asked.

"Houses." Norman waited for a beat and then he chuckled. "Gotcha! You're thinking *house painter*, right?"

"Yes, I was. But you painted . . . ?"

"Cityscapes mostly. I concentrated on urban architecture. Houses, apartment buildings, landmarks . . . that type of thing. Mine were a bit different than most because the frame was always a window. And occasionally the perspective was not from the window itself, but from a point across the room from the window."

Hannah stared at Norman in amazement. She'd seen several paintings of that description in the house Norman had built. She'd assumed they were prints of famous works, or original oils purchased for their investment potential. "The belfry?" she asked referring to the painting she'd noticed hanging in his study.

"The bell tower at Notre Dame. I painted it after a trip I took as a student. It's my last one."

"But it's beautiful. I love it. Why did you stop painting?"

"I'm a lot like Kyle. I realized I wasn't good enough to make a decent living at it, so I went to dental school."

"That doesn't mean you have to give up painting. You could paint on the weekends, or at night, or whenever. You don't have to stop creating!"

"I might take it up again someday . . . as a hobby. But the fire to succeed as an artist of note is gone."

"But you shouldn't just give up. You should . . ."

"Do you still write poetry?" Norman interrupted her with a question.

"I . . . I . . . no. I haven't written anything since I left college."

"Point made," Norman said.

"Point taken," Hannah replied. "I just wish that . . ."

"Another time. Don't you want to hear why Kyle flunked Professor Ramsey's Intro to Poetry class?"

Hannah nodded, pulling herself out of her self-indulgent dream, where they traveled to wonderfully scenic places so that Norman could paint and she could write. "Tell me," she said.

"Kyle told me his girlfriend broke up with him right before Christmas. She said she was in love with Professor Ramsey."

"Oh, no!" Hannah said, feeling sorry for the jilted student.

"They'd both enrolled in his Intro to Poetry class, and Kyle convinced himself that it was just a passing thing and she'd come around as soon as she saw that he still loved her. The first day of class rolled around, and Kyle managed to sit next to her, but she wouldn't even speak to him. That was the way things went for the first week of class. Kyle kept trying, and she kept refusing to have anything to do with him. He said he had to watch her flirting with Ramsey and that it was really hard to take."

"I can imagine that! Poor Kyle."

"And then Professor Ramsey started singling her out for things, keeping her after class, and inviting her to visit his home campus at Macalester. Kyle could tell she was falling completely under his spell, and he just couldn't stand to watch it any longer."

"So he started skipping classes, even when there were tests?" Hannah guessed.

"That's about the size of it. Once he realized that Professor

Ramsey was returning his girlfriend's overtures, he stopped going to class altogether. It was just too painful to watch them interact. He would have dropped the class, but it was too late to drop, so he just took the failing grade."

"That's really sad."

"I know." Norman gave another little sigh. "He was very stoic about it. And he was also very convincing."

"Convincing?"

"He convinced me that he still loved his girlfriend and he was hoping to get her back now that Professor Ramsey was dead."

"Did he tell you the name of his girlfriend?"

"No. I asked, but he didn't want to say. And I didn't think I'd better push it or he'd clam up and stop answering my questions."

Hannah was silent for minute, digesting all that she'd learned. "He's certainly got a motive, especially if he thinks he can get his girlfriend back now that his rival's dead. What about Wednesday night? Does he have an alibi?"

"Yes, and it's a good one. There's no way Kyle could have killed Professor Ramsey since he was hundreds of miles away from the scene of the crime. He flew out to Arizona State University on Wednesday morning to watch his sister graduate, and his parents were with him. They were all having dinner at T. Cooks at the Royal Palms Hotel when Professor Ramsey was killed."

COTTAGE CHEESE COOKIES

DO NOT preheat oven—This dough
needs to chill in the refrigerator
overnight.

2 cups softened butter*** *(4 sticks, 16 ounces, 1
pound)*

1 and ½ cups brown sugar *(pack it down in the
measuring cup)*

2 cups white *(granulated)* sugar

4 large beaten eggs *(just whip them up in a glass
with a fork)*

1 teaspoon baking soda

2 teaspoons baking powder

½ teaspoon salt

4 teaspoons vanilla extract *(that's 1 Tablespoon plus
1 teaspoon)*

2 cups cottage cheese *(one-pound container) (I used
small curd)*

1 cup chopped pecans *(you can use walnuts or any
other nut, if you prefer)*

1 cup cocoa powder *(I used Hershey's)*

5 and ½ cups all-purpose flour *(don't sift—just
scoop it up with the measuring cup and level it
off with a knife)*

———————

approximately 1 cup powdered *(confectioner's)*
sugar for rolling dough balls

***That's room temperature butter, unless you're working in an unheated kitchen in Minnesota in the winter.

Hannah's 1ˢᵗ Note: If you have an electric mixer, use it. This recipe makes about 12 dozen cookies and your arm may get tired. You can also cut the recipe in half if you like.

In a large mixing bowl, mix the butter with the brown sugar and the white sugar. Beat them together until they're light and fluffy.

Add the eggs and mix until they're thoroughly incorporated. If you're using an electric mixer, you don't have to whip them up in a glass first. You can just add them one by one, mixing after each egg is added.

Mix in the baking soda, baking powder, and salt. Stir until they're completely mixed in.

Pour in the vanilla extract. Stir it in thoroughly.

Stir in the cottage cheese. Keep mixing until it's thoroughly incorporated.

Mix in the chopped pecans. *(Marge says you can also add raisins, if you like.)*

Add the cocoa powder in quarter-cup increments (*don't worry about measuring accurately—just add it in 4 parts*). Mix it in after every quarter-cup. Cocoa powder is very

difficult to clean up, so don't add it all at once or it will poof out the sides of your bowl and make a real mess.

Add the flour in half-cup increments. *(It can also make a mess if it poofs out the sides of your bowl.)* Mix after each addition.

Give the bowl a final stir, cover it with plastic wrap, and stick it in the refrigerator to chill overnight.

When you're ready to bake:

Preheat the oven to 350 F., rack in the middle position.

Spray cookie sheets with Pam or another nonstick cooking spray. You can also use parchment paper if you prefer.

Roll small balls of dough about one-inch in diameter. Roll the balls in powdered sugar and place them on the cookie sheets, 12 to a standard-size sheet. Press them down slightly when you position them so that they won't roll off on the way to the oven.

Hannah's ^{2nd} Note: When Lisa and I bake these cookies at The Cookie Jar, we use white, granulated sugar for rolling instead of powdered sugar. That way we don't confuse them with our Black And White Cookies.

Bake the Cottage Cheese Cookies at 350 degrees F. for 10 minutes. They'll spread out all by themselves. Leave them on the cookie sheet for 2 minutes and then remove them to a wire rack to cool completely.

Hannah's 3rd Note: Put on a pot of coffee while the first pans of Cottage Cheese Cookies are baking. And check the refrigerator to make sure you've got plenty of icy cold milk for the kids. Everybody's going to gobble these up and ask for more.

Yield: 12 dozen *(depending on cookie size, of course)* yummy and addictive cookies that everyone in the family will enjoy.

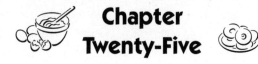

Chapter
Twenty-Five

She'd stared at the page of suspects for five minutes now, and nothing new had occurred to her. There were Bradford's ex-wives, but Mike had eliminated both of them as potential killers. Mayor and Stephanie Bascomb had been cleared, and so had Kyle Williamson. There was Samantha Summerfield, who'd been heard arguing with the victim, but Mike had talked to her driver and then confirmed her alibi. It was possible that Mike might find and interview several students and colleagues at Macalester who weren't shedding any tears for the murdered professor, but Hannah doubted any of them had driven to Lake Eden to kill him.

Her coffee mug was empty. Hannah got up to refill it and returned to her perusal of the names on her list. Their strongest suspect to date was Tim Pearson. Bradford had claimed Tim's work as his own and then failed to keep his end of their bargain. Hannah couldn't blame Tim for putting such a permanent end to their academic relationship. Unfortunately, murder was unpleasant, immoral, and illegal, even in the hallowed halls of higher learning.

With the exception of Tim, there was only one other person on Hannah's list, the one who appeared on every one of her suspect lists. It was *Suspect U*, the unidentified suspect who'd murdered the victim for an unknown motive.

Hannah was sitting there, staring down at the two suspects she'd hadn't crossed out when Lisa came in from the coffee shop.

"Marguerite Hollenbeck's here to see you," she announced. "She says she has cookies for you."

Hannah was always glad to see one of her neighbors from the condo complex, but this was a neighbor bearing cookies. Wasn't that a little like taking coals to Newcastle, or to put it in more modern parlance, bringing a picnic to a restaurant?

"Shall I send her back to see you?" Lisa asked.

"Yes, please."

"Good. I can hardly wait to hear about her cookies."

Hannah was still trying to come up with the best simile when Marguerite came into the kitchen. "Hi, Marguerite. Lisa said you brought cookies for me?"

"Yes. You probably think it's like bringing a Holy Bible to a minister, but these are special cookies."

Marguerite had out-similied her with her church reference. Hannah fetched them both coffee from the kitchen pot, and they sat down at the workstation. Marguerite was smiling and Hannah knew precisely how her mother would describe it in Regency terms. It was *the smile of the cat that had got into the cream pot.* "What makes them special?" Hannah asked the question that Marguerite was obviously waiting to hear.

"They're Watermelon Cookies."

"What?!"

"They're Watermelon Cookies. Remember that night in our garage when you were pacing back and forth, trying to come up with a recipe, and I came home from church?"

"I remember," Hannah said, relieved that Marguerite had never figured out the real reason she'd been in the garage. She'd been meeting with Mike, who'd been pulled off a murder case, to listen to his advice on solving the crime. If they'd been caught, Mike would have been severely reprimanded. Hannah had used the first excuse she could think of when Marguerite had heard her talking to someone. Instead of admitting she'd been talking to Mike, she'd said she was talking to herself, trying to work out a recipe for watermelon cookies.

"I mentioned that to my friend, Brandi Archer, when she called me from Chicago. I said I told you I didn't think watermelon cookies would be very good anyway, and she said she had a recipe for watermelon cookies and they were delicious. Of course I asked for the recipe. It came in the mail yesterday, and I baked them this morning for you."

"That's really sweet of you," Hannah said, vowing never to admit that her story had been a complete fabrication. "Are they good?"

"I think they're excellent. Try one and see what you think."

With that said, Marguerite lifted the lid of the box to expose its contents. Nestled there in wax paper were several dozen pink cookies.

"They're pretty," Hannah said, and then she reached out for one. Although she agreed with Marguerite's initial assessment that watermelon cookies couldn't possibly be good, her neighbor had gone to all this trouble and she simply had to try one.

Marguerite continued to smile her smile as Hannah bit into the cookie. She waited until Hannah had taken the second bite, and then she said, "What do you think of them?"

"Good!" Hannah said, completely shocked at the layers of flavor she'd just experienced. "Crisp like a sugar cookie, sweet and satisfying, and they taste like sun-ripened watermelon." She stopped and took another bite, swallowed, and asked the important question. "How did you *do* that?"

"Watermelon Kool-Aid. Brandi said you can make them in any flavor. She's really fond of lime. Would you like the recipe?"

"I'd love to have the recipe. Are they difficult to make?"

"Not at all. You have to roll them out like Christmas cookies, but that's not hard. And you have to be careful not to let them brown. Brandi warned me not to overbake them." Marguerite opened her purse and pulled out a recipe card. "I copied the recipe for you. Are you going to bake them here for The Cookie Jar?"

"Does Reverend Knudson stand behind a pulpit?" Hannah asked, making up her own church reference on the spot.

Marge and Patsy were waiting on customers, Lisa was handling the cash register, and Hannah was in the kitchen feeling like a fifth wheel when there was a knock at the back door.

"Hi, Hannah," Michelle said when she opened it. "I'd like you to meet a friend of mine, Tim Pearson. Tim and I are dying for coffee."

"You've come to the right place." Hannah opened the door a bit wider and motioned them in. She poured them coffee while they took seats at the workstation, and then she asked, "Cookies?"

"I've heard about your cookies," Tim said. "I've been meaning to get here, but I've been so busy, I haven't had a chance."

"How about something with chocolate?" Michelle suggested, and Hannah noticed that Tim's face lit up in a smile. Another chocoholic. She liked him already.

Hannah turned around to look at the contents of the baker's rack. "I've got Triplet Chiplets."

"Perfect!" Michelle turned to Tim. "You're really going to love these cookies. It'll give you another reason to celebrate."

Hannah delivered the cookies and picked up Michelle's cue. "What are you celebrating, Tim?"

"My new job as assistant professor in the English department at Lake Eden Community College. I found out on the way here with Michelle. Professor Sidwell called me on my cell phone to tell me that the selection committee had reconsidered and I got the job."

"Good for you!" Hannah said.

"It's all because Professor Sidwell stuck up for me. You have no idea how depressed I was when he called me on Wednesday afternoon to tell me that I'd lost the job to Tiffany. What he didn't tell me was that he was going to pull Tiffany's academic records and reconvene the committee. I think he didn't want to get my hopes up."

Michelle turned to Hannah. "Poor Tim was so upset after Professor Sidwell's call on Wednesday, he drove to Minneapolis to be with his fiancée. They had dinner with her parents that night and Tim stayed over until the next morning. I talked to Judy on the phone right after Tim called to give her the good news, and she was really excited. She told me that both of them had been really sad on Wednesday night because they thought they'd have to wait to get married."

"I'm really happy everything worked out for you, Tim." Hannah said, catching on to the fact that Michelle had checked out Tim's alibi with Judy.

"Tim starts teaching fall session, and the wedding's set for the middle of August," Michelle told her. "Professor Sidwell's sure he can find a job for Judy at the college."

"Wonderful!" Hannah said, giving Tim a warm smile as she went to get him two more cookies. She'd known from the get-go he wasn't the killer. Anyone who finished two chocolate cookies in less than a minute couldn't possibly be capable of murder.

She was just crossing Tim's name off her suspect list when her sister barreled through the door separating the kitchen from the coffee shop. "This is it!" she said. "I'm finished!"

Hannah took one look at her usually immaculate sister and knew chocolate was in order. Andrea's eyes were wild, her hair was escaping the neat French knot she'd fashioned at the nape of her neck, and she'd chewed her lipstick half off. Since Andrea would never appear in public this way unless she were dying or a crisis was on the horizon, Hannah led her to a stool at the workstation, poured her a soothing cup of coffee, and set a whole plate of Brownies Plus within easy reach.

Andrea reached for a brownie and ate it. And then she

reached for another. Hannah waited until her sister had eaten three of the chocolate-laden cookie bars before she asked her question. "What's wrong, Andrea?"

"It's Tachyon. They're ruining my life!"

"They offered Bill an even better deal?" Hannah guessed.

"Yes! Those . . . those home wreckers! Those family breaker-uppers! Those . . ." Andrea stopped and gave a shuddering sigh. "I just don't know what to do, Hannah. I can't fight this kind of thing."

"What kind of thing?"

"What they offered Bill this time. They said that if I didn't want to move, they'd fly him back home every other week-end so he could spend time with us. They promised him first-class tickets and a car service to drive him to and from the airports."

"Oh boy, do they want him!" Hannah breathed.

"I know! I just don't know how he can resist something like this. It's really an incredible job offer."

Hannah thought about it for a minute. "You're right. It *is* an incredible offer. What is Bill going to do?"

"I don't know. He told them he'd give them his decision by Monday. I think he's going to take it, Hannah. I really do!"

"Without consulting you?"

"Of course not. He *did* consult me and I told him to do what he thought was best for all of us. What else could I say? He knows how I feel about moving."

"You've done all you can," Hannah said, reaching out to touch her sister's hand. "But . . ."

"What?" Andrea asked, noticing Hannah's frown.

"I'm not sure, but . . ." Hannah stopped to think about it for another moment. "There's something wrong. I'm sure of it. It's not that Bill isn't worth all these perks. It's just that . . ."

"What?" Andrea interrupted, leaning forward.

"It's just that no big company should offer that much for a single employee. Sure, Bill's qualified, but there must be other qualified people who'd jump at the opportunity. Did you or Bill think to check them out to see if the offers he's getting are legitimate?"

"No, but they've been calling him for over a week now. They must be serious."

"Has Bill ever called them back?"

"I . . . I don't think so. I think they're always the ones to call him." Andrea stopped and began to frown. "What do you think is going on?"

"I'm not sure. The question I'd be asking is, *Is Tachyon really calling Bill?* And if the answer is no, I'd be asking, *Who could be playing this kind of horrid joke on Bill, and why are they doing it?*"

Andrea sat back and looked dazed. She was silent for several long moments. "You could be right. We never thought of anything like that."

"Have Bill call Tachyon and see if they've called him."

"I'll run out to the station to see him right now!" Andrea exclaimed, jumping up from her stool. "Have I ever told you what a great sister you are?"

Hannah smiled. "Yes, but I never get tired of hearing it."

WATERMELON COOKIES

Preheat oven to 325 degrees F., rack
in the middle position.

1 package *(.16-ounce)* watermelon *(or any other fla-vor)* Kool-Aid powder *(Don't get the kind with sugar or sugar substitute added.)*

1 and ⅔ cup white *(granulated)* sugar

1 and ¼ cups softened butter *(2 and ½ sticks, 10 ounces)*

2 large eggs, beaten *(just whip them up in a glass with a fork)*

½ teaspoon salt

1 teaspoon baking soda

3 cups all-purpose flour *(pack it down in the cup when you measure it)*

½ cup white *(granulated)* sugar in a bowl

Hannah's 1st Note: When Brandi makes these cookies, she rolls them out on a floured board and uses cookie cutters. Rolled cookies take more time than other types of cookies, so Lisa and I modified Brandi's recipe for use at The Cookie Jar.

Mix the watermelon Kool-Aid with the granulated sugar.

Add the softened butter and mix until it's nice and fluffy.

Add the eggs and mix well.

Mix in the salt and the baking soda. Make sure they're well incorporated.

Add the flour in half-cup increments, mixing after each addition.

Spray cookie sheets with Pam or another nonstick cooking spray. You can also use parchment paper if you prefer.

Roll dough balls one inch in diameter with your hands. *(We use a 2-teaspoon cookie scooper at The Cookie Jar.)*

Roll the cookie balls in the bowl of white sugar and place them on the cookie sheet, 12 to a standard-size sheet.

Bake the Watermelon Cookies at 325 degrees F. for 10 to 12 minutes *(mine took 11 minutes)* or until they're just beginning to turn golden around the edges. Don't overbake.

Let the cookies cool on the cookie sheets for no more than a minute, and then remove them to a wire rack to cool completely.

Yield: Approximately 6 dozen pretty and unusual cookies that kids will adore, especially if you tell them that they're made with Kool-Aid.

Hannah's 2nd Note: Brandi's mother baked these cookies to send to school on birthdays. She used a number cookie cutter that matched Brandi's or her sister's age that year.

Chapter Twenty-Six

Hannah's sides hurt from laughing so hard. Mayor Bascomb was riding a donkey named Harry. Hannah knew that because the donkey's name was stenciled on the donkey-sized sun hat he wore, complete with slits for his ears to poke up from the straw.

The mayor had hit a nice double to left field, but the left fielder, Gus York, couldn't seem to get his donkey traveling any faster than an ambling walk. Meanwhile, the mayor's donkey had stopped cold in his tracks between first and second base. Harry's head was down, his tail was swishing from side to side in a show of bad temper, and despite the mayor's encouraging shouts of "giddyup, boy" and "c'mon, Harry," he was living up to his stubborn stereotype.

Two members of the team in the field did not have to ride donkeys. The pitcher stood on his own two feet, and so did the catcher. The batter didn't sit on his donkey to hit, but he was required to mount in order to "run" the bases.

The teams had two donkey wranglers. One was Ken Purvis, who'd admitted to Hannah that he'd grown up in the Cities and knew next to nothing about farm animals, and the other was Doug Greerson. As the president of the Lake Eden First Mercantile Bank, Doug had dealt with some stubborn people, but he didn't have much experience with donkeys.

Hannah watched as Doug pulled on Harry's reins and Ken

pushed from behind. It seemed to have no effect at all. She would have thought that Doctor Bob, the local vet, would have been the logical choice for a wrangler, but he was known as a prodigious hitter and the mayor had wanted him in the lineup.

"Take a look at Petunia," Michelle said, nudging Hannah. "I want to know what you think of her hat."

Hannah glanced at Petunia, the donkey that Joe Dietz was riding at third base. She was wearing a big, wide-brimmed hat of white straw with large orange and yellow flowers arranged around the crown. "That's the most . . ." Hannah was about to say *ridiculous* when she realized that Delores, who was sitting on the other side of her, was also wearing a white straw hat with orange and yellow flowers arranged around the brim. "That's the most beautiful hat of them all," she said instead, giving Michelle a look that promised retribution in one form or another.

It seemed to take forever, but Gus York finally reached the ball that the mayor had hit. He was about to hop off his donkey, Custer. Custer, who had taken his namesake seriously and truly looked as though this game were his last stand, decided to wake up and smell the roses. Literally. With Gus hanging on for dear life, Custer began to move faster than Hannah had thought a donkey could move, across the baseball diamond, past the stands, streaking across the parking lot, and coming to a skidding stop at the rose garden the school grounds team had planted outside Mrs. Baxter's classroom.

After a hasty conference with Doctor Bob, the two donkey wranglers headed off to retrieve the absent team member. They made a stop at the concession stand and then hurried to rescue Gus. And in a shorter time than anyone had believed possible, Ken and Doug brought Gus and his donkey back to the field by walking in front of Custer and feeding him bits of apple turnover.

"Does anyone want anything from the concession stand?" Hannah asked.

"Nothing, thank you, dear," her mother responded.

"No thanks," Michelle said.

"Okay then . . . I'll be back in a couple of minutes. I want to see how the apple turnovers are selling."

Hannah made her way down the steps of the bleachers and headed for the concession stand. She was almost there when someone called her name. She turned to see Andrea carrying Bethany, followed by Tracey who was in charge of the diaper bag and the booster seat.

"Hi, Aunt Hannah," Tracey said, giving her a big smile. "Everybody loved your Imperial Cereal. Karen and I divided it up so everybody around us had a taste."

"Did you tell them you made it?"

"Yes, but I don't think they believed me. Maybe I'll have to invite them over and do it in front of them next time."

"Good idea," Hannah said with a smile, and then she turned to Andrea. "Did you find out any more about Tachyon?"

"Not yet. Bill's in a conference and I didn't get a chance to talk to him. That's why I'm here with the kids. Everybody knows he's overseeing the murder investigation, but it wouldn't be good for the sheriff's whole family to miss such an important charity function."

"Mother's in the stands with Michelle. They're in section three, four rows up. There's plenty of room if you want to join us. I'm just going to see how the turnovers are selling."

"Okay. We'll go up there and see you later." Andrea motioned for Tracey to follow her, and they headed off toward the bleachers. Hannah went in the opposite direction to the large concession stand.

"How's it going?" she asked Bonnie Surma, who was working behind the counter.

"Just fine. Your turnovers are a big hit."

"That's good. Are you running out?"

"We would have run out an hour ago, except Lisa brought us another ten dozen. Would you like one?"

"No thanks. I've pigged out enough already today. Just a black coffee for me."

"But I'd like an apple turnover," a voice behind her spoke and Hannah turned to see Sherri Connors.

"Hi, Sherri. You look like you're feeling better."

"Oh, I am! That medicine Doc Knight gave me settled my stomach and I haven't . . . well . . . you-know-what in forty-eight hours. The only thing is it made me so hungry I can't seem to stop eating." Sherri accepted the plate with her turnover and gave a little shrug. "I probably shouldn't, but I'd like a hotdog, too."

"One hotdog coming up," Bonnie said, handing over Hannah's coffee. She took a hotdog off the revolving spit that kept them hot and placed it inside a bun. "Ketchup or mustard?"

"Mustard. Four or five packets, please."

"How about pickles?"

"Yes, I just love pickles. And a . . ." Sherri hesitated, eyeing the array of bottles on the shelf behind the counter. "I'll have a root beer to drink."

"And this is my treat," Hannah said, handing several bills to Bonnie.

"Oh, but you really shouldn't . . ."

"Yes, I should," Hannah cut off Sherri's objection. "We're celebrating the fact that you're feeling good enough to eat."

Once Sherri had picked up her tray, Hannah followed her over to the picnic area under the trees. They chose a table and sat down.

"Mmmm," Sherri said, biting into the turnover. "This is so good! But it's dessert, so I'd better eat my hotdog first."

Hannah watched as Sherri made short work of the hotdog, opening the packets of mustard, making a yellow pool on her plate, and dipping in the hotdog as she ate it. She took a large swallow of root beer and smiled at Hannah. "It's so good to eat again. You have no idea. I was beginning to think I'd never be able to enjoy food again."

"I'm glad you're enjoying it," Hannah said, smiling back. And then she watched Sherri attack her apple turnover.

"Oh, this is heaven!" the young dancer exclaimed after her second bite. "Tender, and flaky, and sweet, and good. This is the best apple turnover I've ever had."

And then, as Hannah observed her, a thoughtful expression crossed her pretty face. "I wonder how it would be with . . . I know it sounds crazy, but . . . I'm going to try it and see!"

Sherri dipped the apple turnover in her pool of yellow mustard and took a bite. She chewed, smiled delightedly, and looked up at Hannah. "It's good! You really ought to try it sometime."

Hannah didn't say anything, because alarm bells were clanging in her mind. Doc Knight had said Sherri didn't have the flu or food poisoning. He'd remarked that it was a pity, but she'd be all right in a week or so. That information coupled with Sherri's current meal of dill pickle slices eaten with gusto, a whole hotdog devoured in four bites, an apple turnover dipped in yellow mustard and declared delicious, and a sick stomach that wasn't sick anymore led Hannah to one conclusion.

"Sherri," Hannah leaned close across the table. "Maybe this isn't exactly a polite question to ask, but I have to know. Are you pregnant?"

Sherri's face turned white and her hands began to tremble. "Please don't tell anyone," she begged, and Hannah saw her blink back tears. "I should be so happy, but now I just don't know what to do!"

"Please don't cry. I'll help you any way I can," Hannah promised, reaching out to pat Sherri's hand. "You have options, you know. There are places you can go, people who will help you. If you can't keep the baby, you can give it up to a reliable agency for adoption."

"No!" Sherri cried. "I'll never do that! Look what happened to Perry and me. I'll never let my baby grow up without a mother and a father."

"How about the baby's father? Do you love him?"

Sherri nodded, and when she spoke her voice was husky. "Oh, yes! And he said he loved me. He promised me we'd always be together."

"Can you marry him?"

Sherri shook her head and that action seemed to bring about a flood of tears. They rolled down her cheeks and fell on the table, making dark, painful-looking splotches on the wood.

"Help me understand," Hannah said, reaching out to touch Sherri's hand again. "You love the baby's father, but you can't marry him?"

Sherri made a soft, strangled sound in the back of her throat. "Yes," she gasped.

"He's already married?"

"No!" Sherri covered her eyes with her hands. "No, no, no!"

"He's not married, but you can't marry him."

"Yes! I thought I could, but I can't marry him . . . not now!"

And with that anguished cry, Sherri was up and fleeing, her dancer's legs churning across the parking lot and around the corner of the school building, leaving Hannah to sit there wondering what she could possibly do to help her young friend.

Chaper
Twenty-Seven

Hannah sat there for a long time after Sherri had fled, attempting to decide the right thing to do. Since she didn't know the name of the baby's father, she had to forget about contacting him. She had to go to the person who cared most about Sherri's welfare, her twin brother, Perry. He'd be shocked when Hannah told him about Sherri's pregnancy, but he loved his sister and together they could work out some way to help her.

A quick survey of the bleachers confirmed that Perry was not at the Donkey Baseball fundraiser game. Hannah was just crossing the road to the parking lot to get her cookie truck and drive to the college apartment he shared with Sherri when she remembered his job schedule. Perry worked on the city maintenance and grounds crew every Friday afternoon. This was Friday afternoon and he'd be at work somewhere right here in Lake Eden.

Almost as if she'd willed it, a city maintenance truck pulled into the school parking lot. Hannah hurried over to talk to the driver, intending to ask him where Perry was working, when Lady Luck smiled upon her. The driver was Perry.

"Hi, Perry," she said, approaching the open driver's window. "You're just the guy I need to see."

"Hold on a second." Perry looked apologetic as he pointed

to the cell phone on his dash. "I've got to take this call. It's work."

"Go ahead," Hannah said, stepping back slightly. Because the window was open, she could still hear the call, but it was the polite thing to do.

Perry answered the phone, listened for a moment, and then he spoke. "I'll run out there right now, before I finish that street sign. You say you need the distance between the first five light posts and the gate?"

There was another silence while Perry listened to the reply. "Okay. I'll call it in as soon as I measure."

When he'd clicked off the phone, Perry turned to Hannah. "Sorry. That was another assignment for me. I have to run out to Spring Brook Cemetery. We're putting in motion lights and they need to confirm a measurement someone made this morning."

"I understand, but I really need to talk to you, Perry."

"How about later this evening? They need this measurement right away."

"This is something that shouldn't wait. It concerns Sherri."

"Oh. Well . . . you can ride along with me if you want to. We can talk while I'm measuring, and then I can bring you back here."

"That'll work fine," Hannah said, walking around to the passenger side of the truck and climbing in.

She hadn't thought it was a good idea to bring up the subject of Sherri's pregnancy while Perry was driving. Hannah waited until they got to the cemetery and took the road that separated the new side of the grounds from the old.

Perry parked under a towering oak and went around to the back of the truck to get out his equipment. Hannah stashed her purse under the passenger seat and got out of the truck to wait for him.

It was shady and much cooler than it had been at the school

baseball field. A breeze was blowing from the direction of the brook, and trees dotted the carefully manicured grass. A stately elm spread its leaves like an umbrella over the top of a grassy knoll, tall pines pierced the sky in a bid for a celestial home, and a silver maple rustled its delicate leaves beside the alabaster statue of an angel. The grass lay like a thick green carpet over rolling hills, and even with the headstones to remind her of its purpose, Hannah could see why teenagers might want to park in this beautiful place.

She turned to look at the family mausoleums on the older side of the cemetery. The one directly across the road, a pink granite edifice with crumbled stone columns in front, was in bad repair. The granite blocks that made up the building had separated slightly as the ground had settled, and from where she was standing, she could see a triangular-shaped wedge of the dark interior. It was a real pity the gravesite hadn't been maintained. The bas-relief carving of cherubs on the front was lovely.

Perry got out of the truck with his rolling tape measure, the kind the flooring salesman had used to measure her condo for new carpets. "Do you mind if we talk while I measure?" he asked.

"Not at all. It's really beautiful out here."

"I know. That's why we have to secure the place with motion lights. People are just dying to get in."

Perry grinned, Hannah groaned at one of the worst jokes she'd ever heard, and they set off for the gate. Once they got there, Perry zeroed his measuring device, set it on the ground, and began to walk to the first light post. "So why do you want to talk about Sherri?" he asked her.

"She's in trouble, Perry."

"How is she in trouble?" Perry asked, not looking up at her. He kept his eyes on the rolling measuring tool, making sure the wheels were in contact with the ground as they walked.

They'd covered half the ground to the first light post, an

ornate metal base with filigree at the top that supported a large globe. Hannah knew that there was no time to waste if she wanted to accomplish a plan to help Sherri. "I don't know if you know this, and I hope it's not too much of a shock, but Sherri's pregnant."

Perry arrived at the first light post and stopped to jot down the measurement. "I know," he said, walking on toward the second light post. "Doc Knight told me right after he examined her."

Hannah drew a deep breath of relief and let it out again. The fact that Perry knew made things a lot easier.

"So is that all you wanted to tell me?" Perry asked.

"No. There's got to be something we can do to help Sherri."

"Help her how?"

"I'm not sure. That's why I wanted to talk to you. When I saw her just a couple of minutes ago, she was distraught and frightened."

"Oh. Well, I'll take care of it."

Hannah began to frown. Perry was answering her, but he wasn't really communicating. It was clear he wished she'd leave well enough alone. "The only thing is," Hannah said, wondering how she could persuade him that she really did want to help both of them. "I'm sure you'll do your best, Perry, but you may need some help. I'm really worried about Sherri's mental state."

"Why?" Perry reached the second light post and jotted down the measurement. Then he checked his rolling device again, and walked on toward the third light.

"I'm worried because she needs someone to help her through the days ahead. It won't be easy."

"She's got me. That's all she needs."

Hannah stopped walking as Perry came to the third light post and jotted down yet another measurement. She really didn't like his attitude. She reminded herself that she had to make allowances for the fact he'd grown up alone, with no father or mother to guide him, and he'd learned to rely only on himself. It was clear that he was determined to take care of Sherri and that was admirable, but she wished he'd accept outside help when it was offered.

Perry was moving toward the fourth light post and Hannah hurried to catch up. "I'm not trying to be nosy, Perry. Really I'm not. It's just that Sherri told me she wants to keep her baby, and that'll be very difficult for her. She said giving the baby up for adoption was out of the question."

"She's right about that." Perry's voice was hard. "Most of the kids at the Home were put up for adoption, but they didn't get adopted. They stayed right there until they were old enough to go."

Hannah waited until Perry had stopped to write down the measurement at the fourth light post, and then she tried again. "Isn't there any possibility that Sherri could marry the baby's father? She said she loved him."

"No. There's no possibility at all."

"But she said he loved her, too. I don't understand."

They walked in silence to the fifth light post, where Perry jotted down the measurement. Then he turned to her with a hard smile. "He never loved Sherri. He was getting ready to cut her loose anyway. I warned her. I told her that he was a jerk and not to listen to him. I pointed out that we were only inches from making it, that the movie deal was our ticket out of here. So what did my stupid sister do? She got pregnant and waved that movie deal goodbye. She actually believed him when he said that she was his inspiration, and they were like Elizabeth Barrett and Robert Browning."

Hannah's mind screamed a warning. *Run! Run away now!* But her feet seemed glued to the ground. "You killed Bradford Ramsey?" she asked, already knowing the answer.

"I did the world a favor . . . at least the female half. He used women and then he threw them away. You should have seen his face when he saw the knife. He knew what was coming and he knew he deserved it, but he still sniveled like a baby and begged me not to do it!"

As she looked into Perry's glittering and frenzied eyes, the signal from Hannah's mind finally reached her feet. She whirled and ran as fast as she could over the hilly ground, not caring where she was going as long as it was away from the Bradford's killer and danger.

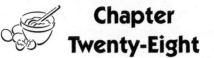

Chapter
Twenty-Eight

He was gaining on her, which was no surprise. Hannah chided herself for one fleeting moment about not keeping up her exercise regimen at the gym, but kicking herself mentally would do no good now. Perry was ten years younger and about a thousand times more athletic than she was at her best. Her only hope was outsmarting him.

Hannah darted around two weeping willow trees. The selection was quite appropriate for a cemetery, but she certainly didn't stop to dwell on that thought. She emerged from the green canopy that had hidden her for a few seconds and dashed across the road that divided the historic section of Spring Brook Cemetery from the resting place of the more recently deceased.

Of course he'd seen her. She'd expected that. But since it was physically impossible for her to outrun him, it might be possible for her to lose him among the crumbling old mausoleums and huge statuary.

She knew this part of the cemetery fairly well from her bicycle trips to the edge of town as a child. Hannah recognized the Ezekiel Jordan mausoleum with its four colors of granite and its grouping of seraphim artfully arranged by the steps leading up to the door. Since it hadn't been erected on a hilltop or even a gentle rise of land, the first mayor of Lake Eden had been laid to rest in a structure with a floor built of granite slabs that were three feet thick.

No place to hide in the first mayor's crypt. It would be locked anyway. The city preserved the graveside of its founder and the key would be under lock and key.

The key would be under lock and key, her mind repeated as she ducked under another weeping willow and jumped over a low crumbling wall. Hannah gave her mind a piece of her mind, which earned her another censure from her grey cells as she darted around a massive statue of virgin and child. This was no time to criticize her use of English. It was a time to look for a hiding place . . . and fast!

The Pettis family mausoleum was directly in front of her. Hannah remembered a missing block of granite at the back, providing access to the crypt itself, where brave kids used to hide in games of Hide and Seek. Hannah had not been a brave kid. But she wasn't being chased by a killer back then, either. She raced around the building, heading for the farthest corner, and stopped dead in her tracks. The hole had been repaired. She couldn't hide here.

She peeked out cautiously and saw him standing about a half-block away, looking toward the west and shading his eyes from sun. Had she lost him? Should she stay here as quiet as a mouse and wait until he gave up and walked back to his truck?

Who are you kidding? Hannah's mind said, and this time she agreed that it would be a bad decision. He'd search this whole area for her and find her huddled here. And then he'd pull out the knife, perhaps even the same one that he'd used on Bradford, and make sure she never told anyone what she knew.

Hannah shuddered. She wasn't quite sure what horrified her most, the idea that he would kill her or the thought that she'd be stabbed with Bradford's knife. In any event, she wasn't going to hang around to find out.

Carefully and quietly, she began to work her way west,

hoping the bright sun that was midway between its apex and the horizon, would blind him to her presence. She'd passed the second mausoleum when she saw it, a way that she could hide from Perry. It was the Henderson family mausoleum. She knew that because Bud Hauge had repaired the metal walleye and attached it to the front of the structure. But it wasn't the walleye that had caught Hannah's attention. It was the door at the side of the structure. The padlock that normally secured it was open and the door was very slightly ajar.

She really didn't want to go in. There was nothing less appealing than a dark final resting place furnished with cold granite slabs that were decorated with spider webs and slithery, slimy things, and inhabited, if you could call it that, by dead mouldering bodies. Hannah swallowed hard, repressed a shiver, and corrected herself. The only thing less appealing than the inside of the Henderson crypt was being cornered by the man who intended to make her into one of those same mouldering bodies!

Hannah pulled the door open. It took all the courage she had to step inside, but she told herself that the dead could hurt her a lot less than the living and to get on with it.

Once she'd shut the door behind her, Hannah felt faint with fear. She stood there breathing heavily for what seemed like hours until she heard another sound, a sound that made her blood run cold. It was the click of a padlock closing outside the door. Perry had discovered her hiding place and locked her in!

A sudden dizziness came over her. It made her lose all sense of direction. She knew her feet were resting on the floor . . . or were they? Was up really up? Was down really down? It was the sort of total disorientation people must feel in a sensory deprivation chamber.

She had to sit down and get her bearings. But where? Even though she'd been here for several minutes, her eyes had not adjusted and it was still as black as a tomb inside. *Black as a tomb?* her mind asked. *Just where do you think you are?*

Of course she ignored it. Her mind wasn't being very help-ful at the moment. She had to concentrate on the positives in her situation. Yes, she was locked in, but she wouldn't think about that. She was alive and unhurt, and that meant she had options. She couldn't see, but she could still feel.

Tentatively, Hannah reached out into the darkness. Her left hand encountered a hard slightly-rounded surface. It was only a bit above chair height, and she sat down. It was a lot better than sitting on the floor with the spiders and the other crawly things, and it would be fairly comfortable if she re-moved the object that was jabbing her from her rear pocket. What could it be, anyway? She'd left her purse in Perry's truck, and the only thing she had with her was . . .

Her cell phone! Hannah stood up in a flash and retrieved her cell phone. Why hadn't she thought of it sooner? It was her salvation, her escape from danger, her passport out of here. She flipped it open, glanced at the display, and gave a moan of dismay. There were no bars, and the screen read *No Sig-nal*. Spring Brook Cemetery was in a dead zone.

The cemetery is in a dead zone, her mind repeated, *how appropriate.* Hannah had to admit it did make sense. Why would they install a cell phone tower in the cemetery? It wasn't as if the residents would be making many calls.

She couldn't sit here and do nothing, hoping that someone had seen her get into the truck with Perry and would ask the right questions to track her to Spring Brook Cemetery. She was responsible for her own survival, and that meant she must find a way to get out of the mausoleum. She needed to ex-plore her surroundings and find something she could use as a weapon if Perry came back. And if he failed to come back, she had to look for something she could use to force the wooden door open.

If only she had her flashlight! Hannah thought about it longingly for a moment, and then she remembered the cell phone in her hand. It wouldn't make calls, but there was a light on the display. The light stayed on for only a minute and then it went off, but it would go on again every time she closed the phone and flipped it open again.

The search began with the area to her immediate right. Hannah flipped on the phone and used the lighted display to shine a dim light on a red wool hunting jacket and a hunting cap with earflaps. For a moment she was puzzled, but then she remembered that she was in Winnie Henderson's family crypt, and Winnie had told Delores that she'd buried her husbands with their sporting equipment.

Too bad there weren't any guns, but Winnie hadn't been that foolish. Three might be knives though. Hannah re-flipped her phone to look through the hunting coat pockets and came up with a hunting knife in a leather sheath. It was a weapon and she would use it on Perry if she had to, but it might also be useful as a tool to carve her way through the wooden door.

Her next discovery was a drawstring pouch. Hannah had just pulled several cigar-shaped objects from the pocket when she heard a car enter the cemetery and drive up the road.

It was a warm summer afternoon. Unless the driver had air-conditioning, the windows of the car would be rolled down. If it was Perry's work truck, calling out for help would do no harm since he already knew her location. If, on the other hand, it was a carload of teenagers looking for privacy at the cemetery, they might hear her and come to her rescue.

The car pulled up and stopped. Hannah waited a moment and then she called out. "Help! I'm locked in the Henderson crypt! Help me, please!"

There was a moment when nothing happened, and Hannah was just wondering if she should call out again when she heard a young female's panicked voice. "I heard something from that grave over there! Turn around quick! Let's get out of here!"

Hannah uttered a series of phrases she hoped her nieces

would never learn from her, and sighed as the engine turned over, the tires squealed, and the driver burned rubber on his way to the gates.

They hadn't heard her words . . . only the sounds. And they'd fled rather than attempt to find out what it was. What if no one heard her, and no one came? Hannah shivered and goose bumps peppered her arms. The light on her phone would give out eventually, and then she would be entombed here in the dark. Alone. Forever.

Visions of someone, years from now, opening the mausoleum to bury another member of the Henderson family and finding her body jolted Hannah into action. She picked up the knife and used the display on her cell phone to light her way to the crypt door. She worked for long minutes, twisting the tip of the blade this way and that, attempting to carve a hole in the wood, but the door was too thick to penetrate easily. She tried again with more force, slamming the blade into the wood, when she heard something snap. She'd broken the blade! It had probably rusted over the years and now it was useless to her.

How long will it take to starve? Hannah's mind asked, presenting the question like a numbered item on a multiple choice test. *One month, two months, more than three months, or none of the above?* Her mind listed the lettered answers.

"None of the above," Hannah answered aloud, startling something with wings that flew up toward the ceiling. It could have been a bird, or perhaps a bat, but she really didn't want to know. "I'm going to get out of here or die trying!" she said. And then, when the words echoed back to her, she warned her mind, "Don't you dare make a joke about that!"

It was then that she heard a second car approaching. She made her way to the door, put her mouth close to the place she'd been attempting to pierce with the knife, and prepared to shout at the top of her lungs. But as the car drew closer, she heard a low boom, and then another boom, followed by several others in an unmistakable rhythm. They were listening to music, and the windows were closed! Hannah cursed the day the car stereo had been invented as the rhythmic booming of the bass faded away in the distance and her hopes dwindled with it.

She was about to sit down again and try to think of something she could do to call attention to her plight, when she remembered that Herb would be patrolling the cemetery. His cruiser had no air-conditioning, and Lisa had told her that he never listened to music when he was on patrol. Herb's windows would be wide open and perhaps she could call out to him as he drove by. But what if he didn't hear her? What then? Somehow she had to make sure he knew she was here.

Since her mind seemed to be perfectly empty of any suggestions on just how to do that, Hannah picked up the last treasures she'd found and shined her cell-phone-turned-flashlight on them.

The first cigar-shaped object was a duck call. It said so right on the side. Hannah blew it once to test it and the thing near the ceiling fluttered again. She reached for the second, larger tube. This one was also marked, and it read *Moose Call.* That wouldn't really do her any good since it was highly unlikely a moose would hear it and crash through the door to the Henderson family mausoleum. The third object, the smallest of the three that was shaped like a whistle, intrigued her. It was not marked, but Hannah picked it up and blew.

Nothing happened. She blew it again and still there was no sound. She was puzzled for a second or two, but then she knew what it was. She couldn't hear the sound because it was too high-pitched for human ears. It was a dog whistle and it was the most important discovery she'd ever made.

Hannah used her phone light to check her watch. Herb should be driving into the cemetery in less than five minutes. She moved near the door, where there might be a slight crack that would make it easier to hear, and prepared to blow Dillon's code on what she prayed was a dog whistle.

The minutes ticked by with agonizing slowness. What if

Mayor Bascomb had called off Herb's patrol for some reason? What if Dillon had a stomach upset and Herb left him at home? What if the dog whistle was broken? Since she couldn't hear it anyway, how would she know? What if no one ever found her and Norman married someone else? And Mike married someone else? And Delores, Andrea, and Michelle grieved for a while and then treated Hannah's disappearance like an old mystery, a cold case that no one was able to solve? What if . . . there he was!

Hannah heard the car crunch across the gravel at the cemetery gates. It drove in, very slowly, and Hannah listened to the sound of the engine approaching. When she thought it was directly opposite the Henderson family mausoleum, she raised the whistle to her lips and blew three short blasts. Then she paused for a couple of beats and blew two more blasts. And then she waited.

"Dillon!" she heard a faint cry in what sounded like Herb's voice. "Get back here!"

Hannah raised the whistle to her lips again. Three short blasts, a pause, and then two more. And no more than ten seconds later, she heard paws scrabbling frantically at the mausoleum door.

There was another shouted cry from Herb for Dillon to come back, and Hannah knew she'd better make sure he didn't return to his master. She gave another three blasts on the whistle, waited the required several beats, and blew two more.

"Dillon! What are you doing?" Herb shouted, and this time his voice was much closer

"Help!" Hannah shouted. "Help me, Herb!"

"Hannah? Are you in there?"

"Yes!" Hannah shouted, almost dizzy with relief. "I'm locked in!"

"Hang on, Hannah! I'll get you out! I've got bolt cutters in the cruiser. I'll be right back."

Hannah knew Herb had to leave for a minute or two in order to rescue her, but she still felt abandoned. The fearful feeling began to come back, but it was quickly dispelled by a little sound outside the door.

"Dillon?" she called out, and she was rewarded by an answering bark. "Stay with me, Dillon," she said, and she heard him paw at the door.

"I'm back," Herb shouted out. "Just a second, Hannah. All I have to do is . . . there we go!"

Hannah heard a loud snap and a moment later, the heavy wooden door creaked open. Sunlight poured in, and for a few moments she was confused. It was still daytime! The sunlight was so bright it hurt her eyes, and she blinked like a mole coming up from its hole. And then a little white dog barreled up to her and she caught him in her arms.

"What happened?" Herb asked, as Dillon licked Hannah's nose.

"Perry killed Bradford and he locked me in here. Call it in, Herb. He's crazy and they've got to catch him!"

"I'm on it," Herb said. "Can you get back to the cruiser by yourself?"

"Yes. Go!" Hannah smiled as she received another doggy kiss on her cheek. She kissed Dillon back on the top of his head and stuffed her lifesaving cell phone back in her pocket. And then she stepped out into the light with Dillon following closely behind her.

They hurried through the cemetery and up to the cruiser where Herb was making the call. Hannah opened the passenger door and patted her lap for Dillon to jump up. When he did, she gave him another nuzzle on the head. "Good boy!" she said.

"Dispatch found Mike," Herb reported, turning to her. "He was heading straight out to the college apartments anyway."

"Why?"

"Michelle called him on his cell phone when you didn't come back from the concession stand. She said she didn't know if it was important, but she remembered where she'd heard

Kyle Williamson's name before. Sherri Connors introduced him as her boyfriend when they were rehearsing the Christmas Follies at the college. Mike was heading out there to interview Sherri about him."

"So I was a step ahead of Mike," Hannah said, not sure if that was a bad or a good thing.

"That's right. Mike said to hang tight, he'll catch up with you later at home to take your statement."

"Good," Hannah said, and then she turned back to Dillon. "You're such a good boy, Dillon. When I get back to the condo, I'm going to bake a special cake just for you!"

Chapter
Twenty-Nine

It was the most unusual cake she'd ever made. Hannah mixed up the frosting, spread some between the layers to hold them in place, and frosted the top and sides. This process was made doubly difficult by the intrusion of an orange and white cat, who was clearly mesmerized by her actions.

"Now don't be jealous," Hannah told Moishe. "This cake is for Dillon because he saved my life. When I come home from the party at the Lake Eden Inn, I'll figure out how to make you your own cake."

Despite her pacifying promise, Moishe's whiskers touched the frosting in several places before Hannah was through putting on the finishing touches. He'd never been this interested in her culinary efforts before! Perhaps it was the cream cheese in the frosting. Moishe loved cream cheese. Hannah found the wrapper, scraped off the little smears of cream cheese that were clinging to the inside, and held out her finger for Moishe to lick.

"Okay," Hannah said, intending to head to the bedroom to get dressed, but thinking better of it. Moishe wanted the cake and it was out on the counter, a small jump for him and a large disaster for her.

The microwave. Hannah opened the door, stashed the cake inside, and closed it. Moishe was a smart cat, but he hadn't learned how to open the microwave yet. . . . or at least she hoped he hadn't.

"Better safe than sorry," Hannah mumbled, just as Michelle came into the kitchen, all dressed and ready to go. "Will you do a favor for me?"

"Sure. What is it?"

"Carry Dillon's cake down to the cookie truck while I get dressed. It's in the microwave and I don't trust Moishe."

"Moishe can open the microwave?"

"I don't think so, but you never know with him. If he can figure out a way to get to his food in a locked broom closet, I wouldn't put a simple thing like opening a microwave past him."

Hannah pulled into Lisa and Herb's driveway and parked. She glanced down at her purse, recovered from the floorboards under the passenger seat of Perry's city maintenance truck, and handed it to Michelle. "I'll be right back."

"This is so sweet of you, Hannah!" Lisa looked delighted as she accepted Dillon's cake. "The only thing is . . . I'm not sure dogs like cake."

"He'll like this one. It's a Good Doggy Cake. The frosting is cream cheese and liverwurst, and the three layers are ground chicken, ground beef, and ground turkey."

"Oh, my!" Lisa was clearly impressed. "In that case he's going to love it. I'll give him a piece for dessert tonight and tell him it's from you."

Hannah gave Lisa a hug and hurried back out to her cookie truck. Once there, she pressed the pedal to the metal, which didn't have the same effect that racecar drivers spoke of, and they arrived at the Lake Eden Inn fifteen minutes later than the time stated by their mother when she invited them for dinner.

"I guess we're not so late after all," Hannah said to Michelle as they followed the waitress to a long table in the center of the dining room. Delores was already seated at the head of the table with Mike seated next to her around the corner. There were place cards, as usual, and Hannah headed over to Mike, knowing that her mother always sandwiched her in between Mike and Norman.

"Hello, darlings!" Delores greeted them. "You're on the other side, Michelle, next to Tracey when Andrea and Bill get here. And Hannah? You're next to . . ."

"I know," Hannah interrupted her mother.

"I have something for you in my car," Delores said, and then she smiled. "Actually, it's for my grandcat. It's that umbrella stand you wanted for Moishe. Andrea bought it at the auction for you."

"Great!" Hannah was pleased. The giant gargoyle-like mice might keep Moishe amused for a while. "I hope she didn't pay too much."

"She paid a dollar. No one else bid on it. I only have one caveat before I hand it over to you, dear."

"What's that, Mother?"

"You hide it in the closet when I come over. It's the most hideous thing I've ever seen."

Hannah was saved from making that promise by the arrival of Andrea, Bill, and Tracey. Once everyone had been properly greeted, they took the places Delores indicated, and then Bill turned to Hannah.

"Thank you, Hannah," he said.

"For what?"

"For planting the seeds of doubt in my mind. I was so bowled over by Tachyon's offer, I didn't even think to question it. You were absolutely right. They called me. I never called them."

"Was the offer legitimate?" Hannah held her breath. She wasn't sure whether she hoped it was or it wasn't.

"Tachyon never heard of the person who offered Bill the job," Andrea answered. "It was all a lie."

"And now that Professor Ramsey's killer is behind bars, I've got Mike and Lonnie making inquiries to find out who made the calls and why," Bill picked up the explanation. "That idea you had about someone who wants to discredit me is a good one."

"We're going to tap Bill's home phone," Mike said. "We think we might be able to trace the call if Bill keeps him on the line long enough."

Bill laughed. "You don't have to worry about that. He was pretty long-winded."

"I hope you get him!" Andrea said to Mike. "I just about went crazy thinking we'd have to move."

"Me too," Tracey said. "I hope you get him, Uncle Mike!"

There was a series of faint musical notes, and Andrea reached into her purse for her cell phone. "It's Norman," she said, glancing at the display. "I wonder why he's calling me? I'll run out to the lobby and talk to him. The reception's better out there."

Hannah thought she knew why Norman was calling Andrea. Her own cell phone was still plugged into the charger in the kitchen.

"I have some news," Michelle said. "Sherri Connors called me this morning. She's back with Kyle and they're getting married."

"Even though the baby's not his?" Delores asked.

Hannah could tell her mother regretted the question the moment after she'd asked it. She glanced at Tracey and frowned.

"It's okay, Grandma," Tracey said, jumping to her feet. "I'll just go find Mom in the lobby so you can talk about those things."

As Tracey rushed off, Delores just shook her head. "I forget she's just a child," she said.

"I'm not sure she is," Hannah commented, and then she turned to Michelle. "Kyle doesn't mind that the baby's not his?"

"He says as long as the baby's Sherri's, that's enough for him. And since they're getting married right away and he'll be listed as the husband on the birth certificate, he'll be the baby's legal father."

Andrea came back into the dining room, followed by Tracey. "Norman's on his way, but he had an unexpected visitor, somebody he knows from dental school. I told him his friend was welcome to join us. I hope that was okay."

"Of course it is," Delores said. "We'll just set up an extra chair next to Norman. Now would everyone like to know why I arranged this little party?"

"Because Perry's locked up and I'm still alive?" Hannah guessed.

"Partially, dear. Would anyone else like to guess?"

"Because Sally has pork with baby asparagus and honey mustard glaze on the menu?" Mike asked.

There was laughter around the table, and Hannah turned to her brother-in-law. "Aren't you going to guess, Bill?"

"That wouldn't be fair. Andrea and I already know."

"So do I." Tracey said. "But I can't tell. I promised Grandma."

"Tell us, Mother," Hannah urged.

"All right then. Carrie and Earl called me from Rome last night. They thought it would be fun if I flew to join them for the last week of their honeymoon. All four of us are going to explore the city together. They already booked us a room next to theirs."

There was silence around the table. Delores had been seen with three eligible men in the past week. Was she going to go to Rome with Joe Dietz? Bud Hauge? Doc Knight? It was clear no one wanted to ask her.

Hannah knew she was stuck with that unenviable duty when everyone turned to look at her. "Okay. I'll ask. Who's *us*, Mother?"

Delores nodded at Tracey, and Tracey jumped up from her seat. "It's me! I'm going to fly to Rome with Grandma. Isn't that exciting?"

The waitress arrived right on cue with two chilled bottles

in an ice bucket. There was champagne for those who wished to imbibe, and sparkling apple juice for those who didn't. As the glasses were filled with one or the other, the conversation turned to Rome and what Tracey could expect to see there. They were just talking about the famous fountain when Norman walked into the dining room with an attractive dark-haired woman on his arm.

"*That's* his friend from dental school?" Mike asked.

"He didn't tell me she was a woman," Andrea said, looking over at Hannah apologetically.

Hannah knew what to do. She pasted a perfectly composed, perfectly polite smile on her face. Maintaining her composure shouldn't be that difficult for someone who'd just been locked in a mausoleum and almost starved to death. But it *was* that difficult. She wasn't sure exactly where her heart was located in her chest, but she knew it hurt a lot.

"Hi, everyone," Norman said, stepping forward to greet them. "I'd like you all to meet my new partner at Rhodes Dental Clinic, Doctor Beverly Thorndike."

GOOD DOGGY CAKE

Preheat oven to 350 F., rack in the
middle position.

½ pound lean ground beef
½ pound ground chicken
½ pound ground turkey
8-ounce package cream cheese
4-ounce package liverwurst

You will need 3 pie plates, or 3 layer cake pans to make this cake. *(I used disposable pie pans.)*

Spray the 3 pans with Pam or another nonstick cooking spray.

Press the half-pound of lean ground beef into the bottom of the first pan, spreading it out evenly.

Press the half-pound of ground chicken into the bottom of the second pan, spreading it out evenly.

Press the half-pound of ground turkey into the bottom of the third pan, spreading it out evenly.

Bake the ground meat in the 3 pans at 350 degrees F. for 25 to 30 minutes.

Use a turkey baster to suck out the grease and dispose of it. Let the meat cool completely in the pans.

When the meat is cool, it's time to make the frosting. Place the cream cheese and the liverwurst in a medium-

sized, microwave-safe bowl. Heat them together on HIGH for 30 seconds.

Stir the cream cheese and the liverwurst together into a paste. If they're still too solid to stir, give them another 20 seconds on HIGH in the microwave.

Take one disk of meat out of its pan and place it on a cake plate. Spread a little of the frosting on top.

Take another disk of meat, put it on top of the first, and spread a little more frosting on top.

Take the third disk of meat, put it on top of the second, and spread a little more frosting on top. Cover this disk completely with frosting since it'll be the top of your cake.

Use a spatula or frosting knife to spread frosting on the sides of your cake.

If you'd like to decorate your cake, use little Milk Bones. They come in colors. Arrange them artistically on top of the cake. *(Actually your lucky doggy recipient won't really care if they're artistic or not.)*

Keep this cake **REFRIGERATED** until you serve it to your favorite canine.

Hannah's Note: This cake is very rich. It's the frosting. Dole it out to your dog in small pieces.

Yield: Enough for the "good doggy" and five furry friends.

APPLE TURNOVER MURDER
RECIPE INDEX

Baking Conversion Chart

These conversions are approximate, but they'll work just fine for Hannah Swensen's recipes.

VOLUME:

U.S.	Metric
½ teaspoon	2 milliliters
1 teaspoon	5 milliliters
1 tablespoon	15 milliliters
¼ cup	50 milliliters
⅓ cup	75 milliliters
½ cup	125 milliliters
¾ cup	175 milliliters
1 cup	¼ liter

WEIGHT:

U.S.	Metric
1 ounce	28 grams
1 pound	454 grams

OVEN TEMPERATURE:

Degrees Fahrenheit	Degrees Centigrade	British (Regulo) Gas Mark
325 degrees F.	165 degrees C.	3
350 degrees F.	175 degrees C.	4
375 degrees F.	190 degrees C.	5

Note: Hannah's rectangular sheet cake pan, 9 inches by 13 inches, is approximately 23 centimeters by 32.5 centimeters.